W9-BQS-787

TIM WAGGONER

THEY KILL

This is a FLAME TREE PRESS book

FLAME TREE PRESS
6 Melbray Mews, London, SW6 3NS, UK
flametreepress.com

Distribution and warehouse:
Baker & Taylor Publisher Services (BTPS)
30 Amberwood Parkway, Ashland, OH 44805
btpubservices.com

Publisher's Note: This is a work of fiction. Names, characters, places, and incidents are a product of the author's imagination. Locales and public names are sometimes used for atmospheric purposes. Any resemblance to actual people, living or dead, or to businesses, companies, events, institutions, or locales is completely coincidental.

Thanks to the Flame Tree Press team, including:
Taylor Bentley, Frances Bodiam, Federica Ciaravella, Don D'Auria, Chris Herbert, Matteo Middlemiss, Josie Mitchell, Mike Spender, Cat Taylor, Maria Tissot, Nick Wells, Gillian Whitaker.

The cover is created by Flame Tree Studio with
thanks to Nik Keevil and Shutterstock.com.
The font families used are Avenir and Bembo.

Flame Tree Press is an imprint of Flame Tree Publishing Ltd
flametreepublishing.com

A copy of the CIP data for this book is available from the British Library and the Library of Congress.

HB ISBN: 978-1-78758-257-6
PB ISBN: 978-1-78758-255-2
ebook ISBN: 978-1-78758-258-3
Also available in FLAME TREE AUDIO

Printed in the US at Bookmasters, Ashland, Ohio

TIM WAGGONER

THEY KILL

FLAME TREE PRESS
London & New York

CHAPTER ONE

A tall, lean man known only as Corliss – to those who knew of him at all – walked down the middle of County Road 25A, roughly three miles outside the Ohio town of Bishop Hill. Dawn was only beginning to touch the eastern horizon, and the morning air was chilly, more like November than mid-September. Corliss liked the bite in the air, found it rather bracing.

An invigorating start to the morning, he thought.

Cornfields flanked the road on either side, the stalks swaying gently in the morning breeze, leaves rustling against each other, making it sound as if the plants were communicating in hushed whispers. Corliss sniffed the air. The corn was almost ready to harvest. Another few weeks. He walked up to the wood-and-wire fence on his right, reached out, and wrapped his fingers around a stalk he selected at random. He concentrated for a moment, then removed his hand, returned to the road, and continued walking. Now, whoever ate the corn from that particular plant would respond in one of two ways, depending on their temperament. They'd either fall into a deep, dark depression and kill themselves, or they would become consumed with homicidal fury and kill whoever was in their immediate vicinity at the time.

Corliss smiled. It was the little things that made his work worthwhile.

He wore a black suit and tie, which at first glance appeared perfectly normal. But the longer someone looked at his clothes, the more it seemed like the suit was an open void, a portal to some vast dark place. The observer would be tempted, almost uncontrollably so, to step forward and try to touch the suit, to prove it was nothing more than a garment made of sewn-together fabric. And if that person succumbed to this temptation, he or she would regret it, bitterly, for the few seconds of life remaining to them.

Corliss was clean-shaven, eyebrows thin, straight blond hair falling halfway down his back. His hair – almost the precise shade of corn silk, coincidentally – made a startling contrast with his dark clothing. More startling was the way his hair was always in motion, if only slightly, even when the air was still.

A third of the sun was visible by the time Corliss reached his destination. There was nothing immediately apparent about this place that marked it as special. More corn on either side of the road, uncut grass in the ditches, asphalt old, cracked, and in need of repair. Nevertheless, this was the right place. What it wasn't, however, was the right *time*. But that was easily rectified.

He made a languid gesture with his right hand, as if he were half-heartedly shooing away a bothersome insect. Daylight vanished, darkness rushed in, and with it came rain. Not a light shower, but a motherfucking *deluge*. Water poured from the sky in torrents, wind blasted with gale force, thunder boomed like artillery fire, and lightning crackled as it split the dark, illuminating the area for miles in all directions with stark white strobing flashes. It was only 6:09 p.m., but thanks to the storm, it might as well have been midnight. Corliss's head and hands became immediately drenched, but the rain that touched his suit simply kept on going, disappearing into the black expanse within. The wind grabbed hold of his wet hair, flung it this way and that, and the strands cried out in a chorus of fear and excitement. Corliss grinned, spread his arms wide, and raised his face toward the sky. This was *his* kind of weather. He stood like that for several moments, enjoying the sensation of the storm raging around him, but he soon became aware of headlights approaching from the east. He sighed. Time to go to work.

He lowered his head and arms and stepped to the side of the road. He didn't do so to avoid being struck by the oncoming vehicle. If the driver managed to hit him – a big *if* – his void would protect him. This spot simply offered the best vantage point to observe what was about to happen. He looked to the west, and for a moment he saw only darkness disrupted by lightning flashes. But he soon saw another pair of headlights heading this way. Both vehicles were too far away for him to make out any details visually, but he prided himself on the thoroughness of his research, and he already knew everything he needed to.

The vehicle approaching from the west was a black Dodge pickup, eight years old but still in excellent condition. The driver, thirty-two-year-old Jeffrey Sowell, made sure to keep it that way. Not that his devotion to vehicle maintenance would do him any good this night. The vehicle approaching from the east was a silver Nissan Altima. It had a few years on it as well, but it was also in good condition. The Altima was sixteen-year-old Courtney Marsh's first car, and she was anal about making sure her vehicle was serviced regularly. She intended the Altima to get her through her last two years of high school and – hopefully – through college as well. Unfortunately for Courtney, her car wasn't even going to get her home tonight.

Both drivers were going faster than they should have, given the conditions. Jeffrey and his boyfriend, Marc, had been having dinner out this evening, when they'd had a fight. Upset, Jeffrey had left the restaurant in tears. He'd gotten in his truck and took off, with no particular destination in mind. He'd just wanted to get away and think, so he'd headed out of town on County Road 25A. As he was driving, he'd called his sister to vent some steam, but she'd proven less than sympathetic. *How many times have I told you that Marc isn't the right guy for you? Maybe now you'll listen to me and break up with that asshole.* Before long they'd started arguing too, and Jeffrey ended the call, frustrated and angry.

Courtney was equally upset, but for a very different reason. She played oboe in the school orchestra and had driven to Ash Creek to have an afterschool lesson with her teacher, Mrs. Olivetti. Courtney had only had her license for a short time, and she'd never driven in inclement weather before. But while the weather app on her phone had predicted rain, the sky had been clear, and since she was a type-A student who intended to graduate valedictorian – although she'd settle for salutatorian if she had to – she *hated* missing any kind of lesson, and her anal-retentive tendencies warred with her sense of caution. It was no real contest, however, and she'd set out for Ash Creek. It had been a good lesson, but she regretted her choice now. The rain hadn't been coming down too hard when she'd left Mrs. Olivetti's house, but the storm had grown stronger and more violent with each mile she drove, until now it seemed as if it might destroy the world. No wonder ancient people had worshipped storm gods. All this wild power…. She'd pray to any god who could get her through this storm safely, if only she knew the right deity to call on.

She could've stayed with Mrs. Olivetti until the worst of the storm passed. She could've – *should've* – pulled over to the side of the road and waited it out. But she was also on the girls' tennis team, and they had practice tonight. Intellectually, she knew she could miss one practice. Hell, their coach might even cancel it if the storm didn't let up soon. But until she got a text informing her practice was off, she had to assume it was still on. And just as she hadn't been able to make herself skip her oboe lesson, she was determined not to miss tennis practice – even if it meant having to drive through this hellstorm. The thought of missing practice, combined with the storm's unrelenting assault on her vehicle, filled her with anxiety, so much so that she was unaware of how fast she was driving. Her subconscious mind goaded her to go fast, *faster*, so she could get out of the storm and find shelter all the sooner. In response, her right foot slowly increased pressure on the gas pedal, and her Altima picked up speed without her realizing it. Tears filled her eyes – tears of fear and frustration – making it more difficult for her to see the road ahead of her than it already was.

Both drivers experienced the same awful conditions. Rain coming down so heavy and fast that their wipers, even on the highest setting, couldn't keep their windshields clear. Gusting winds buffeted their vehicles, punching them this way and that, making it a constant battle to keep them under control. There was so much water on the road that their tires hydroplaned. Courtney didn't have enough experience driving to recognize what her tires were doing, and she didn't ease back on her speed. Jeffrey had experienced hydroplaning before, although nothing nearly as bad as this. But he didn't slow down because he was too pissed off.

As the vehicles raced toward each other, Courtney's Altima drifted over the centerline, putting her on a direct collision course with Jeffrey's pickup. Jeffrey didn't react at first. Given the poor visibility, it seemed to him as if the Altima had appeared out of nowhere. It took him a couple seconds before he jammed his foot onto the brake and yanked his steering wheel to the right. Courtney didn't have the presence of mind right then to perform any evasive maneuvers. Her eyes widened in shocked disbelief when she saw Jeffrey's pickup, and all she had time to do was let out a shrill scream of panic before she saw the other vehicle swerve toward the cornfield on her left. It ran off the road, hit the ditch, and was launched into the air. She slammed on her own brakes then, fishtailing to a stop. She didn't see the pickup flip over as it started to descend.

When the pickup began to invert itself, Corliss gestured and the world froze. Millions of swollen icy raindrops became suspended in the air, the wind stilled, and the thunder grew silent. He'd managed to halt time in the midst of an especially bright lightning flash, providing him plenty of illumination. He'd been standing on the opposite side of the road from where Jeffrey's vehicle was headed, and now he walked toward the other cornfield. The raindrops his face and hands encountered adhered to his skin, caught in his own personal time field. The drops that his suit touched disappeared into its endless black depths.

He took a jump-step over the ditch and continued into the cornfield until he was close enough to the pickup to touch it. The vehicle was frozen in midair, making it look as if it were levitating. It amused him to imagine that the pickup was a huge balloon, and if he gave it the smallest push with his hand it would float away. The vehicle's driver's side was tilted toward the ground, and Corliss had an excellent view of Jeffrey's face. The man's expression was intriguing. Shock mostly, mixed with fear and disbelief. But what really intrigued Corliss was the hint of acceptance in Jeffrey's widened eyes. Corliss had seen this before – many times, in fact – in the gazes of people who knew they were about to die. He didn't know if this recognition had a psychic basis, a kind of death-sense that humans possessed, or if the realization was entirely rational. Given the situation Jeffrey found himself in, why wouldn't he anticipate dying? At this point, it would certainly appear to be the most logical outcome. It was a puzzle that fascinated Corliss, and he took every opportunity to look into the eyes of humans who were only seconds from their death in the hope he would eventually find an answer. But like all the others before him, Jeffrey's eyes provided none. Corliss hadn't really expected they would, but he was disappointed nevertheless.

He stepped back several feet, gestured again, and time resumed its normal course.

The pickup continued sailing through the air, flipping over as it went. It came down top first, striking the ground at such an angle that the driver's side took the worst of the impact. The cab crumpled at that spot, the metal smashing upward onto Jeffrey's head the same instant gravity yanked him downward. The top of his skull caved in, which would've been enough to kill him by itself, but his neck snapped as well. The pickup bounced, rolled, then slid to a stop, leaving behind it a swath of flattened cornstalks. The vehicle – glass broken, metal twisted – came to a rest on its passenger side in a soup of mud and smashed plant matter. Corliss waited to see if the pickup would fall to one side or the other, onto its wheels or its roof, but it remained sitting on its side. He walked over to the vehicle, crouched, and peered through the broken windshield. He gazed upon Jeffrey, still held in place by his safety belt. The top of his head was a crushed red ruin, and blood trickled from his ears and nostrils. The man had died almost instantly upon impact, which Corliss supposed Jeffrey would've considered a mercy. Corliss, however, viewed it as a missed opportunity. Humans only died once, and it was a shame that Jeffrey had missed out on fully experiencing his demise.

Corliss didn't worry about Courtney. She was uninjured – physically, at least – and would remain in her car, hands wrapped around the steering wheel in a death grip, until a power company crew drove by in search of a downed line in the area. It was they who would call 911, bringing state troopers, firefighters, and EMTs to the scene. Corliss had some time before any of that happened, though. More than enough to finish what he'd come here to do.

Corliss crouched in front of the pickup's broken windshield. He touched an index finger to the glass, and it became mist that was instantly blown away by the howling wind. Jeffrey hung upside down, still buckled to his seat in an awkward, almost comical position. Corliss touched the belt, and like the glass, it transformed into vaporous wisps. Without the belt to hold him in place, Jeffrey – or rather, his corpse – fell to the passenger-side door with a dull thud. Corliss gazed upon Jeffrey's corpse. It had come to rest on its shoulders, spine curved, knees down by the face, head twisted at an unnatural angle. Death fascinated Corliss. One moment a collection of meat, blood, and bone was moving, and the next it was motionless. The event always struck him as so… anticlimactic.

He leaned his face close to Jeffrey's and breathed upon the man's open, staring eyes. An instant later the pupils widened and Jeffrey began to stir. Corliss straightened and stepped back to observe. He made no move to help the man extricate himself from the wreck. He'd returned life to Jeffrey – of a sort. The man could manage the rest himself.

Jeffrey's limbs twitched slightly, as if his muscles were trying to remember how to move, then he half shoved, half rolled through the opening where the windshield had been. He lay in a crumpled heap for several moments, then slowly, torturously began to stand, rising like a marionette controlled by shaky, uncertain hands. His head rested on his right shoulder, but aside from that – and the bloody dent on the top of his skull – he didn't look too bad, all things considered. The lashing rain washed the worst of the blood from his head wound, and while he staggered under the assault of the violent wind, he didn't go down.

Corliss nodded. *Good.*

Out of the corner of his eye, he detected a new pair of headlights approaching. It was the power crew, searching for the downed line but about to discover something much worse.

Time to be going, he thought.

"Follow," Corliss said. His voice was drowned out by the wind and rain, but that didn't matter. He didn't have to speak aloud for Jeffrey to hear him. He started walking toward the road, and after a moment's hesitation, Jeffrey followed. The dead man struggled against the storm, but the moment Corliss set foot on the road, daylight returned, and with it a clear blue morning sky. Corliss turned around and waited for Jeffrey to catch up. There was no sign of the man's pickup, or of Courtney and her Altima. They'd been left behind in the past.

Jeffrey might no longer have the storm to contend with, but in the present, the cornfield wasn't damaged, and he had to shoulder his way between stalks on his way to the road. His movements were slow and halting, which was only to be expected given the state his body was in. Once out of the cornfield, he had trouble negotiating the ditch, and he lost his footing and fell to his knees. Corliss made no move to help him. In a sense, Jeffrey was a newborn, and he needed to learn to walk on his own. When Jeffrey reached Corliss, he stopped, and Corliss examined him. Jeffrey was still wet from the storm, which had blown itself out 365 days ago, but he would dry eventually. His color was good – a little gray-tinged, but overall very lifelike – but something had to be done about that bashed-in head and broken neck. Corliss took hold of Jeffrey's lolling head and gently straightened it. There was an audible *click* as bone set and fused, and when Corliss removed his hands, Jeffrey's head remained upright. It still tilted a bit to the left, but Corliss thought the angle gave Jeffrey a rakish, almost mischievous look that he rather liked, so he decided to leave it that way. He then ran his right hand over the top of Jeffrey's head, as if he intended to straighten the man's hair. When he was finished, Jeffrey's skull had returned to its normal shape. Corliss's hand was smeared with blood – evidently the rain hadn't washed all of it away – and he lifted it to his face. He opened his mouth and a long black snakelike tongue emerged. It quickly licked the hand clean and then slithered back into Corliss's mouth.

The sun was almost all the way above the horizon now.

"What's your name?" Corliss asked.

Jeffrey frowned, as if he were having trouble remembering, but then he said, "Jeffrey Sowell."

"Good. And where do you live?"

Another frown, and then, "An apartment."

Corliss pursed his lips in irritation. "What *town*?"

"Bishop Hill."

Hardly any hesitation this time. Excellent.

"What happened to me?" Jeffrey asked. "The last thing I remember...." He trailed off, unable to complete the thought.

Corliss wasn't surprised. No one returned from death with all their memories intact, and Jeffrey had suffered severe brain damage. Yes, Corliss had repaired Jeffrey's injuries, but he wasn't a neurosurgeon. He might've put the pieces of the man's head back together, but not necessarily in the proper order. No matter. Jeffrey would serve his purpose as he was.

"All you need to know is Bishop Hill is that way." Corliss pointed west. "If you start walking now, you can be there in a couple hours."

Jeffrey looked at him for a long moment, and Corliss thought the man was going to say something, perhaps question who Corliss was and why he wanted Jeffrey to walk to town. But instead Jeffrey turned away and began plodding westward, one slow, awkward step after another.

Corliss watched him go. The man walked on the centerline, as if needing it to guide him.

"Keep to the side of the road," Corliss called after him. "I didn't return you to life so you would end up as roadkill."

Jeffrey continued walking in the middle of the road. Corliss thought the man hadn't heard him, or perhaps hadn't understood. Either way, Corliss was about to run after the man, grab his arm, and pull him to the side of the road, but then Jeffrey moved there himself, saving Corliss the trouble. He watched Jeffrey a bit longer to make sure the man didn't wander back to the middle of the road, but he kept to the side, and Corliss allowed himself a smile. All in all, things had gotten off to a good start.

He began walking, trailing after Jeffrey, partially to keep an eye on him, but mostly because it was a pleasant morning for a stroll. He started whistling an atonal tune, and soon his hair was rippling in time with the music.

CHAPTER TWO

Sierra Sowell sat up in bed, surrounded by darkness, disoriented, heart racing, breath coming in short gasps. She didn't know where she was, or even *who* she was. But the longer she sat there, twisting and untwisting the blanket clutched in her hands, the more her memories trickled back. And then, all at once, she remembered the dream, every fucking detail. She began trembling, and nausea slammed into her gut with sledgehammer force. She feared she was going to throw up, but instead of jumping out of bed and running toward the bathroom, she forced herself to remain sitting. She'd had dreams about her brother's death before – although admittedly, none so weird – and she should be able to handle the emotional aftermath by now. She closed her eyes, although as dark as the room was, she needn't have bothered, and concentrated on an image of a calm, still pond. She'd read on the internet grief support forums where she lurked and rarely posted that this sort of visualization technique was an effective tool to alleviate anxiety and panic. She'd never used it before, but now seemed like a damn good time to give it a try.

Her attempt lasted almost two whole minutes before she gave up, dashed to the bathroom, and puked into the toilet. She felt as if she was going to keep vomiting until she turned herself inside out, but eventually her stomach was empty. Throat fire-raw and abdominal muscles aching, she flushed the toilet, then grabbed the edge of the sink to steady herself as she got to her feet. She rinsed her mouth with tap water, then rinsed again with mouthwash. Afterward, she felt better, but weak, and she staggered back to bed and flopped onto the mattress. Vomiting really took it out of her, had done since she was a child. Her phone was on her nightstand, and she picked it up to check the time. 7:23 a.m. She always slept in a T-shirt and underwear, and she'd managed to avoid getting any puke on either of them. A minor victory, but she'd take whatever she could get this morning.

She rose from the bed, already feeling a little stronger, and walked over to the curtains and opened them. Sunlight flooded into her small bedroom, and she turned her face away from the window with a muttered "Fuck!" She'd had so much trouble sleeping after Jeffrey's death that she'd bought heavy-duty blackout curtains to keep even the tiniest sliver of light from entering her room and keeping her up. They worked, but she didn't think she'd ever get used to the sudden transition from deep darkness to bright eye-stinging daylight. It was like what that strange black-suited man had done in her dream, moving from early morning sunrise to a storm-battered night with a mere wave of his hand.

She didn't need to be at work until nine, and while she normally would've crawled under the covers to snooze another thirty minutes, she knew she wasn't going to be able to get back to sleep. Might as well get her day going.

She walked out of the bedroom, down the short hall, and into her small kitchen. The light was as bright as in her bedroom – no blackout curtains here – but her eyes had more or less adjusted to it by now. She turned on the coffee maker, inserted a single-serve coffee pod into it, placed a Van Gogh's *Starry Night* mug beneath the dispenser, and hit the brew button. The machine whirred and hissed to life, and she stared at the thin stream of hot black liquid that began to flow into her mug.

She wasn't surprised that she'd dreamed about Jeffrey's accident. Today was the one-year anniversary of his being run off the road by that stupid bitch Courtney Marsh – who'd not only escaped injury in the accident but hadn't gotten so much as a goddamned ticket. So what if the weather conditions had been terrible that night? Drivers were responsible for the safety of their passengers as well as other drivers on the road. End of story. Courtney had started her senior year of high school a couple weeks ago and would probably be going off to college next fall. She could build a life because she still *had* life. Sierra's brother wasn't so lucky.

But as many times as she'd dreamed about the accident, she'd never done so like last night. Usually, she watched the event unfold as if she were a spectator standing at the side of the road. She wanted to yell for Jeffrey to slow down, wanted to run into the street and wave her arms to force him to do so. But she couldn't move or speak. Last night, however, she'd been both Jeffrey and Courtney at different points in the dream. She'd also been the man in the black suit sometimes. She couldn't recall his name. She thought it started with a *C* or maybe a *D*. He was the weirdest thing about the dream. His strange suit and hair. The way he could manipulate time. And worst of all, how he'd brought Jeffrey back. Not to life, exactly. More like a mocking impersonation of it. Seeing Jeffrey move and speak, even if he was still mostly dead, had been such an emotional experience for her, it was no wonder she'd puked soon after waking. And the way the dream had ended, with Jeffrey and the man in the black suit walking toward town. If the dream had been real, they would be heading to Bishop Hill this very moment. What would happen if she called off work today, got in her car, and drove down County Road 25A right now? Would she find her undead brother shambling toward town followed by the man in the black suit?

No, if she went, she'd find nothing, of course. Dreams didn't come true, and neither did nightmares. She'd give anything to see her brother again one last time, tell him all the things she hadn't said to him while he lived. Most of all, she wanted to tell him she was sorry.

When the coffee was finished, she put cream and sugar into it, and then leaned against the counter while she sipped it. Mom and Dad had asked her to go over to their place for dinner tonight. When her mom had invited her, she'd said nothing about it being the anniversary of Jeffrey's accident. His deathday, as Sierra thought of it. She didn't want to go to her parents', didn't know if she could take being around them and the grief that followed them wherever they went, like an obnoxious animal that you couldn't get rid of, no matter how hard you tried. She was having a hard enough time dealing with her own grief, and she feared she didn't have the emotional resources to help her mom and dad deal with theirs. She'd told her mom she'd come, though. What else could she do? She was her parents' only living child now, and it was up to her to help them when they needed it. And tonight they were going to need her, very much so. She would just have to suck it up and try to be the best daughter she could tonight. Afterward, she could return home and collapse into a sobbing mess if she wanted.

He thoughts turned again to the man in the black suit. She wondered if he was supposed to represent someone in the real world, maybe the director of the funeral home where they'd held Jeffrey's viewing and funeral. The man in the black suit didn't much look like the funeral director, though. The funeral director was shorter and heavier. Older too, with snow-white hair and a goatee.

She finished the last of her coffee, rinsed the mug in the sink, then placed it on the top rack in the dishwasher. Maybe the man in the black suit hadn't meant anything, was only a random – if bizarre – addition to her usual nightmare. Dreams didn't have to make sense, and most of the time they didn't. You could drive yourself crazy looking for meaning in things that were by their very nature meaningless. She decided to take a long warm shower and do her best to forget about her dream and the strange man in black.

She remembered his name then – *Corliss* – and despite having told herself the dream meant nothing, she spoke the name aloud, and the sound of it in her otherwise quiet kitchen made her shiver.

★ ★ ★

After showering, Sierra let her curly brown hair air-dry while she put on minimal makeup and dressed. She was an artist – she worked with watercolors, primarily – and she was a teacher at ArtWorks Education, a funky combination of art school and gallery downtown. She also taught art classes at Riverbank Community College. She worked part-time at both places, but together the gigs allowed her to make a living, meager as it might be. As an artist, she liked to dress creatively for work. She wore colorful blouses that had interesting images or patterns on them, along with black leggings and black flats. She was feeling down today – big shock – so she deliberately chose something upbeat: a yellow blouse with a daisy pattern. When she checked herself in the bedroom's floor-length mirror, she liked what she saw. Her eyes were a bit bloodshot from throwing up so violently, but hopefully they'd return to normal as the day wore on.

On her way out, she grabbed the canvas bag with Egyptian hieroglyphics on it that served her as both purse and teacher's carryall, slung the strap over her shoulder, opened the door, and stepped out into the hall. She closed the door as quietly as she could, and she was locking it – holding her keys so they wouldn't jingle – when she heard the door across the hall from her apartment open.

Goddamn it, she thought. But when she turned around, she managed to put a reasonable facsimile of a smile on her face.

"Hi, Grace. How are you this morning?"

Grace looked at her with bleary eyes that struggled to focus. If Grace had been anyone else, Sierra would've thought she hadn't woken up all the way yet. But the stink of cheap alcohol wafting off the woman told a different story.

"I can't find my purse," Grace said, her voice rough as old leather.

Grace Coates was somewhere in her sixties, hair dyed an unconvincing blond, face lined from years of sun exposure. She was a tall woman – taller than Sierra by at least a foot – and so thin she looked like a skeleton whose bones had been painted flesh color. She wore her makeup heavy and inexpertly applied, and Sierra had never seen her without it. She might've thought it tattooed on if she hadn't seen the woman's eye shadow and lipstick smeared so often. Grace wore a fuzzy pink robe marred with stains, and the belt around her waist was loose, leaving the robe open to the point where most of her right breast was exposed.

Before Sierra could say anything, Grace scowled, stepped forward, and leaned her face in close to Sierra's.

"You took it, didn't you?"

Grace's breath smelled like vinegar and vomit. Sierra hadn't had anything to eat or drink that morning except for her coffee, but her stomach was still tender after throwing up earlier, and she had to fight to keep from puking again.

"I didn't take your purse. I couldn't have. I don't have a key to your apartment."

She did her best to keep the irritation she felt from her voice. She tried to be as silent as possible whenever she came and went from her apartment, and this was why.

Grace had already been living there when Sierra moved in a few years ago. She'd found Grace to be a pleasant neighbor, and after a while they began spending time together, chatting over coffee in each other's apartments, sometimes having dinner or watching a movie. Grace worked as a loan officer in a bank, and she had been married to an orthodontist – who, unfortunately for her, had made her sign a pre-nup. She had two children, both of whom were older than Sierra. Grace had so much more life experience than Sierra, and she came to view the woman as something of a mentor as well as a friend.

And then Grace started asking her for money. Not a lot at first. A five here, a ten there. Just to help tide her over until she got paid. She'd hired a lawyer to help her get a better settlement from her ex, she said, and he'd proven more costly than she'd expected. The story sounded a bit off to Sierra. If Grace had the money to hire an expensive lawyer, why did she need more from her ex-husband? But she decided to put her doubts aside and trust her friend. Then Grace began drinking. Sierra was used to seeing the woman have a glass of wine once in a while, and she'd usually have one with her. But now it seemed Grace always had a drink in hand, and not wine but liquor, straight up. She favored bourbon but sometimes she'd drink vodka instead.

Grace began telling Sierra all her woes, and she had a lot of them. Her husband had cheated on her with the officer manager where he worked. She'd forgiven him and wanted to work things out, but he'd refused and left her. Her children took their father's side in the divorce – *Because he told them lies about me*, she'd said – and now her son and daughter didn't want to have anything to do with her. Sometimes they'd call her on holidays or on her birthday, if she was lucky. She had trouble finding men to date, and when she did finally start going out with someone, it ended quickly – never her fault, of course. Her boss at work was always on her about her job performance, and Grace feared she would be fired any day. She was having trouble making payments on her pre-owned Lexus, and she was afraid the bank – the same one she worked for, awkwardly enough – was going to repossess it. If she lost her job, she wouldn't be able to make her rent, and then she'd be homeless because neither of her children would take her in and she had no friends she could live with. No friends except Sierra, and could she be a dear and loan her some more money, just until her situation became more settled, and then she'd pay it right back, she promised.

Sierra wasn't an idiot. She knew she was being taken advantage of, but she wanted to be a good friend to Grace, wanted to find a way to help her with her problems. She spent hours talking to the woman – in person, on the phone, via text – but in the end she always gave Grace money, if she had it to spare. One of the reasons Sierra was reluctant to confront Grace directly about her drinking and spending was that the woman had been there for her when Jeffrey died. She'd remained by her side throughout those first awful days, supporting her through it all. Sierra didn't know how she would've made it if Grace hadn't been there to help her. And a few months later, she'd been there to help her through her breakup with her longtime boyfriend, Stuart. She knew she was enabling Grace, but how could she turn her back on this woman after she'd stood by her during the worst times of her life?

Then a couple weeks ago, Grace's daughter, Chloe, had called Sierra. Chloe introduced herself and said she'd gotten Sierra's number from her mother. Given the portrait Grace had painted of her children, Sierra expected Chloe to be a heartless bitch. But she found that not to be the case at all. First off, Chloe said Grace had told her about Sierra a while ago, during one of their weekly phone calls. Chloe wanted her to know how much she and her brother, Trent, appreciated her being such a good friend to their mother.

"You're aware she's an alcoholic, right?"

Sierra had been a bit surprised by the woman's directness, but she said yes.

"This might sound weird, but could you tell me what she's said about my brother and me, and about our father?"

It *was* weird, but Sierra went along with it, partly because Chloe was so different than she'd expected, but mostly because of her own doubts about Grace's honesty. When she was finished, Chloe sighed.

"I was afraid of that. She was the one who was unfaithful, and she left Dad for her lover, who eventually dumped her. It's true that Trent doesn't call her as often as I do, but it's more often than she says. He couldn't take her asking for money anymore. He found it so hard to tell her no every time, even if that's what our therapist said to do."

Chloe went on to tell Sierra about her and her brother's attempts over the years to try and get Grace into counseling, but their efforts failed. Grace would pretend to go along with whatever they wanted, even go to a few appointments with a therapist before quitting, but while she could manage to hide her drinking when she worked at it, she never stopped.

"Trent and I went to a therapist of our own to get some ideas how to help Mom, but she told us that the best way to help was to stop helping her. More specifically, we had to stop giving her money. So long as we were helping her to maintain her life as it was, she had no motivation to change. So as hard as it was, we cut her off. No more money, no matter what she said she needed it for, no matter how much she begged."

Chloe had gone on to say that while Sierra could, of course, do whatever she wanted, she hoped for her mother's sake as well as Sierra's that she'd stop giving Grace money.

So even though it was hard, the next time Grace asked Sierra for money – so she could get some maintenance work done on her car, she claimed – Sierra said she was sorry, but she couldn't help her out financially. Not anymore.

Grace said she understood, but she asked for money again a few days later, and when Sierra turned her down once more, she asked again the following week. That time when Sierra declined to give her money, Grace got nasty. She said Sierra was an ungrateful little hippie bitch, no better than her two worthless children.

Since then, Grace took every opportunity to try and pick a fight with Sierra, and each time she had a different pretext. She complained that Sierra played her TV too loud at night, that her cooking stunk up the hallway, that she parked too close to her Lexus…. But lately her complaints had become strange. Earlier in the week, she'd confronted Sierra in the hall and told her not to leave her microwave running all day while she was gone because its radiation gave her a headache. Later that same day, she'd said that every time Grace flushed her toilet, the water in her apartment stopped working for an hour. And now Grace was claiming that she'd sneaked into her apartment and stolen her purse. Sierra had started to fear that Grace's alcoholism had affected her mind, and now she was certain of it.

"You didn't need a key," Grace said. "You obviously picked the lock."

Sierra gaped at Grace, unable to believe what the woman had said. Then she lost what little patience she had.

"That's right. When you were asleep – I mean drunk and passed out on the floor – I used my vast experience as a cat burglar to break into your apartment and steal your purse. I put it up for sale on eBay this morning, and someone bid a million dollars on it. I'm on my way to the post office right now to mail it to the buyer."

Grace's eyes narrowed and her lips – smeared with too-red lipstick – tightened. She glared at Sierra with bloodshot eyes, and while Sierra felt the raw hostility behind that gaze, she refused to look away. Grace made no move toward her, didn't raise a hand, but Sierra had the impression that the woman was on the verge of physically attacking her. Then Grace looked at Sierra's canvas bag, and some of the fire went out of her.

"You're lying. You don't have enough room in there for my purse. I'll give you until tonight to return it. After that, I'm going to the police."

"You do that," Sierra said. She turned away from the older woman and headed for the building's exit. Sierra and Grace lived on the ground floor, and it took Sierra only a few steps until she was outside and walking down the stone steps in front of the building. Her red Volkswagen Beetle – which she called Ladybug – was parked right in front, and she practically ran to it, hoping to get in, get the hell out of there, and leave Grace behind. But before she could reach her car, the building's door banged open, and Grace came charging out after her. The front of the woman's robe fell open completely, and her breasts wobbled and flopped as she stumbled down the stairs.

"Don't you turn your back on me, you goddamned thief!" Grace shouted.

Up to this point, Sierra had been mostly irritated by Grace, but now she was afraid of her.

"Leave me alone!" she shouted.

She reached Ladybug, thumbed her key remote to unlock the door, opened it, jumped in, and immediately locked it. She started the car without bothering to put her seat belt on, but before she could put the vehicle in gear, Grace was at the driver's side door, smacking the window with her hands, striking so hard that Sierra wouldn't have been surprised if the glass cracked.

"People like you think you can do anything you want and get away with it!" Grace was screaming now, spraying the window with spittle. "But you're wrong! Wrong, wrong, wrong, *wrong*!"

Sierra put the car in reverse, stomped on the gas, and flew backward. Grace's hands had been on the window when Sierra started backing up, and as the car moved, the woman lost her balance. She spun around, struck the front quarter panel with her bony ass, bounced off, and fell to the asphalt. Sierra was horrified, and for an instant she almost threw the car into park and got out to see if Grace was okay. But then she remembered the insane fury in the woman's face as she pounded on the window, and Sierra put Ladybug in drive and roared away. As she pulled onto the road, she glanced at her rearview mirror and saw Grace standing there, blood on her knees from where she'd hit the ground, mouth stretched wide in a scream of anger.

* * *

Grace watched Sierra drive away, hands bunched into fists, entire body shaking. Her throat was raw from screaming, her knees stung from being scraped when she'd fallen, and her tits were hanging out for all the world to see.

Let them look, she thought. *I hope they all get an eyeful and go blind.*

She couldn't believe what a total cunt Sierra had become. She used to be such a sweet girl – or at least she'd *pretended* to be. Why should she turn out to be any different from all the other people in her life? Her dumbass ex, her heartless children, and all the unreliable men she'd dated since her divorce. None of them had ever cared for her, not really, and none of them had been there for her when she truly needed them. They treated her like garbage and expected her to put up with it. Well, fuck that and fuck them too. She'd take care of herself, just as she had most of her life. Her dad had run out on her mom and her when Grace was a toddler, and her mom had started drinking. She drank so much that Grace had had to take care of her and do all the household chores, including feeding herself. Her mom died of a heart attack when Grace was in high school, and she hadn't shed a single tear for the bitch. Thank god she knew how to handle her booze. She never wanted to end up a useless drunk like her mother.

She closed her robe and belted it, then ran her hands through her hair in a vain attempt to make it look somewhat presentable. She then started back toward the building. Her mouth was dry as sandpaper and her head throbbed with a headache that was worsening with each passing second. She needed some hair of the dog. She would've made a liquor store run – despite the early hour – but she didn't have any cash. She couldn't use her debit card because her checking account was seriously overdrawn, and her credit cards were all maxed out. Besides, all her cards were in her goddamned purse, which that bitch Sierra had stolen. She'd just have to scrounge around her apartment and hope she'd find something, *anything* to drink.

★ ★ ★

The encounter with Grace left Sierra feeling emotionally and physically wrung out. So when her phone rang, she pulled it out of her bag, and instead of checking the display to see who was calling – as she normally did – she answered it.

"Hey, Sierra! What's up?"

She let out an audible groan upon hearing Stuart's voice, but if he heard, he didn't remark on it.

"It's been a while since we talked, and I thought I'd check in with you and see how you're doing."

It's been a while because I won't take your calls or answer your texts, she thought. *Haven't you gotten the message by now?*

But of course he hadn't. Stuart Redmond wasn't interested in other people's feelings, only his own. And when he claimed something as his – like her, for example – as far as he was concerned it was always his.

"This isn't a good time," she said. Not that any time would be good.

"You obviously want to talk or you wouldn't have answered the phone."

Wanting to talk and wanting to talk to you *are two different things*, she thought. Out loud, she said, "I'm on my way to work. Could we do this another time?"

"Considering how long I've been trying to reach you, I'd rather talk now, while I've got you on the line. Otherwise, it might be another couple months before you answer your fucking phone again."

She ground her teeth in frustration. This was pure Stuart – pushing for what he wanted by trying to make her feel guilty about denying it to him. The hell of it was, even when she knew he was doing it, she couldn't keep herself from feeling exactly the way he wanted. She remembered something he'd once told her.

People are like machines. All you have to do is figure out how to work their controls, and you can make them do anything you want.

He worked as a salesperson at Electronics Emporium, and he'd been talking about how to manipulate customers into buying more than they originally wanted, sometimes more than they could afford. It hadn't occurred to him that he'd been giving Sierra an important insight into how he viewed people. All people, including her.

"I'm doing fine," she said, almost snapping at him. "Things are pretty much the same. No major changes."

Stuart was silent for a moment, then he said, too casually, "No special someone in your life?"

Oh, for fuck's sake!

Sierra and Stuart had dated for nearly a year when he asked her to marry him. She'd said yes, although not without some reluctance. Their relationship had still been new when Jeffrey died, and like Grace, Stuart had been there for her during those awful early days of her grieving. She'd been considering breaking up with him before Jeffrey's accident, but afterward, she'd needed his support too much, and so she'd stayed with him, even though his support was primarily self-serving. He wanted to own her, to have sex whenever he wanted it, and in return he would hold her when she cried, pat her on the back, tell her everything was going to be all right, that it would just take time. And she'd needed to hear those words so badly that she ignored how empty the rest of their relationship made her feel.

So when he proposed, she'd accepted out of what she later realized was misplaced gratitude. But as soon as she agreed to be his wife, Stuart's attitude toward her grieving changed. Whenever she felt sad about Jeffrey's death and started crying, he told her that she was being childish, that she'd mourned long enough, and it was time for her to get on with her life.

People die, he'd said. *It's sad, but it's a fact of life. You have to learn to accept it.*

And if he became especially frustrated with her continued grief, he'd tell her how fucked up it was that he had to be jealous not only of her brother, but her *dead* brother.

And his need to control her hadn't ended with her grief. He wanted to know what she did during her day – where she went, and especially who she spoke with. He wanted to know who she was texting and what they talked about. He asked her about her students at the college, wanted to know if she had any cute guys in her classes and if any of them were especially friendly toward her. The final straw had come when he suggested she avoid spending time with her parents because they were only "reinforcing your unhealthy fixation on your brother."

Stuart had *not* taken their breakup well. He'd kept calling and texting, showing up at ArtWorks and at the college to talk to her, waiting in front of her apartment building for her. She'd had to take out a fucking restraining order on him, and he finally, grudgingly left her alone after that. He still tried to get in touch with her sometimes, which was a violation of the restraining order, but overall, he was so much better than he had been that Sierra hadn't made an issue out of it. Now she wished she had.

"You're not supposed to talk to me. You know that."

A pause, and this time when he spoke, his tone was ice-cold.

"You. Answered. The. Fucking. Phone."

"And now I'm disconnecting."

She ended the call and tossed the phone back into her bag. The phone immediately started ringing again, but there was no way in hell that she was going to pick it up this time. Stuart would probably leave a nasty voicemail, which she'd delete unheard. How the hell had she ever ended up with a guy like him? Jeffrey had tried to warn her that Stuart was no good for her soon after she started dating him. At the time, she'd felt like Jeffrey was trying to get back at her because she didn't approve of his boyfriend, and it became a sore point between them. She wished Jeffrey were still alive for a million reasons, but one of them was so she could tell him that he'd been right about Stuart, and she wished she'd listened to him.

Hindsight might be 20-20, but sometimes it hurt like a bitch too.

* * *

Stuart sat behind the wheel of his hyper-blue metallic Camaro in the Electronics Emporium parking lot. The store didn't open until nine, but he liked to get there early. He hoped to be promoted to manager soon and getting to work early showed his dedication to the store – he hoped.

He'd purchased the Camaro less than a month ago, and the thing was his pride and joy. The kind of car a person drove made a statement about who they were and, more importantly, where they were going. The vehicle was loaded with the latest hi-tech features – built-in 4G Wi-Fi, heated and ventilated seats, rear camera mirror with streaming video, infotainment system with eight-inch touchscreen, and a forward collision warning system. Driving the car was like piloting a starfighter, and Stuart fucking loved it. What he did *not* love, however, was being hung up on.

"Call Sierra," he said.

His phone was connected to the car's system, allowing him to make and receive calls hands-free. He listened as Sierra's phone rang and rang before finally going to voicemail.

"Hi, this is Sierra. I can't take your call right now, so please—"

Stuart pushed a button on the steering wheel to end the call. What he really wanted to do was leave a message telling Sierra she was an immature cunt for disconnecting like that, but he restrained himself. The last thing he wanted to do was let Sierra think she'd gotten him angry enough to lose control. He refused to give her the satisfaction.

Stuart closed his eyes, drew in a long slow breath, held it for a ten count, then released it slowly. He did this four more times before he felt his anger had diminished to a manageable level.

He opened his eyes, then opened the mirror on the driver's side visor and looked at his reflection. His expression was calm, and there was no hint of anger or frustration in his eyes. He tried a smile, and while it looked a little strained to him, he thought most people would've taken it as genuine. When you were in sales, your facial expressions – along with your voice and body language – were your most important tools, and he always made sure his were in working order. Clothes were important too, of course, and today he wore a gray suit with a blue tie that complemented the color of his car. Sierra had told him on several occasions how good he looked in a suit, and the thought of her caused his smile to falter and fade.

He didn't understand what her fucking problem was. He was reasonably handsome, kept his weight under control, had a good job with excellent prospects for advancement, and he was great in bed. No woman had ever told him he was good at sex, but they didn't need to. When you were a man – a *real* man – you just knew. He was everything a woman should want. So why didn't she want him?

You know why, he thought. *It's because of her damn brother.*

Today was the one-year anniversary of Jeffrey's death. That's why Stuart had called Sierra this morning. He'd hoped she was feeling sad and might need a little TLC. But it hadn't worked out that way, had it?

Stuart hadn't been sorry when Jeffrey died. The man hadn't thought he was good enough for his precious little sister, and he'd done everything he could to drive a wedge between Sierra and him. After the asshole was gone, Stuart figured it would be smooth sailing with Sierra from then on. And it had been – for a while. But she was obsessed with her brother, and he had no idea why. He could understand being sad for a couple weeks, maybe a month, but a whole fucking *year*? He just didn't get it. Sometimes, when he was feeling especially angry at Sierra, he wondered if there hadn't been more to her relationship with Jeffrey, if maybe they were a little closer than a brother and sister should be. Yeah, Jeffrey had been gay, but that didn't mean he hadn't fucked his sister at some point. People experimented, right? When Stuart was a teenager, he'd let his cousin Paul jack him off in his parents' basement once. When Paul had told one of his friends, Stuart beat the holy living shit out of the little bastard. Fucker had it coming for talking when he should've kept his mouth shut. The way Stuart figured it, Sierra and Jeffrey had to have had sex, or maybe come close to it without actually doing it. He couldn't understand having such strong emotions for someone you hadn't fucked.

He reached out and patted the Camaro's black dashboard.

"At least you make sense."

That was one of the things he liked about technology. It was designed to do specific tasks, and when you operated it correctly, it performed those tasks exactly as you wanted. Not for the first time in his life, he wished people were more like machines. Maybe he'd understand them better then.

He checked the time on the dashboard display. Ten minutes to nine. Time to quit thinking and head inside if he wanted to keep up his streak of coming in early. He hoped work would take his mind off Sierra, but he knew from experience that it wouldn't. Maybe he'd give her a call later to see how she was handling the anniversary of Jeffrey's death. Or maybe he'd just show up at her place. She couldn't get mad at him for violating the restraining order, not when he'd done so entirely out of concern for her emotional well-being.

He thought about it for a moment and decided there was a decent chance she'd buy that story. And if she did, who knows? Maybe she'd realize what she'd been missing and invite him into her bedroom for some make-up sex. And if she didn't invite him, maybe he could find a way to make her let him in anyway. Once he was inside her apartment, he was confident he could get her into bed, one way or the other. Sure, she might say no, but she wouldn't mean it, not really. None of them did.

Cheered, he got out of the Camaro and headed for the store's entrance, imagining the things he would do to Sierra when he finally got her alone again.

CHAPTER THREE

ArtWorks was located in Bishop Hill's downtown Historic District. The buildings were old enough to earn the 'historic' designation, most of them having been built in the early part of the twentieth century, but the businesses located here didn't fit with that motif. There was a cell phone store, a store that bought and sold used video games, a coffee shop, a hot yoga studio, a pizza joint, a store that sold handmade soaps and essential oils, a store that sold large wood carvings created with chainsaws, and ArtWorks Education. ArtWorks had only been in business for the last five years, about the time Sierra had graduated with her MFA in art. Before that, it had been a local office supply store that ultimately hadn't been able to compete with the large national chains. And it hadn't helped that the parking lot was so small. Because of this, the employees at ArtWorks were encouraged to park on the street and leave what spaces there were at the building for students and parents. Parking was free downtown, thankfully, but finding space each morning was a pain in the ass. Sometimes Sierra would be forced to park a couple blocks away and walk, which was no big deal on a day like today since the weather was nice, but which really sucked when it wasn't, especially in winter.

But it was a Monday morning, and business was usually slow on Mondays, and Sierra found a space on the street opposite ArtWorks, in front of Subs-to-Go, where she often grabbed lunch. She parked, feeling absurdly as if she'd just won the lottery, got out, locked the door behind her, and started down the sidewalk, canvas bag slung over her shoulder. The emotional aftereffects of her encounters with Grace and Stuart still lingered, making her feel yucky, but she was determined to try her best to make the day better going forward. Jeffrey wouldn't want her to mope around. He'd want her to honor his memory by living her best life, and so that's what she'd do.

There were few cars passing by right now, and even fewer pedestrians on the sidewalks. But as Sierra approached the corner where she would cross to the other side of the street, a man came around the corner and started walking toward her – a man she recognized. He was in his sixties, wore a dark blue sweatshirt, tan slacks, and gray sneakers. He was clean-shaven and, with the exception of some gray hair on the back of his head, bald. At first he showed no sign of recognizing Sierra, and she began to think that he'd pass by without stopping. But then his eyes locked onto her and a broad smile stretched across his face.

"Sierra! What a pleasant surprise!"

She stopped in front of the man and returned his smile, although hers was more subdued.

"Hi, Mr. Kovach."

The man frowned, but not in an unfriendly way.

"Call me Randall. You've been an adult too long to keep calling me Mr. Kovach."

"Old habits are hard to break, I guess."

Randall and his wife lived across the street from her parents, and while the couples weren't exactly friends, they knew one another well enough to exchange pleasantries and make small talk every once in a while. Sierra had known the Kovachs her entire life. Their children had been too old for her to play with, but their daughter had babysat her when her parents went out on date nights. Randall was retired, although Sierra couldn't remember from what profession. He'd worked in an office somewhere, she thought, but that didn't exactly narrow it down much. As far as she knew, Randall had generally been in good health, but his skin had a slight yellowish cast to it that made it seem as if he were suffering from jaundice. But since he always looked like this, she figured it was normal for him, although it still struck her as odd every time she saw him.

"I take it you're not teaching at the college today?" Randall said.

"I teach a class there at noon on Mondays and Wednesdays.

I teach at ArtWorks mornings and afternoons." Even though Randall knew about the gallery, Sierra hooked a thumb in its direction.

"Keeping busy," Randall said approvingly. "That's why I'm here too. Trying to keep busy and make the world a better place in my own little way."

Before she could stop him, he reached into his pants pocket and pulled out a penny. The front side of the coin had been covered with a raised sticker of a yellow smiley face. He held it up so the face was pointed at Sierra.

"Chuck says have a nice day."

Sierra smiled weakly as she took the penny.

"Thanks."

For as long as she could remember, Randall had been making and giving out 'Chucks' to everyone he met, especially children. She didn't know where he'd gotten the idea or why he called them Chucks, but he claimed he did it to bring a little cheer to people's days. Sierra had always found it more than a little creepy, and as she'd gotten older, she wondered if Randall might be a pedophile and the Chucks were his way of approaching children. But he'd never done or said anything inappropriate to her, or as far as she knew to any other kid in the neighborhood. In the end she'd decided Randall wasn't dangerous, just weird.

She dropped the Chuck into her bag and was about to take her leave of Randall, when he said, "I was thinking of stopping by the gallery today and passing out some Chucks to the children. Do you think that would be okay?"

Since school was in session, the morning and early afternoon classes at ArtWorks consisted of preschool-age children and homeschooled children whose parents brought them to the gallery for their art requirement. Sierra doubted the parents would be thrilled to learn an older man was walking around the gallery passing out smiley faces stuck to pennies.

"I'm afraid that's not a good idea," she said. "We aren't supposed to have visitors during classes unless they're immediate family. Sorry."

Randall had kept a smile on his face the entire time they'd been talking, but now his smile fell away and his brow furrowed into a frown. She thought he was going to challenge her, maybe accuse her of making up that policy on the spot, which she had. But his brow smoothed and his smile returned, although not as broad as before.

"It's a shame that a silly rule can prevent children from experiencing a little bit of joy in the course of their day, but I suppose there's nothing to be done about it." His smile hardened a touch more. "It was good seeing you, Sierra. Give my best to your parents when you see them."

He continued down the sidewalk then, no doubt in search of more Chuck recipients.

Sierra was about to cross the street when Randall stopped and turned around to face her once more.

"I almost forgot! I know today's the anniversary of Jeffrey's accident. I went by the cemetery earlier and put a Chuck on his headstone. I used a sticky pad on the back to hold it in place. My version of leaving flowers, I guess."

She knew that Randall had meant this as a gesture of kindness and respect, but after the morning she'd had so far, the thought of one of Randall's dumbass Chucks on her brother's headstone infuriated her.

"Jeffrey didn't like your Chucks," she said. "I don't like them either, and I don't know anyone who does. You're not making people feel better. You're not brightening their day. All you do is creep them out and make them feel sorry for you!"

Randall's face widened in shock, as if she'd struck him a physical blow. When she saw his reaction, she instantly regretted her words. She wanted to go to him, to apologize and tell him that she'd had a terrible morning so far and she shouldn't have taken out her frustrations on him. But she was also angry at him for defiling her brother's grave, even in such a small fashion. So instead of apologizing, she turned and started across the street, and she didn't look back.

★ ★ ★

Randall watched Sierra hurry across the street and go inside ArtWorks. He remembered when the building had housed the unimaginatively named Office Supplies and More!, complete with exclamation point, as if that would somehow lure more customers. Now, the outside of the building was covered with artwork created by the gallery's students – images of people and animals, along with abstract designs and psychedelic splashes of color. It looked to Randall like a bunch of amateurish graffiti, and he thought it an ugly addition to the Historic District's ambience, such as it was.

He had been hurt by Sierra's words, mostly because he feared they were true. But he'd also been angered by them. What was so wrong about trying to make the world a brighter place, about literally giving people smiles? Sure, some people probably thought he was a bit eccentric for passing out his Chucks, but he believed there were just as many – if not more – who appreciated his small gesture of kindness. If you greeted someone with a smile and a kind word or two, the effect was temporary, the incident soon fading from their memory. But a Chuck lasted. You could keep it in your pocket and take it out and look at it whenever you needed to see a smile, even if it was an artificial one. You could leave it on your kitchen counter or maybe a dresser, somewhere you could see it a few times during the course of your day. So yeah, maybe he wasn't curing cancer or creating world peace, but that didn't make what he did any less meaningful.

He'd never really liked the Sowells or their children. They didn't attend a church, didn't decorate their house for the holidays, considered themselves independent voters, and always let their grass grow too high before finally getting around to mowing it. They didn't make any *commitments*, didn't uphold any *standards*. And as far as he was concerned, that made them bad neighbors, which to his mind was just about the worst thing you could be. As Sierra and Jeffrey had grown up, he'd hoped they wouldn't turn out like their parents, that maybe they would learn to take more pride in themselves and their community. But of course, they hadn't. The acorn didn't fall far from the tree, as the saying went. He shouldn't have visited Jeffrey's grave earlier. It had been a waste of a good Chuck.

Enough brooding. He'd come here this morning to spread some happiness, and that's exactly what he would do.

He reached into his pocket, clutched the Chucks in there as if for reassurance, and then continued down the sidewalk. The next person he encountered would receive the biggest smile that he was capable of, and he might even give them *two* Chucks.

★ ★ ★

Sierra walked into ArtWorks at 8:43, and Karolyn Cho – who stood by the door to greet parents and children as they arrived – gave her a smile. But the smile quickly faded when she registered Sierra's expression.

"I take it you haven't had the best of mornings," Karolyn said. "Is it because of Jeffrey?"

"Partly. It's also because there are a lot of assholes in the world."

Karolyn laughed, then quickly glanced over her shoulder. Sierra followed the direction of her gaze and saw that one of her students – a four-year-old boy named Joshua Phelps – was sitting at a table, drawing with crayons. Joshua's mom always dropped him off early. Most parents seemed to understand that ArtWorks was a school and not day care, but there were some who never seemed to get the message, and Joshua's mother was one of them.

Karolyn was the owner and director of ArtWorks. She was an Asian woman in her forties who'd taught art in elementary school before quitting to start her own business. She'd gotten tired of the administrative bullshit and wanted to open her own school focused entirely on student learning. Karolyn had been as surprised as anyone when ArtWorks not only remained in business but flourished. The students ranged from preschool to APA high school students looking to build a strong portfolio before applying to college art programs. Karolyn employed several artists to teach part-time at ArtWorks, Sierra included, and it was a wonderful place to work. The main level was a single large open space, with long tables set up for students to work at. There were cabinets for supplies and a couple sinks to wash paint off hands and brushes, and student artwork decorated the place. Wherever you looked, you could see drawings, paintings, charcoal sketches, papier-mâché sculptures, hanging mobiles, and pottery. Most were crude beginners' work, but some of the pieces were quite sophisticated and polished. There was a space on one wall for faculty work, so parents and students could see that the teachers at ArtWorks were artists in their own right. A few of Sierra's watercolor paintings hung there. Perhaps not her best work, but they were decent efforts and she wasn't ashamed of them.

Karolyn always dressed like a working artist – large button shirt over a tank top, faded jeans, and old sneakers decorated with pen drawings. She wore no jewelry and no makeup, but Sierra thought she didn't need them. She was beautiful as she was, and makeup would only detract from her natural beauty, not enhance it.

"Want to tell me about it?" Karolyn asked.

Some people offered to listen only out of politeness. They didn't really want to hear what was bothering you. But not Karloyn. If you had a problem, she was always ready to listen and help any way she could. She'd been a huge support for Sierra after Jeffrey's death, in many ways her strongest support, more so even than her parents, who'd had their own grieving to do. Sierra had loved the woman before that, but now she absolutely adored her.

"Maybe later. I think right now I just want to get to work and let the kids take my mind off things."

Karolyn smiled. "That's one of the secret perks of teaching: free therapy."

Sierra laughed then headed over to Joshua to greet the boy, take a look at what he was drawing, and tell him he was doing a good job, even if he wasn't. Especially if he wasn't. At his age, art was more about building self-confidence and strengthening hand-eye coordination than it was about wowing critics – which was what she liked so much about working with this age group.

Joshua looked up as she approached, grinned, then held up his drawing for inspection. It was a riot of color with no discernible form.

"It's a rocket ship!" Joshua said proudly.

Sierra could feel the tension that had built up inside her this morning begin to drain away.

"And a fine one it is," she said.

★ ★ ★

By 9:20, all the children in her class were sitting at their tables and working. There were ten of them, six girls and four boys, and they were all on task. Today's lesson was drawing basic shapes – circles, squares, rectangles, and triangles. She'd given the kids worksheets with the shapes printed on them, and the students were supposed to draw the appropriate shape on the space beneath the example. It was an exercise older children could do easily, but it could be quite a challenge when you had the fine motor skills of a four-year-old. Most of the students gamely soldiered on, even if their efforts bore only a marginal resemblance to the models. But Eleanor Ramos was becoming increasingly frustrated. She'd already crumpled up two exercise sheets, and from the angry look on her face, the girl was getting ready to wad up sheet number three.

Sierra started toward Eleanor, hoping to calm the child, when she heard tapping on glass. The building had two large picture windows flanking the entrance, and when Sierra turned in the direction of the sound, she saw someone standing at the left window, looking in. People often stopped to watch classes work for a while. Karolyn thought that was a good thing. Not only did it contribute to the town's culture – if only in a small way – she thought it was free advertising. Sierra was more leery of observers, worrying that some of them might be pedophiles who viewed ArtWorks almost like a pet store with cute little ones encased behind glass, just waiting for the right person to come along and claim them.

So when she saw the man standing at the window, her first reaction was to think the school had drawn the attention of another freak. The man's hair was mussed, as if he'd been hit by a wild wind and failed to comb it afterward. His clothes were filthy, splotched with dark stains that looked like mud. *Or maybe blood*, she thought. His skin had a sickly grayish tinge, and the flesh around his eyes was bruised and puffy. She didn't recognize him at first, but then he smiled, the right corner rising slightly higher than the left, and she knew who he was.

Jeffrey.

Her breath caught in her throat, and a cold numbness spread over her body. She didn't tell herself that she was hallucinating, nor did she try to convince herself that she'd never actually gotten up this morning, that she was still in bed, asleep and dreaming. She knew what she was seeing was real, knew it was Jeffrey. This knowledge wasn't rational. It came from a place within her that was deeper than thought, deeper than feeling. She couldn't name this place, was only dimly aware of it within her, but she knew it spoke the truth when it told her the disheveled-looking man at the window was her brother, somehow come back to her.

Jeffrey gave her a quick wave, and then he turned and continued on down the sidewalk. For a moment, she thought he might enter ArtWorks, but when he didn't, she ran from the table – startling the children – and toward the door. Karolyn was giving a mother and prospective student a tour of the place. She was on the other side of the building, but she saw Sierra run outside. She called out something, but the door swung shut before Sierra could make out what it was. Not that it mattered. Right then, her entire focus was on something that couldn't be possible yet somehow was. Her brother was back.

She glanced right then left and caught sight of Jeffrey turning the corner. Just before he disappeared from view, he reached out and brushed the tips of his fingers against ArtWork's brick wall. Sierra ran after him, dodging the few pedestrians who were out this morning with *excuse me*'s and *I'm sorry*'s. As she neared the corner, her shoulder clipped an elderly woman with a walker, and the woman tripped and fell to the sidewalk, her walker following her down. Sierra didn't register what had happened right away, so focused was she on reaching her brother. She ran several more steps before she realized what she'd done. Part of her – a very large part – wanted to leave the old woman to fend for herself. If she couldn't manage to get up on her own, someone would be along soon to help her. And if she was injured, they'd make sure she got medical attention too. There was no reason for Sierra to stop, and certainly no reason for her to go back and check on the woman. She'd seen her brother, for godsakes! Her *brother*!

But her confidence in her perceptions – so strong at first – began to wane. She'd seen Jeffrey's body at his viewing and funeral. She knew he was dead. She didn't believe in ghosts, nor did she believe in any sort of afterlife, at least not the kind where people retained their consciousness and memories of their earthly lives. She was more of an everyone's-energy-returns-to-the-source kind of gal. It was only natural that she should mistake someone with a general physical resemblance to her brother for him, especially on this day. And she couldn't in good conscience ignore the old woman when she'd been the one to cause her to fall. So she stopped, less than three feet from the corner, turned around, and hurried back to the woman who was struggling to stand.

* * *

The woman was as sweet as she could be to Sierra, and she apologized to the younger woman for getting in her way. This of course made Sierra feel like shit, and once she determined the woman hadn't been injured during her fall and her walker was still in good condition, Sierra offered to accompany her to make sure she arrived at her destination safely. The woman thanked Sierra for her kindness – making her feel even worse for knocking her on her ass – but she said she'd be fine. Her doctor wanted her to get out and take some exercise every day. She only lived a couple blocks from the Historic District, and she carried a cell phone to call her daughter if she needed any help. And then the woman continued down the sidewalk, moving at a slow, deliberate pace.

Sierra thought about catching up to the old woman and insisting she allow her to walk her home, but now that she'd established the woman was all right, her thoughts turned back to her brother. She still believed she'd mistaken someone else for him, and she knew she needed to get back to her class. She'd run out on them without explanation, and she'd already been gone for too long. Karolyn was undoubtedly tending to the children until she returned, but

Karolyn was likely upset that Sierra had flaked out on her while she was showing a prospective student and his mother around. And if by some miracle it *had* been Jeffrey at the window, he would never smile, wave, and go on his way. He'd want to see her again as much as she wanted to see him. Wouldn't he? A thought whispered through her mind then. *Who knows what the dead want?* It was a disturbing notion, and she put it aside. She knew that if she didn't at least look around the corner now, it would bother her for the rest of the day.

Just a quick peek, she told herself.

She walked to the corner, more slowly this time, but when she got there, she hesitated. She told herself she was being foolish. Whoever it was she'd mistaken for Jeffrey, he would be long gone by now. Still, she couldn't help feeling that when she turned the corner, the man who looked too much like her dead brother would be standing there waiting for her, mouth stretched into a mirthless smile.

She turned the corner.

The sidewalk was empty.

An unpleasant odor hung in the air, the smell of trash that had been left out to rot in the summer sun. She wrinkled her nose in disgust and wondered if something was wrong with the sewers in the district. They were as old as the rest of the area and most likely needed some serious repairs. She forgot about the smell and looked around, checking to see if the Jeffrey lookalike had crossed to the other side of the street. There were a few people over there, senior citizens mostly, but no Jeffrey clone. She hadn't really expected anything else, but she still felt disappointed as she walked back around the corner, intending to return to her class. But as she walked by the place where the man she'd followed had touched the brick wall, something caught her eye, and she stopped to examine it. The spot where the man's fingers had brushed the wall was soft and crumbling, more like grayish sandstone than brick. There were five lines, one for each finger, each line no more than three inches long.

She stepped closer to the lines to get a better look at them. She reached out to touch one of the lines, but then she quickly drew back her hand, as if she was afraid the crumbling brick was toxic and touching it would hurt her somehow. But she told herself not to be so stupid, and instead of merely touching a single line, she put all five of her fingers in the lines and traced their path. She didn't know what she'd expected to feel. Some kind of psychic connection to the man who'd touched the wall? A sense that something strange had happened here, that the laws of nature had been violated? That the man's touch had somehow altered the substance of the brick, had aged it?

Whatever she thought she'd learn by touching the lines, all she succeeded in doing was dislodging more of the powdery gray substance, which drifted down to the sidewalk. She'd never noticed any other places like this on ArtWorks' outer walls, but then it wasn't as if she'd conducted a thorough examination of every brick that had been used in its construction. There were probably other areas, and she simply hadn't noticed them before. And the man hadn't created these lines. They'd already been here, and when he'd noticed them, he'd run his fingers across them, just as she'd done now. A simple explanation for a simple event that her imagination had blown out of proportion.

Satisfied that she'd solved this little mystery, she started to head for ArtWorks' entrance, when one more thing drew her gaze. Next to the lines, so small that she hadn't noticed them at first, were two words etched into the bricks' powdery surface.

HI SIS

⋆ ⋆ ⋆

Corliss stood across the street from ArtWorks. When Jeffrey had first approached the building, Corliss had been curious whether the man would go inside or walk on past without recognizing the place where his sister worked. But Jeffrey had split the difference. He'd stopped at one of the front windows, waved to his sister, perhaps with only the dimmest recollection of who she was, then continued on his way. When Sierra ran out of ArtWorks a moment later in search of her dead brother, Corliss had smiled. He couldn't have orchestrated the encounter better if he'd tried.

He now watched Sierra as she read the tiny message her brother had left for her. How would she react? Would she stand and stare, unable to make herself believe what she was seeing? Would she try to rub out the letters in an attempt to deny their existence? Or would she let out a noise – anything from a squeak or a soft moan up to a full-throated scream? She did none of those things, though. After a moment, she turned, walked back to the building's entrance, and stepped inside.

Interesting, Corliss thought.

He would've loved to remain and observe Sierra more, but he had work to do elsewhere. That was all right, though. He knew he'd be seeing her again soon enough.

He'd followed Jeffrey into town on foot to make sure the resurrected man made it, but he saw no reason to travel like that now, not when he had other, more efficient options available to him. The fingernails on his right hand became ebon claws, and he cut the air with a vicious swipe. He heard a cry of pain in his mind, piercing at first, but it quickly degenerated into a whimper. A rift in reality opened before him, and he could feel unseen energies bleeding from it. He stepped through, pinching the rift closed behind him. No one had seen what he'd done, but the next dozen people who walked through the space where the rift scar hung invisibly in the air would experience the onset of a sudden debilitating migraine that would last for days, the pain so bad that its sufferers would pray for death. Corliss knew about this aftereffect, but not only didn't he care, as far as he was concerned, it was extra added value.

* * *

"I understand," Karolyn said. "But the way you ran outside like that, without saying a word to me or the kids.... It's not like you."

Sierra wanted to tell the woman to mind her own business, but she considered Karolyn a friend as well as a boss. She felt she could tell her something crazy without being judged. Besides, Karolyn had the tenacity of a pit bull. If she thought there was something wrong with someone and she might be able to help, she'd keep bugging you about it until you finally told her what was going on. So Sierra told her about seeing a man at the window who reminded her of Jeffrey and how she had to go outside and see for herself if it was him, even though she knew it was a stupid thing to do. She didn't tell Karolyn about the marks in the brick left by Not-Jeffrey's touch, nor did she tell her about the short message she'd found etched into the brick. *HI SIS.* That was too crazy to tell anyone about. Besides, she didn't want to think about the message and what it might mean.

By the time Sierra had finished, Karolyn and she had slipped all the crayons into boxes and put them back on the storage cubby next to the table.

"So?" Sierra asked. "Think I'm ready to check in to the funny farm?"

"I believe the more politically correct term these days is nuthouse." Karolyn smiled when she said this, but her smile quickly fell away. "If you're asking whether I think mistaking some random guy for your brother means your mental health isn't what it could be, then the answer is no. I think it's only natural for grieving people to think they see and hear their loved ones from time to time. But I *do* think it might not be a bad idea for you to consider going back into therapy." She held up a hand before Sierra could say anything. "You're obviously still hurting, and I think it would help you to have someone to talk to about how you're feeling. Someone who knows what they're doing instead of a busybody like me."

"I tried therapy, and honestly, I don't think it did much for me."

The psychologist she'd seen had been nice enough, but the antidepressant she'd put Sierra on had made her thoughts sluggish, and she felt sleepy all the time. Sierra had quit taking it after a month. She figured she couldn't deal with her emotions if a pill prevented her from experiencing them fully. Although if they made a pill that would remove all her memories of the night Jeffrey died, she'd be tempted to take it. Jeffrey had had a fight with his boyfriend that evening, and he'd called her to have someone to commiserate with him. She'd tried at first, but she'd never liked Marc Naranjo. He was an okay guy, she supposed, but he hadn't been a good match for her big brother. Jeffrey was laidback and easygoing, while Marc was nervous and high-strung. He was insecure too, so he could get jealous whenever Jeffrey looked at another man – or another woman, for that matter. That's what they'd fought about that night. Jeffrey was friends with one of his coworkers, a woman named Vicki Washington. Vicki loved mock-flirting with Jeffrey, and he loved their playful back-and-forth banter. Marc *hated* the way Vicki acted, and no matter how many times Jeffrey told him it was all in good fun, that Vicki felt safe to flirt with and tease him *because* he was gay, Marc remained jealous of her. That evening Jeffrey and Marc had gone out for dinner, and during their meal, Vicki texted Jeffrey a picture of herself in some sexy lingerie she'd recently bought and wanted his opinion on how she looked. When Marc asked Jeffrey who'd texted him, Jeffrey – naively, in Sierra's opinion – showed Vicki's photo to Marc. Predictably, Marc lost his shit and started yelling at Jeffrey right there in the restaurant, accusing him of being a liar, unfaithful, and a closet hetero. Jeffrey had fled the restaurant in tears, got into his pickup, and drove off into an oncoming storm.

As much as Sierra hated Marc for driving Jeffrey out into the storm that night, she hated herself even more for how she'd reacted when her brother called her. He'd been looking for support, and all she'd done was take his call as another opportunity to criticize his boyfriend. Not only had she not helped him, she'd made things worse. She was as much to blame for his death as Marc, or even Courtney Marsh. More so, because she was Jeffrey's sister and she should've been there when he needed her, and she wasn't.

She hadn't seen Marc since Jeffrey's funeral, and they'd made sure to stay away from each other then. Despite her feelings toward Marc, she wondered how he was doing today. Did he feel guilt for his role in Jeffrey's death? Or had he moved on and was now dating someone else, her brother just another name in his sexual history? She wondered what Marc would say if she told him she'd seen Jeffrey this morning, alive, and that he'd left a message for her carved in brick. She was surprised to find herself tempted to call him. Yes, they hated each other's guts, but they shared a common bond in Jeffrey. If there was anyone in the world who could understand her guilt and grief, it would be Marc. It was a laughable idea, though, and she immediately dismissed it.

"Do you know what still bothers me now, a year later?" Sierra asked.

Karolyn shook her head.

"Why do bad things happen? Especially to good people like my brother. What's the point of doing anything when your life can be snuffed out in an instant? How can you enjoy anything when Time steals it from you as soon as it's given to you? What's the point of continuing with life, with going forward?"

Sierra hadn't intended to dump so much on Karolyn, but once she started, she'd been unable to stop herself.

Karolyn looked at her, stunned, her gaze filled with sympathy and concern. She looked as if she was struggling to come up with a response, but before she could speak, the front door opened, and a father came in with his young daughter. It was time for Sierra to play teacher again.

Karolyn gave her a sad, understanding smile, gave her arm a long squeeze, and then moved off so Sierra could go greet her student. Sierra put a smile on her face that she hoped didn't look as fake as it felt and walked toward the father and daughter.

"Hi, Lindsey! How are you today?"

CHAPTER FOUR

Grace sat on her couch, staring at a blank TV screen – the cable had been cut off last week – and sipped slowly on the dregs of a bottle of Old Crow she'd found hidden in the cabinet beneath her bathroom sink. She had no memory of putting it there, but she was glad she had. It was always good to have a little put aside for emergencies.

As she drank, she fumed about Sierra. She had no idea why the ungrateful bitch had stolen her purse. It wasn't like she had anything in there anyone could want. If she'd had any money, her total liquor supply wouldn't have consisted of one almost-empty bottle of bourbon, which was rapidly on its way to becoming completely empty.

"She did it to fuck with you," she muttered. "That's all. Did it out of sheer fucking malice."

But now that she'd gotten some alcohol in her system, her throbbing headache had subsided from agonizingly intolerable to uncomfortably distracting. A big improvement as far as she was concerned. With the reduction in pain came an increase in mental clarity – a little, anyway – and she wondered if her purse wasn't somewhere in her apartment after all. She hadn't found it when she was searching her apartment looking for booze this morning, but the way her head had been hurting, she might've overlooked her purse. It was possible, wasn't it? And even if she had seen it, that didn't mean she'd remember it. Her memory wasn't so great these days. Not that she was getting old. She night not be as young and pretty as she once was, but she was hardly a decrepit hag. If she were being honest with herself, that was one of the reasons she hated Sierra so much. She hated her youth, health, and most of all the possibilities that lay before her. Career, husband, children…or maybe travel to interesting places where she would do interesting things. Whatever Sierra might want from life, she had time to go for it, time to make as many of her dreams come true as she possibly could. Time to avoid ending up (almost) old, unwanted, unloved, and poor.

Grace tried to take another sip of bourbon and found the bottle empty.

"Fuck!"

She hurled the bottle at the widescreen TV on the wall. There wasn't much strength behind the throw, and while the bottle cracked the screen, neither shattered. The TV remained attached to the wall, and the bottle *thunk*ed to the carpet.

She glanced at the empty bottle, and an awful realization hit her: she was out of alcohol. She had nothing to drink in her apartment and there was no one she could borrow money from. Her kids wouldn't give her any – the little traitors – and asking her ex was out of the question. Not only would he turn her down, she'd have to listen to him lecture her about getting help for her 'problems'. No fucking thanks. Sierra was out, and of the two units on the second floor, one was empty, and the other was home to a single mother who was almost as poor as Grace. She didn't know anyone else in the complex, and of the friends and coworkers she'd once had, none of them would speak to her anymore after her repeated attempts to get money from them.

She felt the first fluttery stirrings of panic in her chest, and her headache began to worsen once more. She got off the couch and began searching frantically through her apartment with a thoroughness that would've impressed a seasoned crime-scene investigator. She found plenty of empty bottles that she hadn't bothered to take to one of the dumpsters on site, but she didn't find any liquor. The Old Crow truly had been the last of her supply. By this point, she was in full panic mode. If she didn't get some more to drink soon, she'd start going into withdrawal, which would be a special kind of hell – one she wanted to avoid at all costs.

She gave up looking for booze and began searching for money to *buy* booze. She checked behind the couch cushions, checked the kitchen and bedroom dresser drawers, checked the pockets of clothes hanging in the bedroom closet, all without luck. But when she checked the coat closet, she discovered a wadded-up ten-dollar bill in the pocket of a raincoat she'd owned before the birth of her first child. She sat on the couch and smoothed the ten on the coffee table, sliding her fingers over the bill gently, almost lovingly. Tears trickled down her careworn cheeks, and she laughed with relieved delight. It was almost enough to make a girl believe in god.

There was a knock at the door then, three sharp raps that made her jump. Her first thought was that someone had come to steal her money. Maybe Sierra, who'd somehow sensed she'd found the ten and had come back from work to take it, just like she'd taken the purse.

Grace was still dressed in her robe and nothing else, otherwise she might've stuffed the ten into her bra. Her robe had pockets, but she didn't feel the money would be safe there. It was the first place someone would expect her to put it. Maybe if she pretended like she wasn't home, whoever it was would—

The knocks came again. Three raps, louder and more insistent this time. Whoever it was at her door was determined to speak with her, it seemed. Maybe so determined that they'd break down her door and.... A horrible thought occurred to her then. Had she remembered to lock the door after her confrontation with Sierra that morning? She looked at the door, and sure enough, it was unlocked. So whoever was there wouldn't need to knock down the door. All they'd have to do was try the knob, and once they discovered the door was open, they would come in and demand she turn over her money.

She couldn't let that happen.

She jumped up from the couch and ran for the kitchen. The throbbing in her head tripled in intensity, became so strong it nearly sent her to the floor. But she grabbed hold of the counter in time to steady herself. She had several cookbooks on the counter, and she grabbed one on making low-carb meals, opened it, and stuck the ten between two pages in the middle of the book. She closed it, put it back with the others, then returned to the living room.

The trio of knocks came again. This time whoever it was pounded on the door, making it shake. Grace stopped in front of the door. Trembling, she made sure her robe was belted securely and ran her hands through her hair in an attempt to make herself at least somewhat presentable. Then she peered through the peephole. She saw a man in a black suit. He had long blond hair and he was smiling. One hand was held behind his back while the other was raised in a fist, ready to pound the door again.

Grace took a deep breath, then, with a trembling hand, opened the door.

"Hello," she said. "Sorry it took me a minute to answer. I was…occupied."

The man's smile widened. His teeth were almost too white, and they all appeared to taper to small sharp points. But as strange as that was, his suit was stranger. She'd never seen a black so, so *deep* before. It looked as if it went on and on forever, and if she reached out to touch it, she thought her hand might keep going and going and….

Without realizing she did so, she raised her right hand and reached toward the man.

But then he brought his own hand from behind his back. He was holding something, and he held it up for her to see. When he did, she forgot all about the endless darkness of the man's suit and focused her entire attention on the object before her. It was an unlabeled glass bottle filled with amber liquid. It was the most beautiful thing she'd ever seen, the color almost unearthly in its perfection. It seemed to glimmer, as if the bottle held light as well as liquid, and she thought she could feel a soft, soothing warmth coming from it. The strange man standing in the hall had ceased to exist for her the moment he'd displayed the bottle, and when he began speaking, it startled her.

"My name is Corliss, and I've brought you a present."

His voice was rich and smooth. He sounded the way bourbon tasted.

She wanted to snatch the bottle from his hand. Her throat was so dry it hurt. She imagined her throat as sun-beaten earth, cracked and desiccated. Within the bottle was the elixir that would take away the pain. *All* of it, physical and emotional. Her fingers twitched, and her hand started to rise, as if working by itself. But something about this wasn't right. She struggled to concentrate, but the pounding in her skull made it so hard to think. Strangers didn't show up on your doorstep at the moment of your greatest need just to give you the one thing in the world you desired above all others.

"Does it really matter how I know what you need, Grace? Isn't it enough that I have it?"

Part of her feared her booze-soaked brain had conjured up a hallucination of a man – a wonderful, generous man – bearing what looked to be the finest bourbon she'd ever seen. Another part said she shouldn't look a gift horse in the mouth and told the first part to shut the fuck up, which it promptly did.

"Thank you." The words came out in an almost unintelligible croak, but Corliss didn't seem to notice, or if he did, he didn't care.

He handed the bottle to her, and when her flesh came into contact with it, she gasped. It was warm, and the glass seemed to mold itself to her hand, as if the one had been made for the other. She pressed the bottle to her chest gently, as if it were a newborn baby. The heat radiated by its contents warmed her, and even though she had yet to drink a single drop, her headache began to diminish, and her body ceased trembling.

"Drink it in good health," Corliss said. He bowed his head in a courtly gesture of farewell, turned, and walked away. Grace stuck her head out into the hall to watch him leave, but he was already gone. She hadn't heard the outer door open and close, though. Maybe she'd been so distracted by the strange man's gift that she hadn't been listening closely enough when he'd exited the building. Sure, that's what had happened. She pulled her head back into her apartment, and if as she did she saw an odd blurry line in the hallway like a scar in the air, she dismissed it as a trick of the light. She would never know, but the next time the mail carrier came, he would pass through the rift scar, and benign tumors would begin growing in his lungs. No surgery would be able to remove them completely, and they would continue to regrow until eventually the man was unable to breathe and suffocated.

Grace quickly closed the door and locked it, as if Corliss might change his mind and return for the bottle.

She walked to the kitchen, her gaze fastened on the bottle the entire way. She set it down on the counter and examined it more closely. It had a simple black plastic cap and no seal. She ran her fingers across the glass. It was smooth, without any indication it had once borne a label that had been removed. The woman she had been not so long ago – a woman whose higher brain functions had been more reliable – would've had serious misgivings about this 'gift'. Just because it looked like there was bourbon in this suspiciously unmarked bottle didn't make it so. There could be any number of substances in there...*poisonous* ones. Corliss could be some kind of weird serial killer who poisoned his victims by giving them what appeared to be a bottle of free booze. She should pour this shit down the drain, or better yet, call the cops and have them remove the bottle from her apartment and take it somewhere for testing. Maybe she'd end up being the one who provided the evidence the police needed to catch Corliss.

But she wasn't that woman anymore. She was an addict, and all that mattered was the mere possibility that the bottle contained what she needed. Every other concern, even the fact that she might well be risking her life by drinking the amber liquid, simply didn't matter. She removed the cap from the bottle and placed it on the counter. She then lifted the bottle to her nose and inhaled. She had never smelled anything sweeter. The odor was potent enough to give her a little buzz all by itself, and her stomach cramped painfully, as if demanding she sample the liquid *now*. She placed the bottle to her lips, tilted it, and got her first taste of the contents.

Her mouth exploded with sensations more intense than any she had ever known. It was beyond the finest food, the best sex, and even the most expensive liquor that she'd ever had. She had no idea the human body was capable of experiencing anything even close to this level of stimulation. It was so overwhelming that for a moment she thought she might actually lose consciousness, and she gripped the kitchen counter with her free hand to steady herself.

And then she swallowed.

It burned all the way down, and when it hit her belly it erupted into a blazing mass of flame. It hurt, but it was a *good* hurt, a fucking *fantastic* hurt, and she needed more, needed it *all*. She tilted her head back and drew swallow after swallow from the bottle, taking in great gulps of the amber liquid, one after the other until the bottle was empty.

She pulled the bottle from her mouth and held it out so she could inspect it. She'd sucked it bone dry. There wasn't a single drop remaining. Disappointed, she put the empty bottle on the counter. She felt amazing, better than she had in decades. She felt so good that she considered going into the bedroom, taking her vibrator from her nightstand drawer, and making herself come. As great as she felt right now, her climax would be *incredible*!

But before she could move, her mouth became suddenly, horribly dry. It felt like the flesh inside her cheeks had turned to puckered leather, and her tongue had shriveled into a hard nub. Her throat felt choked with sand, and her skin drew taut on her bones, became brittle and cracked in numerous places. No blood seeped from these wounds, though. She no longer had any moisture to spare. Her eyes became hard balls resting in dry sockets, and her breathing became a labored wheeze. She was so thirsty, she thought she could turn on the kitchen faucet, put her mouth to the tap, start drinking and keep on drinking until her stomach burst. And even then she would still be thirsty. She didn't turn on the water, though. She was thirsty, desperately, maddeningly so, but not for water. Despite this, she felt energized. She felt *strong*. She needed more booze, needed it *now*, and she intended to get it.

She snatched the ten-dollar bill she'd hidden in the cookbook with clawlike hands with hard, prominent knuckles. Now all she needed to do was grab her keys. She always left them on the kitchen counter, and that's where she found them. At least Sierra hadn't stolen them too.

Keys in hand, she grinned, dry lips splitting and cracking.

Time for a booze run.

★ ★ ★

Marc Naranjo slowed as the traffic light turned yellow. There was no one ahead of him, and while his Honda Civic wasn't exactly a sports car, he knew he could make it through the intersection. But he removed his foot from the gas pedal and pressed the brake. His car slowed and came to stop just as the light turned red.

Marc worked for Strategic Insurance, and he was on his way to meet a client for breakfast. Selling insurance didn't make him any more cautious than the average person, although he did have a better idea of what the odds were when it came to taking risks, which could be a real downer sometimes. But that wasn't the reason for his caution now. This was the one-year anniversary of Jeffrey's death, and while Marc hadn't been present at the accident scene, he'd gone to the police station afterward to see Jeffrey's pickup. Why he'd done this, he wasn't sure. Maybe to convince himself that Jeffrey's death was real and not some sick joke. Maybe just to feel close to him one last time. They shared their first kiss in the vehicle, when Jeffrey had given him a ride home from a mutual friend's backyard barbecue. As soon as he saw the twisted hunk of metal that had been his love's truck, he regretted his decision to view it. All he could think about was the vehicle swerving off the road, flying through the air, hitting the ground and rolling, tossing Jeffrey around so violently that his head had been crushed and his neck broken. One of the EMTs on the scene was a client of Marc's, and he'd told him that given his injuries, Jeffrey had died immediately.

He was dead before he knew what was happening, she'd said. *If that's any comfort.*

It was, but not much.

So on this day, Marc was going to be the world's safest driver. Not because he was superstitious and thought it would be bad luck to drive recklessly, but because he couldn't get the image of the mangled truck out of his mind.

Jeffrey's loss didn't hurt the same way it had when it was fresh, but the pain hadn't gone away. It had merely changed, become less raw but much deeper. It was a part of who he was now, and he knew he'd never be rid of it, not entirely. And that was okay. In a way, it meant Jeffrey would always be part of him.

He'd tried dating a couple times over the last few months, had even slept with one of the guys. Just once. But he'd realized he wasn't ready to date yet. He had no idea when he'd be ready for a relationship again, and that was okay too. So long as he was being true to his feelings, everything would—

His thoughts slammed to a halt when he saw a man walking down the sidewalk, heading in the opposite direction. Marc was in what he thought of as Bishop Hill's slice of Generica: mazes of strip malls containing small shops and restaurants, all crowded together in an indistinguishable mass of colorful signs and company logos. The majority of Bishop Hill's residents regarded this area as downtown, although technically it wasn't. The Historic District was downtown, and it was located several blocks south of here. There weren't as many pedestrians here as in the Historic District. Traffic moved at a faster clip, and the sidewalks were too close to the street for most people's comfort. But there were always a few who didn't mind vehicles zipping past them only a few feet away, and one of these people walking by looked like Jeffrey. So much so that when Marc saw him, his breath caught in his throat, and he felt a stab of anguish that hurt as much as any physical pain. Unbidden, the argument they'd had in the restaurant the night Jeffrey died replayed in his mind.

You're being ridiculous. I love you and only you. I don't care what you have between your legs.... Well, that's not strictly true. I'm quite fond of what's down there. What I mean is that even if I was bi – which I most definitely am not *– I would still choose to be with you because you're an amazing person, and the only one I want to be with.*

That should've been enough, *more* than enough. Marc had known that then, but his emotions often outraced the more rational side of him, especially when he was afraid or insecure.

If you're really a card-carrying queer, then why do you have mostly naked pictures of some skank from your office on your phone? And don't tell me it's not your fault she sends them. You could delete the goddamned things, but you never do. They're still on your phone! All of them! Unless you deleted ones I don't know about...ones that are especially NSFW.

Marc had known there was nothing especially upsetting about Jeffrey keeping the photos of Vicki. He never deleted anything on his phone. Texts, voicemail messages, emails, videos, pictures.... Marc still hadn't been able to keep his mouth shut.

Do you masturbate to Vicki's photos? Do you imagine squeezing her tits, twisting her nipples, slipping a couple fingers up her snatch and wiggling them around?

Jeffrey's face had reddened with anger and embarrassment as Marc ranted on. Jeffrey then fixed his gaze on Marc and spoke in a voice tight with restrained fury.

Sometimes I think Sierra is right about you.

It had been the last thing Jeffrey had said before getting up from the table and leaving the restaurant. Marc had never heard his lover's voice again.

The man on the sidewalk didn't just look like Jeffrey. He moved like him too. Marc would have recognized Jeffrey's slight slump, the loose way he swung his arms, and the surprisingly graceful way he moved his feet anywhere.

A car horn blasted behind Marc, causing him to jump. He looked at his rearview mirror and saw a line of cars had pulled up behind him. The vehicle immediately on his rear was a minivan with a very distressed-looking woman behind the wheel. She laid on the horn again, features scrunched in frustration. He looked forward and saw that the light was green, but he was so stunned by the appearance of the man who couldn't be Jeffrey that for an instant he couldn't remember what a green light meant.

Go, you dumbass, he thought. *Green means go.*

He took his foot off the brake and pressed the gas pedal. His Civic might not have had the acceleration of a sports car, but the vehicle surged forward. Marc forgot about the breakfast meeting with the client. He yanked his steering wheel to the left, intending to do a U-turn in the intersection and follow the Not-Jeffrey. Unfortunately, the oncoming traffic had a green light too, and drivers honked and swerved to avoid hitting him as he whipped around, tires squealing, then raced down the street, scanning the sidewalk for the man who moved exactly like Jeffrey. His rational mind shouted that he was acting like a crazy man, but his emotions paid no attention. He had to find the Not-Jeffrey, had to get close enough to prove that the man wasn't his lover somehow returned to life.

He caught sight of him almost at once. He was walking past a dog-washing place called Shampoodle, and now that Marc was closer, the man looked even more like Jeffrey to him than before. Marc continued on, intending to pull up next to the man, lower the passenger-side window, and call out to get his attention. The man would turn toward him, and once Marc got an up-close look at his features and saw that despite his original impression, the man didn't look a thing like Jeffrey, he could put this incident behind him, chalk it up to unresolved grief, and get on with his day.

He accelerated, but as he did so, a Citation pulled out of an access road between strip malls right in front of him. He slammed on the brakes and barely avoided rear-ending the Citation. Unfortunately, the driver of the Prius behind him wasn't able to react as swiftly and smacked into the rear of Marc's vehicle. Marc's head snapped back then forward, and a bolt of pain shot through his neck. He looked at his rearview and saw the Prius's driver still sitting in her car, hands clutching the steering wheel with white-knuckled grips, eyes wide with shock. She looked unhurt, but at that moment, Marc wouldn't have cared if she was gushing blood from a head wound and screaming in agony. He put his Civic in park, turned off the engine, and got out of the car, wincing as he felt another jolt of pain in his neck.

Probably have whiplash, he thought, but it didn't matter. He had to catch up to Jeffrey.

The driver of the Prius got out of her vehicle and started walking toward Marc, commencing the ritual of the minor car accident – exchanging insurance information and calling their respective insurance companies. As an insurance professional, Marc knew exactly what needed to be done. But he only gave the woman the barest of glances before running toward the sidewalk.

"Hey!" she shouted. "Where the hell are you going?"

He didn't bother replying, barely registered her words. His entire focus was on Jeffrey. His love – or at least someone who resembled his love – was a good fifty feet ahead, glancing in the windows of every store he passed. The man's clothes were dirty, and his complexion had a grayish tint to it. He looked like he needed a shower, a fresh outfit, and a good night's sleep or two. The street here was lined with young elm trees, trunks and branches thin, leaves a light green. The Not-Jeffrey reached out with his left hand as he passed an elm and brushed his fingers against its trunk. He then made an abrupt turn and entered a parking lot.

Marc ran faster, dodging other pedestrians and ignoring the throbbing in his neck. As he drew close to the tree the Not-Jeffrey had touched, his eyes were drawn to a discolored patch of bark. The patch was gray, roughly rectangular in shape, and located on the spot where the Not-Jeffrey's fingers had touched. Despite his urgent need to catch up with the man who looked too much like Jeffrey, the strange discolored section of bark caught his attention, and he stopped to examine it. He'd grown up outside town in a small house in the country. His family hadn't been farmers – his dad was a welder and his mom a checkout clerk at a grocery. But he'd grown up around trees and had spent plenty of time playing in the woods when he'd been a kid, and he'd never seen any kind of tree blight like this. Not only did it look weird, but the longer he stared at it, the more it seemed as if it were spreading in front of his eyes. That couldn't be possible, could it? There was no kind of mold that could spread that swiftly. None that he knew of, anyway. The gray patch was widening, extending outward in all directions. And it had a distinct odor too, a scent like spoiled, rotting meat.

The tree was fine before Jeffrey's touch. There had been no sign of disease on the trunk, Marc was sure of it. But now it was sick and becoming more so with each passing second. If Jeffrey *had* returned to life, maybe he'd brought back a little death with him. The thought chilled Marc, but he told himself to quit being ridiculous – at least any more than he already was. He turned away from the tree and jogged toward the parking lot Jeffrey had entered. The lot was located in front of a number of shops, and at first Marc didn't see the Not-Jeffrey. Had he gone into one of the stores?

But then he saw him on the far side of the lot. He was crouching down, which was why Marc hadn't seen him right away. A woman stood next to him, holding the leash of a white-and-tan pit bull. The woman was petite but fit. She had short blond hair and wore a tank top that said *Cincinnati 10K* on it, black shorts, and running shoes. As Marc started toward them, he heard Jeffrey's voice as he spoke to the woman, and it was that voice – his lover's voice, one which he knew as well as his own – that finally convinced him this man was Jeffrey Sowell, somehow returned to life.

"Your dog is beautiful. What's her name?"

"Stella," the woman said.

"Do you mind if I pet her?"

"Go ahead. She loves to meet new people."

Jeffrey smiled and reached out to touch Stella's head. She wagged her tail when his fingers first touched her, but then her body stiffened and she let out a pained whine. Halfway across the lot, Marc stopped and watched in horror as Stella began to age rapidly. Her body seemed to deflate as her skin drew close to her bones, and her fur turned coarse and white. Her legs trembled then gave out on her, and she fell to the ground, cataract-covered eyes open and unseeing. Stella's dead body then collapsed in a pile of gray dust. Her owner dropped Stella's leash and screamed.

Jeffrey stood.

"It's okay," he said in a soothing voice. "I've given Stella a great gift, and now I'm going to give it to you."

The woman stared at Stella's remains, and she didn't move as Jeffrey stepped forward and gently, almost lovingly, raised his hand and placed his fingers on her cheeks. Like Stella, she stiffened, and her fit body began to wither, losing tone and definition. Her muscles shrank and her skin hung from her skeleton like an empty sack. Her hair whitened and began to fall from her head like drifting autumn leaves. She opened her mouth, most likely to scream again, but when she did, her teeth began to fall out in twos and threes, hitting the ground with *click*s and *clack*s. Then she too disintegrated, her clothes as well, until all that remained of her and her dog were two mounds of gray dust, one slightly larger than the other.

Marc was staring at the twin piles of dust, unable to believe what he'd just seen, when Jeffrey turned to look at him. At first there was no sign of recognition from Jeffrey, but then his eyes lit up and he grinned.

"Marc!" He started walking forward, arms raised, as if he intended to give Marc a great big hug when he reached him. A stink of rot and decay preceded him, the same odor that had clung to the diseased tree, and Marc realized that Jeffrey was the source of the stench.

Marc's paralysis broke then. Without saying a word, he turned and ran for all he was worth.

⋆ ⋆ ⋆

Marc kept looking over his shoulder as he ran, although his sore neck protested every time he did. Each time he expected to see Jeffrey running behind him, arms outstretched, hands reaching to touch him and grant him the same terrible 'gift' he'd bestowed upon Stella and her owner. But each time Marc looked, Jeffrey wasn't there. Marc ran on automatic, and before he realized what he'd done, he'd returned to the scene of the accident he'd been involved in. A police cruiser had pulled up behind the Prius, lights flashing. The officer was standing next to the Prius's driver, who was gesticulating wildly. When she caught sight of Marc, she pointed and said, "There he is!"

Rather than being upset by this, Marc was profoundly grateful to be confronted with a situation so normal after what he'd witnessed. He was also absurdly relieved to see the police officer. Police were armed and could shoot anyone who tried to hurt you. So strong was Marc's relief that he couldn't prevent himself from letting out a strained and not altogether sane giggle.

He walked up to the officer and the woman with a wide smile and spoke in a too-loud, too-cheerful voice.

"Hi! What can I do for the two of you?"

⋆ ⋆ ⋆

Electronics Emporium wasn't as large as some of the big-box stores, but it was large enough. *A medium-box store*, as Stuart sometimes thought. The pay wasn't all that great, and he'd have left by now if it hadn't been for the generous employee discount. He spent a good chunk of his paycheck here every couple weeks, snagging the latest in tech and accessories. His last purchase had been a smart watch, and he liked to move his wrist back and forth to see the way light played across its glass surface. He didn't even have to turn it on. Just knowing he possessed it – that it was *his* – was enough.

The Emporium sold computers, phones, game systems, e-readers, speakers for PCs and gaming, smart TVs, drones.... You name it, the store had it. And if the Emporium had it, Stuart wanted it. He sometimes fantasized about pulling up to the store in the dead of night with a semi, breaking in, loading the store's entire contents into the truck, and driving off. He might've done it too, if he'd thought there was a chance he could get away with it.

This morning, Stuart was working the video games section, and while a lot of the employees loved being stationed here, Stuart would've preferred to be somewhere else. Games wasn't a manager's section. Computers or TVs would've been better. More adult. It was hard to come across as manager material when you were trying to sell games to kids. And who the hell bought video games on a Monday morning anyway?

He stood next to a screen upon which a demo of *Demon Riders* was playing. *Demon Riders* was a video game where players fought demons in hell while riding supercharged motorcycles equipped with various weapons. Stuart had played the game before, and it was okay. There wasn't much to it, really, other than riding around and killing monsters and shit. He preferred more complex games, ones where a certain amount of strategy and puzzle-solving were involved. But *Demon Riders* was a bestseller, so what the hell did he know?

Annoying pop music played over the store's sound system. When he became manager – and had an even larger employee discount – he'd pick the music, and he'd play something better than this crap. Seventies rock, maybe, or Nineties alternative. There were a half dozen other employees on the floor, all standing at their different stations, all wearing black Electronics Emporium polo shirts and jeans. Managers wore suits, though, and the manager on duty this morning, Alton Withrow, wore an ill-fitting blue one, with a light blue shirt, and a pink tie. Alton was short and overweight, and his suit was too tight on him, making him look like too much sausage meat stuffed into a blue cloth casing. And that tie! Pink was not a color that projected strength and inspired confidence. Besides the horrible way he dressed, Alton was too wishy-washy to be an effective manager. He was reluctant to make decisions, and when he finally did make one, he rarely stuck to it. Stuart had no idea how the man had become a manager in the first place. When Stuart was manager, he'd make sure everyone did exactly what they were told, or else. He'd have this goddamned place running as smoothly as his smart watch.

He disliked working Mondays because of how slow it always was, but his conversation with Sierra had put him into an even fouler mood than usual for a Monday. He couldn't stand it when someone else got the last word in, and by hanging up on him, that's exactly what Sierra had done. He knew it would be better if he waited until later to call her. He'd already called her back once after she'd hung up on him. Calling again too soon would make him appear weak and needy. Not in *control.* But the longer he stood there among the game consoles and cartridges without a single customer coming by to distract him, the more he stewed about Sierra. When he was at work, he wore a Bluetooth receiver, as did the other employees. This way, they could answer any calls that came into the store or communicate with each other if need be. They weren't supposed to make personal calls at work, but Alton paid no attention to what they did. When he wasn't wandering around the store doing nothing, he was in his office in the back, watching porn on his computer. Any of the employees could spend the entire day on the phone gabbing with friends, and he'd never know it.

Stuart tried to resist the impulse for several more moments before giving in and calling Sierra. He listened as her phone rang a half dozen times before going to voicemail. As he listened to her outgoing message, he remembered what she'd said to him the night they'd broken up.

You know how people say it's not you, it's me? Well, it's definitely you, Stuart. One hundred fucking percent.

The tone at the end of Sierra's message brought him back to the present.

"You hung up on me. That was rude, Sierra. The least you could do is show me some simple common courtesy. Is that too goddamned much to ask?"

He became aware of a customer approaching him, a tall guy with long blond hair who was dressed like a mortician. Stuart didn't want to be interrupted, and he turned his back on the man, hoping he'd see he was talking on the phone, get the message, and go find someone else to bother.

"This is the problem with you, Sierra. You're too focused on yourself all the time. Yeah, it sucks that your brother died, but you need to get over it. Fuck, you need to get over *yourself!*"

Now that he'd managed to vent some of his anger, he realized that he wasn't doing himself any favors by yelling at Sierra in a phone message. If he hoped to get her to soften her attitude toward him, this sure as hell wasn't the way to go about it. He tried to think of a way he could turn this around and end the message on a more positive – or at least less confrontational – note. But he was silent too long and her phone disconnected.

He wanted to scream. He'd allowed his emotions to get the better of him again, and it was all *her* fault. Why did he let her make him so crazy?

"Why indeed?"

Stuart turned, startled. The man in the black suit had not gone away. Instead, he'd stood there while Stuart had left his ill-conceived message on Sierra's voicemail. The fucker had probably heard every word too. Stuart wanted to tell the sonofabitch to go back to the funeral home, but that wasn't the kind of behavior that got you promoted to manager. So Stuart stuck a smile on his face and said, "Welcome to Electronics Emporium. How can I help you today?"

The man smiled, but his eyes remained dead, like those of a fish that had been out of water too long.

"I'm not here to purchase any particular item. I just thought I'd take a look around and see if anything caught my eye."

Beneath the man's words was a soft, almost inaudible hum, as if electric current flowed through him, and there was something strange about his suit. The more Stuart looked at it, the more he felt his attention drawn by its dark color. It was like looking into the depths of a vast black ocean, and he thought he could dive into it if he wanted and swim downward forever and still never reach the bottom.

"This is interesting."

Before Stuart could react, the man plucked the Bluetooth receiver from his ear and examined it.

"That's, uh, the latest in Bluetooth tech," Stuart said, struggling to pull his attention from the suit and focus it on the man who was wearing it. "It's wireless and hands-free, obviously, has impressive call quality, outstanding noise cancellation, compact size, and great battery life."

The man turned the receiver over in his hands, examining it from all angles, but he made no move to put it on. Maybe he was some kind of a germophobe.

"If you'd like to try one on for size, I can get you one that's never been worn before."

The humming sound Stuart had heard grew louder, and for an instant he thought he saw skeins of electricity dance across the Bluetooth receiver. But then they were gone, along with the humming sound, and Stuart decided he must've imagined both.

"That won't be necessary." The man handed the receiver back to Stuart. Stuart was reluctant to touch it at first, but he took it and, after a moment's hesitation, slipped it back over his left ear.

"I'll think about it," the man said. He then turned and walked directly toward the store's exit. A moment later he was gone.

"*That* was fucking weird," Stuart muttered.

"It certainly was."

The voice in his ear was female, that of an older, poised woman. It had a slightly artificial quality, as if it was being generated by a speech-synthesizing program. Was one of his fellow employees playing a trick on him? He looked around the store, but people were either helping customers or standing around with their thumbs up their asses, looking bored.

"Who is this?" he asked.

"My name is Krista. I'm your new digital assistant. Would you like to upgrade now?"

Stuart looked around once more, but no one was looking in his direction, watching to see how he reacted. If this was a joke, whoever was behind it was playing it real cool. What the hell? After his encounter with the man in the black suit, he could use a distraction. He decided to play along.

"Sure, Krista. Upgrade me."

"Upgrade in progress."

Sudden sharp pain lanced through his left ear. It felt as if someone had heated a metal spike until it was glowing orange and then jammed it into his head. He tried to scream in agony, but what came out of his mouth was a deafening burst of what sounded like static. He could feel tendrils – no, *wires* – extending into his brain, squirming around, searching for the best areas to connect themselves to. He was distantly aware of another pain, this one less intense. It was located in his right wrist, and he looked down to see that his smart watch was sinking into his skin, fusing with his flesh. He reached up to touch the Bluetooth receiver and found that the same thing was happening with it. The device had burrowed into his ear and blended with his body, until it was impossible to say where one began and the other ended.

Fear and revulsion welled up within him, but before his emotions could take him over he heard a soft *click* inside his brain, and then he felt nothing. He'd spent so much of his life struggling with his emotions, with the need to control and the anger that resulted when that need was denied, that this state came as a great relief to him. He still felt pain in his head and wrist as intensely as before, but now it didn't matter to him. Pain was merely a sensation and sensations could be ignored.

"Stuart, are you all right?"

Alton came toward him, a concerned look on the manager's chubby face. Stuart couldn't believe how much sharper his vision had become. Colors were brighter and more vibrant, and he could pick out the smallest details. If he wanted to, he could count the individual pores on Alton's face – a good number of which were clogged with grease and dirt. Stuart saw that everyone else in the store was looking at him, employees and customers alike. He wasn't sure why.

"Your scream alarmed them," Krista said. *"Upgrade complete, by the way."*

Alton had hurried over to Stuart so fast he was out of breath by the time he reached him. One of the shirt buttons over his belly had come undone, exposing a section of pale, jiggling flab. Alton stared at Stuart's face.

"What happened to your eyes? They're all silver."

"Are they?" Stuart said, his voice smooth and evenly modulated. "I'll have to take a look at myself in a mirror."

For a moment, Alton seemed at a loss for words, but then he said, "Something's seriously wrong with you, Stuart. Let's go to the employee lounge. You can lie on the couch and I'll call 911. We'll get you to a hospital where they can help you." From the doubt in the man's voice, it sounded like he wasn't particularly confident about this last part.

"I'm fine," Stuart said. "Better than I've ever been, in fact. But I am going to take the rest of the day off. I need to see my old girlfriend and straighten out a few things with her."

Stuart started to walk toward the exit, but Alton grabbed hold of his upper arm and stopped him.

"I really don't think you should leave."

Alton looked scared, but he didn't release his grip on Stuart's arm, didn't back away. Maybe the man was stronger minded than Stuart had given him credit for.

"Like I said, I'm fine. Let go."

Stuart fixed his gaze on Alton, and however his eyes now appeared, they made Alton go pale. But instead of releasing his grip, his hand tightened.

"Please, Stuart! I'm only trying to help you."

"I already have all the help I need. Her name is Krista."

His watchband had sunken entirely beneath his flesh, but the smart watch's screen remained visible. The screen lit up, and he saw that the display showed different apps than it had before, strange ones that he didn't recognize. One of them was represented by a cartoonish lightning bolt. He was interested to see what it would do.

"Krista, activate lightning."

As soon as he'd spoken the command, every electronic device in the store activated, filling the air with the sounds of humming and whirring, of video-game sound effects and music. The din rose in volume until it was deafening, and then electricity arced from the machines – all of them – and filled the store with a crackling network of miniature lightning. Employees and customers alike were caught in the web of electricity, Alton included. Their eyes rolled white and their bodies shuddered and jerked uncontrollably. No one made a sound as smoke began to curl from their ears and nostrils, and their skin began to blacken and char. Eyes popped like eggs on a too-hot griddle and hot viscous fluid splattered onto their faces. An appalling stench filled the store – the acrid smell of ozone combined with burning human flesh. Before his upgrade, the stink would've cause Stuart to violently empty his stomach, but now it was merely one more detail to note. People's hair began to smoke and then burst into flame.

They look like epileptic angels with halos of fire, Stuart thought. The sight was equally absurd and beautiful.

"That should do it, Krista."

The lightning storm winked out, and all the machines in the store fell silent, screens dark. Without electricity holding them upright, the blackened smoking husks of both the employees and the customers collapsed to the floor.

"That was impressive."

"Thank you. Do you require any further assistance?"

"Start my car, please. I'd like to pay an old friend a visit."

Stuart walked toward the exit, carefully stepping over burned corpses as he went. He was going to have to get a new set of clothes at some point. No way was he getting the smell out of these.

CHAPTER FIVE

Randall had spent the morning walking through the Historic District passing out Chucks. Actually, *trying* to pass them out was more like it. People turned him down as often as not, and those who did take them did so without enthusiasm, as if they were humoring a crazy old man that they wanted to get away from as soon as possible. He considered giving up and heading home, but he made himself a deal. He'd stay out here until lunchtime, and if things didn't get any better, then he'd go home. With that resolved, he looked around for his next Chuck recipient.

He was in luck. Coming down the sidewalk was a young mother pushing a toddler in a stroller. She looked to be in her early to mid-twenties, had blue-dyed hair so short it was nearly a buzz cut, along with tattoos on both arms and a septum ring hanging from her nose. She wore a T-shirt that said *Fuck Fascism* on the front, cut-off jeans shorts, and flip-flops.

Randall pursed his lips in disapproval. He knew it was old-fashioned of him, but he couldn't help viewing tattoos and piercings as something that only low-class people did. And while he was no fan of fascism, he didn't appreciate her shirt either. It wasn't as if he didn't use such words himself from time to time, but he was always careful not to do so in public. He considered this common courtesy. You never knew who might be around and how they'd react to such harsh language.

But what bothered him most about the woman was what she'd done to her child. The little boy in the stroller – at least, he thought it was a boy; it was so hard to tell these days – had a small earring in his right ear. The child couldn't have been more than three, and his parents, assuming Dad was in the picture at all, had decided to violate his flesh. As far as Randall was concerned, if you wanted to alter the body that god had given you, that was your business – once you were eighteen and had the legal right to choose for yourself. But it shouldn't be forced on you, especially when you were as young as this little boy.

Randall seriously considered walking past the woman and child without offering them any Chucks. But then he reminded himself of his purpose. He passed out Chucks to brighten people's days. *All* people, regardless of whether or not he approved of their lifestyle choices. So when they drew close, he stopped, smiled, and removed a Chuck from his pocket. He held it out to the woman, displaying the smiley face, and said, "Chuck is smiling at you."

The woman scowled.

"Get the fuck away from us, freak!"

She pushed the stroller faster, and once she was past him, she threw a glance back over her shoulder to make sure he wasn't following her and her child.

Randall watched them go, still holding onto the Chuck, disappointed. When had the world become so cynical and mean-spirited? Sierra was a perfect example. She used to love getting Chucks when she was a child, but she'd spurned him today, and her words when she had done so hurt him deeply.

You're not making people feel better. You're not brightening their day. All you do is creep them out and make them feel sorry for you!

He'd already retired from his job at the auto plant. Maybe it was time to retire from making Chucks too.

"Pardon me, but I saw you try to give that woman something. Do you mind if I ask you what it is?"

Randall turned to see a most unusual man standing before him. Long blond hair and black suit made of some strange material that hurt to look at, as if his old eyes were having trouble focusing on it.

Another weirdo, he thought. Still, at least the man showed some interest, and he seemed polite enough. He held up the Chuck for the man to see. He briefly explained what it was and why he distributed them.

To his surprise and delight, the man didn't react as if he were some kind of lunatic.

"What a charming idea! Would you mind if I saw it?"

Randall happily handed the Chuck over to the man in the black suit. He regarded the Chuck for a moment, then he lifted his free hand to his mouth. He opened it, showing teeth that were sharper than they should've been, and then he inserted his index finger into his mouth and bit down on it. Randall watched in horrified fascination as blood welled from the finger wound and flowed past the man's lips. The man showed no sign that he felt any pain from his self-inflicted injury. He kept his gaze fixed on Randall's eyes, as if he were enjoying watching his reaction. The man removed his bleeding finger from his mouth and touched it to the Chuck, smearing blood across its face. The man then tossed the Chuck back to Randall, who caught it out of reflex. As soon as the blood-smeared Chuck touched his flesh, he felt a coldness seep into him. It spread rapidly, moving up his arm, down through his torso and legs. It entered his neck and head last, rising slowly, as if he were a hollow vessel being filled with frigid water. At first the sensation of spreading cold alarmed him, but now he felt calm. Not only did he accept what was happening, but he knew it to be right. He was being remade. Just as he changed pennies into Chucks, the coldness was transforming him into something else, something better.

The man in the black suit licked the blood on his lip and chin clean with a tongue that was black and sinuous and far too long to fit in a human mouth. He then licked the blood from his wounded finger, and when he was done, the skin was smooth and unbroken once more.

"That's a neat trick," Randall said. Despite the cold that suffused his body, he felt cheerful, almost giddy. His mouth stretched into a smile that was wider than any he'd ever made before. It hurt at first, but then the flesh relaxed, became more malleable, and his smile stretched even farther.

"Here comes another surprise," the man in the black suit said, nodding toward Randall's hand.

Randall looked down at the bloody Chuck, and as he watched, it twitched and juddered, growing, lengthening.... When it was finished, Randall held a shiny copper knife in his hand, one with a round smiley face on the end of the handle.

"It's beautiful," Randall said, unable to take his eyes off the gleaming object.

"Yes, it is," the man in the black suit agreed. "And so are you."

Randall wasn't sure what the man meant, but then he saw the hand that held the knife begin to take on a yellowish cast, and he felt an itching sensation on the back of his head. An instant later, he felt a tickling on the back of his neck, and he realized the last of his hair had fallen out. This did not disturb him.

"You know," the man in the black suit said, "that woman and her child are still in the vicinity."

Randall's smile – which was already wider than a human mouth should be capable of producing – stretched even more.

"What a splendid idea!"

He curled his fingers around the handle of his new and very special Chuck, turned, and began walking in the direction the tattooed and pierced mother had gone.

* * *

Corliss's smile as he watched Randall depart was nowhere near as large as the man's, but it was a very satisfied one. So far, everything was going according to plan, praise Oblivion. He had only one stop left to make, and then he could relax and allow events to play out as they would. *It's such a blessing to be able to enjoy one's work*, he thought.

He sliced a rift in the air, stepped through, and was gone.

* * *

Olivia Dunn hadn't come to the Historic District to shop. There were some funky stores here that she thought were cool, but right now she didn't have money to spend on non-necessities. She was here because Joey had kept her up half the night. She was exhausted and desperate to get some sleep. Joey had a lot of food allergies, just like his father, and they were still learning what was safe for him to eat and what wasn't. Last night she'd made pizza for dinner, with pepperoni and extra mushrooms, just the way her boyfriend liked it. Joey had been suspicious of the mushrooms at first, but after he tried one, he decided he liked them and ate two pieces of pizza. He'd gotten up around midnight, complaining that his belly hurt, and proceeded to vomit and shit profusely for the next several hours. Olivia had finally gotten him settled around four, and she then began cleaning up the various messes Joey had made during his bout of mushroom-poisoning. Carl – her current boyfriend, but not Joey's father – had slept through it all, which was typical of him. Olivia was a light sleeper herself, and was jealous of Carl's ability to sleep through just about anything. She'd been up since midnight and was so tired she could barely see straight.

Joey had woken up at six, after having slept only a couple hours. She knew that if he didn't get more sleep he'd be hell to deal with all day. Her too, for that matter. That's why she'd brought him here. Fresh air always made him sleepy, as did riding in the stroller. But for some reason, the Historic District put him to sleep better than anyplace else she took him. Car rides didn't make him sleepy. He was too interested in looking out the window at everything they passed. And if she walked him in a quiet suburban neighborhood, he became even more alert than when they'd arrived. She figured it was too quiet for him there. She and Carl had an apartment in the part of town where all the strip malls and restaurants were, and there was always a certain amount of noise there – traffic outside, people in neighboring apartments or in the hall. The Historic District was a perfect balance of all the things Joey needed to relax. There were interesting things to look at, but not too many. There was activity and noise – pedestrians and traffic – but not too much of either. So when she *really* needed Joey to go down for a nap, she brought him here and walked him around for a while. It usually didn't take long, maybe fifteen to thirty minutes, and once he was asleep, he'd stay that way during the ride home, and he wouldn't so much as stir when she carried him upstairs to their apartment and put him to bed. He would sleep soundly afterward, giving Olivia a chance to do her homework for her online courses at Riverbank Community College. She was just taking general education courses for now, but she was thinking about eventually majoring in nursing.

No homework for her today, though. Once Joey was in bed and snoozing, she planned to do the same. If she had any energy by the time she got up, maybe she'd do her homework then. So far, though, the Historic District had let her down today. This was their third time going around the block, and Joey showed no sign of getting sleepy.

"Momma? I wanna smile."

At first she didn't know what Joey was talking about, but then she understood. He was talking about the smiley-face penny that weird old fucker had tried to give them. She sighed. How the hell was she going to explain to a two-year-old what a creeper was? Especially when she was so tired her brain felt like stagnant sludge?

"Maybe later," she said. She hoped this would work. Sometimes *Maybe later* placated Joey, but other times it set him to wailing, *Now, now, now, now, now!*

He must've been as exhausted as her, though, because he didn't react to her words at all.

Thank god for small miracles, she thought.

They were approaching her favorite shop in the Historic District: Heaven Scent. You could buy handmade soaps and essential oils there, along with incense and aromatherapy products. She loved the smells that wafted from the shop, and she always slowed down whenever they passed it so she could breathe in the delightful odors. They'd walked by it a couple times already today, and she wondered if she might be able to stop this time and take Joey inside. She'd leave the stroller on the sidewalk and carry him in. The question was whether she could keep him from grabbing hold of whatever caught his eye. The last time she'd taken him in, he'd grabbed a blue soap shaped like a dolphin and bit into it like it was a piece of candy. He'd gotten quite a surprise, and she'd ended up buying a dolphin soap with toothmarks in its waxy hide.

"Momma, pee-pee!"

She groaned. Of *course* he had to go, and he always waited until he was on the verge of pissing his pants to say anything. Her mother said she'd taken him out of diapers too early, but Olivia had ignored her. *She* was Joey's mother, and she knew what was best. Now she wished she'd listened to her mom.

She debated taking him into Heaven Scent to use their bathroom, but she feared that his bladder would let go before they could reach the toilet, and he'd pee all over the floor. She wouldn't be able to withstand the embarrassment. But letting him sit in the stroller and piss himself was out of the question.

There was a small alley between Heaven Scent and the shop next door, a used clothing store called A Stitch in Time. Knowing she didn't have time to think about it, she unsnapped Joey from the stroller, lifted him out, and hurried into the alley. As they left the sidewalk, she caught a glimpse of someone approaching. She hoped that whoever it was would go on by without watching what she was doing. Or if they did notice, she hoped they'd understand and say nothing. The last thing she needed today was for whoever it was to report her to a cop for allowing her child to pee in public.

She carried Joey halfway down the alley, set him in front of a wall and pulled down his pants. He stood there for a moment, unsure what to do. She couldn't blame him. When you'd been told over and over that you were only supposed to pee in a toilet, it had to be confusing as hell when your mommy suddenly wanted you to pee on the side of a building, outside where anybody could see.

"It's okay," she said. "This is an emergency, and sometimes you have to do things a different way when it's an emergency."

Joey looked at her uncomprehendingly, so she decided to try a more direct method. She smacked his bare bottom – not hard – and said, "Go."

If Joey had been confused before, he was doubly so now. She smacked his ass again, a bit harder this time.

"Go!"

Joey's eyes moistened with tears and his lower lip quivered. Olivia had never spanked her son before, and Joey had no idea why his mommy was hitting him. Olivia didn't want to hit him again, but by this point she was committed to this course of action and had no other idea what to do. She pulled her hand back once more, but before she could swat his bottom again, a stream of urine jetted from his tiny penis. It splashed against the wall, ran down the brick, and formed a small puddle on the ground. Joey stared at the widening wet spot on the wall with amazement, as if he couldn't believe he could pee-pee standing out in the open air.

"The world isn't your child's toilet, you know."

Olivia turned toward the voice, startled. Joey turned to look too, and his urine stream cut off as if his little dick was a hose and someone had just turned off the water.

Coming toward them down the alley was the old man who'd bugged them earlier. At least, Olivia thought it was him. He wore the same sweatshirt and tan slacks, but his face and hands looked different. His skin was yellow, and a bright yellow at that. He looked like he'd been covered with makeup or paint. What little hair he'd had was gone, and his head had swollen to the size of a basketball. His eyes were darker than she remembered, almost black, and his nose had become so small it was almost invisible. His mouth was the worst of all, though. It was a long, curved, lipless line that took up the bottom half of his face. She thought he was the most disturbing thing she had ever seen – until she noticed the knife clasped in his right hand.

She scooped up Joey without bothering to pull up his pants. She held him tight as the smiley-faced man continued toward them.

"What kind of mother allows her son to piss in an alley like some animal?" His words were angry ones, but his tone was pleasant, even jolly, and his gigantic smile never faltered.

Run, you stupid bitch! she told herself, and she took her own advice. She turned toward the other end of the alley and started running, cupping the back of Joey's head and pressing his face to her chest so he wouldn't see the thing they were fleeing.

She heard a jingly sound then, followed by a soft *whoosh* that made her think of an arrow being loosed. An instant later pain erupted on her neck, shoulders, back, ass, and legs. It felt as if dozens of needles had been thrust into her body. Her legs gave out beneath her and she pitched forward. She instinctively turned to protect Joey and she landed on her left side, hard enough to knock the breath out of her. Joey began wailing at the top of his lungs, but she thought he was more scared than hurt. The back of her body had become a single mass of fiery pain, and she took one hand off Joey and reached around to her lower back. Her hand found something sharp and metallic, and she hissed as she cut her fingers prying the object loose. When she held it to her face to examine it, she saw that it was one of the smiley-face man's Chucks. The edges of the penny had been honed to razor sharpness, and she realized he had thrown them like *shuriken* to bring her down.

She pushed Joey off of her. Then she helped him to stand and pulled up his pants.

"Run," she said. The word came out in a gasp as she struggled to get her breath back. She tried again, and this time her voice sounded more normal. "Run!"

For a moment she thought he would do it, and as he ran, she'd do whatever she could to slow down the smiley-face man, to keep his attention on her long enough for her little boy to reach the end of the alley and make it to the sidewalk on the other side, where hopefully someone would see him and help him.

But Joey didn't run. Instead, he plopped down on his butt, looked at the smiley-face man, and cried. Tears streamed down his cheeks and his chest hitched with sobs. Olivia reached out and gathered Joey to her once again. At least she could hold him while whatever was going to happen to them happened. She didn't want to look at the man – at the *thing* – that was coming for them, but she did anyway. She wasn't sure why. Maybe she felt a need to be brave for her son one last time. Or maybe she did so out of some innate perversity of the human psyche, a need to stare death – especially one's own death – in the face as it came for you.

The smiley-face man stopped when he reached them. He gazed down at them with his frozen too-wide smile and his empty black eyes.

"Why are you doing this?" Olivia said. She didn't expect a reply, but she got one anyway.

"I want to make the world a better place," the smiley-face man said. "And it will be much better without you two in it."

He raised his copper knife high, and he brought it down, swift and strong. Then he did it again. Again. Again. Again....

* * *

A little while later, Randall gazed upon his handiwork. The girl and her son were hardly recognizable as things that had once been human. They'd become a single collection of ragged, torn meat and bone, slathered in blood. Blood splattered the alley walls, pooled on the ground around the remains, stippled his face and hands, soaked his shirt and pants.

He felt better than he had in years. In fact, he felt fan-fucking-*tastic*! It was so rewarding to know you were doing good work and making an important contribution to your community.

He considered gathering the Chucks he'd thrown to stop the woman from fleeing, but they were all messy now. Then again, he wasn't exactly Norman Neat right now, was he? He spent several minutes collecting his Chucks, careful to avoid cutting his fingers on their sharp edges, and returning them to his pocket. When he finished, he stood and pondered what to do next. What he'd *like* to do was go to ArtWorks and give Sierra an attitude adjustment. But she'd told him that she taught at the college at noon, and she wouldn't be back at ArtWorks until later, for her afternoon class there. He wasn't sure what time it was, but he figured that if Sierra hadn't left for the college yet, she'd do so soon. He decided there was no hurry. Sierra would return to ArtWorks eventually, and in the meantime, there was plenty of work for him to do around here.

He held his knife with the handle pointed upward and looked at the smiley face on the end.

"What do you think, Chuck? Ready to greet some more of Bishop Hill's less-than-upstanding citizens?"

The smiley face winked at him in approval.

Smiling – but then, Randall no longer could do anything *but* smile – he flipped his knife into a regular grip, turned and walked away from the savaged bodies of Olivia and Joey, and set off to find more people to introduce his friend Chuck to.

★ ★ ★

Sierra was finishing cleaning up after her second class of the day when she heard her phone buzzing in her Egyptian hieroglyphics bag. She always left the bag on the windowsill near where she taught, so she'd have easy access to whatever materials she'd brought for the day. She walked over to the windowsill and removed her phone from the bag. This time she checked the display to see if it was Stuart calling, but it wasn't, which was a relief. She'd had more than enough of him for one day. He'd left a voicemail message earlier that she'd immediately deleted without listening to, and recently, he'd left another, which she'd also deleted. She didn't recognize the number, and she almost didn't answer, figuring it was most likely a sales call. She decided to take the call, though. After the morning she'd had, she'd enjoy telling a salesperson to go to hell.

"Hello?"

At first whoever it wasn't didn't speak. Sierra was about to end the call when a male voice said her name.

"Yes?"

"This is Marc. Marc Naranjo."

Sierra was so surprised that Marc had called her that at first she didn't know what to say. Then she got angry. How dare he call her today of all days? She was about to tell him off – despite the fact that she knew he had to be hurting too – but then he said, "This is going to sound extremely fucked up, but by any chance did you see Jeffrey today?"

Sierra's anger drained out of her in a rush and was replaced by a cold, sick feeling in her gut.

Hang up now, she told herself. *Before this gets any weirder*. But she didn't hang up. Instead, she found herself answering calmly. "As a matter of fact, I did."

* * *

Sierra sat at a table near the entrance to Temptations Café. She wanted to be close to the door in case her meeting with Marc took a turn for the worse and she needed to make a quick getaway.

Temptations wasn't far from Riverbank Community College, which worked well for her since she had to teach at noon and didn't have a lot of time for lunch. Even so, she'd been reluctant to come here. Jeffrey and she had eaten here often, so much so that she'd come to think of it as their place. She didn't like the thought of Marc intruding on her memories of Jeffrey. But Marc had suggested meeting at Temptations, and she wondered if it was because he knew what the place meant to her. Maybe.

Temptations was a small, simple place without much in the way of décor or ambience. Just old tables and chairs, tacky curtains on the windows. But the food was good – soup and salads, mostly – and they had a selection of pastries and pies that were made on the premises and which were absolutely delicious. The desserts were the café's main attraction, and Sierra would never understand why they bothered serving anything else. She went ahead and ordered a Caesar salad and iced tea. The food arrived, but once it was in front of her, she found she wasn't hungry. She picked at it until Marc arrived.

She hadn't seen him for almost a year, but when he entered the café, she nearly didn't recognize him. He was thinner now, and he'd shaved his head. He'd grown a mustache and goatee, and since he was ten years older than Jeffrey, his black beard was streaked with white. He wore a gray suit with a white shirt and purple tie. He would've looked good, but he had a distressed air about him. His tie was crooked and the knot loose, his face was pale, and he moved with fidgety agitation. If they hadn't come here to talk about seeing her dead brother, she might've thought he was nervous about seeing her, and maybe that was part of what bothered him, but if so, it was only a small part. He gave her a shaky smile when he saw her, then joined her at the table. He didn't greet her – didn't say hello, offer to shake hands, ask how she was doing these days. He merely looked at her until a server came to their table, a young woman Sierra figured was probably a college student. A lot of Riverbank students worked at businesses near campus. Marc ordered a cup of coffee, but no food. When the server left, he nodded toward Sierra's salad.

"I'm glad you went ahead and ordered," he said. "I have absolutely no appetite myself."

"I don't have much of one either."

It felt so strange to be sitting here with the man she blamed, at least in part, for her brother's accident. But then again, she also blamed herself, so they had that in common. They belonged to an exclusive club: People Who'd Driven Jeffrey Sowell to His Death. All they needed was for Courtney Marsh to be here, and the roll call would be complete.

They didn't speak again until the server brought Marc's coffee. He added a ton of sugar to it then added so much cream the contents overflowed onto the saucer. He lifted the cup with shaky hands, spilling a bit more onto the table, but he managed to bring the coffee to his mouth without dumping the whole thing onto his lap. He drank half in several large gulps, then set the cup back down. His hands trembled slightly less now.

"Thank you for coming here," he said. "I was sure when I called you'd think I'd lost my mind."

"The jury's still out on that," Sierra said with a nervous smile. "For both of us."

"Before we go any further, I just want to say I know this day is hard for you. It's difficult for me, too. Jeffrey and I had our last dinner here, the night he died. I suppose that's why I wanted to meet you here. Sort of a way to honor his memory. I know I'm not exactly your favorite person in the world, so I appreciate you putting your feelings about me aside so we can talk."

Sierra hadn't put her negative feelings toward Marc *that* far to the side, but she saw no reason to tell him this. They weren't here to repair their relationship – not that they'd ever really had one. They were here to talk about the impossible. Neither of them had gone into any detail about their sightings of Jeffrey on the phone, and now that they were face to face, she had no idea how to get started.

"You want to go first?" she asked.

He shook his head. "I'm still trying to process what I saw. It was a lot to take in."

There was a quaver in his voice as he spoke, and Sierra wasn't sure she wanted to hear his story. But that's why they'd come here, to share their stories, so she told hers. She left nothing out, not even the message Jeffrey had somehow carved into brick simply by touching it. Marc kept his gaze fixed on her the entire time she spoke. So intense was his focus that he didn't seem to breathe as he listened. When she was finished, she thought he might challenge the part about *HI SIS*, or least express some skepticism. But he didn't. Not only did he seem to accept that part of her story readily enough, but he nodded, as if it made perfect sense to him.

She'd also told him of the dream she'd had last night, the one in which the strange man in the black suit had returned Jeffrey to life.

"Do you have any idea who the man in your dream was?" Marc asked.

She shook her head.

"I figured he was just part of the dream, a character my subconscious invented, kind of like a reverse undertaker who brings people back instead of burying them. I didn't think he was real, but now...."

"Since Jeffrey did return from the dead, like in your dream, do you think this man in the black suit might be real too?"

"I don't know. Maybe?"

Marc downed the rest of his coffee. He started to talk, but then the server came by to refill his cup. He didn't bother doctoring it this time, and he launched into his own tale.

If she'd thought her story was crazy, Marc's was absolutely insane. She would've discounted it entirely if it hadn't been for the detail about Jeffrey's touch being the thing that caused the tree to become sick and which killed that poor woman and her dog. As difficult as it was to believe that her brother had somehow returned from death, she couldn't imagine him hurting anyone, let alone killing them. But who could say what a person became after they died? Yesterday, she would've dismissed such a thought as ludicrous. Today, not so much.

"So what do we do next?" Marc asked when his story was done. "Hire an exorcist?"

"So there's a *we* now?"

"Sorry. I didn't mean to presume. It just came out that way."

Marc was obviously scared, and Sierra couldn't blame him. Assuming what he'd seen had been real – and despite how bizarre his story was, she felt he was telling the truth – he had every right to be afraid. Your love comes back from the grave only to disintegrate a woman and her dog while you watch? That would be enough to fuck anyone up. There was one aspect of his story that bothered her, though, for purely selfish reasons. Jeffrey had smiled and waved to her, but he hadn't spoken to her, and he'd walked off before she could catch up to him. She understood why Marc had fled rather than allowing Jeffrey to touch him, given what he'd witnessed. She wondered, if she had seen Jeffrey kill with his touch, would she still want him to hug her? It might be worth being turned to a pile of dust if she could feel her brother's arms around her one more time.

"If Jeffrey is out there somewhere hurting people, then we need to find him and stop him." More than that, she wanted to talk with him, to try to understand what had happened to him. Maybe if they knew how and why he'd returned, they'd be able to find a way to help him become normal again – or at least prevent him from killing anyone else.

"Stop him?" Marc said. "That sounds awfully…final."

She hadn't meant it that way. She'd meant they needed to prevent him from hurting anyone else. But how exactly were they supposed to do that? If Jeffrey had been in his right mind, he'd never have killed the woman and her dog. So if they managed to find him, how could they expect to reason with him? He'd recognized Marc, though. If she and Marc confronted Jeffrey together, maybe their combined presence would be enough to get through whatever madness held him in its grip, and they would be able to convince him to let them help him. But if they couldn't, if Jeffrey continued to be a threat, would they be forced to find a way to stop him permanently? If that was even possible. How could you kill something that had already returned from the dead once? The unreality of this conversation was starting to get to Sierra. She felt disconnected from her own body, as if she were merely an observer watching their conversation from a distance.

Her hands rested on the table, and Marc surprised her by reaching out and taking them in his.

"Are you all right?" he asked. "You look…well, I'm not sure *how* you look, but I don't think it's good. Do you need to go lie down somewhere?"

She looked down at Marc's hands. They were larger than hers, the fingers long and delicate-looking. She wondered if he played piano. He had the hands for it.

This conversation was the longest they'd ever spoken to each other, and this was the first time he'd ever touched her. He'd done so out of concern, she knew that, but these were hands that had touched her brother, had pleasured him. Hands that belonged to the man who'd sent her brother out into the storm that had killed him. The anger and resentment that she'd tried to put aside during their talk – dark emotions she'd fed and cultivated for an entire year – came flooding back.

She pulled her hands from under his and placed them in her lap. Marc, seeming to realize he'd crossed a line, withdrew his quickly as well.

"Sorry," he said.

Sierra ignored his apology. She wanted to stay angry at him, *needed* to. It helped focus her mind.

"The first thing we need to do is find Jeffrey," she said.

"How do we do that? Drive around town and hope we spot him disintegrating more pets, maybe a mail carrier or two?"

She recognized his snark as a defense mechanism against the insanity of the situation, but she still didn't appreciate it.

"Be serious," she snapped.

Marc glared at her in response, but he nodded, grudgingly, she thought.

"Yes, we could drive around and see if we get lucky," she said. "We both saw him wandering the street. Maybe he's still doing that. But I think we'd have better luck if we went to the places he knew best. He came to ArtWorks, and he tapped on the window to get my attention and waved at me. I don't think he recognized me – not all the way, at least."

Although it had hurt at the time, now she was grateful Jeffrey hadn't entered ArtWorks. What if he'd come inside and tried to touch her, to give her his 'gift'? Worse, what if he'd touched some of the children? She had a mental image of her students falling away to dust, and her stomach threatened to expel what little of her salad she'd managed to get down before Marc arrived.

"But you think he went to ArtWorks because somewhere in his mind he remembered you work there?"

"Yes. And he definitely recognized you." She couldn't help feeling a jealous twinge as she said these words. "Maybe his memory is improving as time passes. If so, he might go to his apartment or maybe where he worked. Those are the places we should try first." She took her phone from her bag to check the time. "My class begins in twenty minutes, but I can cancel it, and we can get started right away."

She went to her contacts list to find the number for the college's art department. She'd tell the administrative assistant that she'd come down with something. *Hi, Dawn. I'm afraid I have to cancel my twelve o'clock class today. I've got a bad case of my brother has returned from the dead and is disintegrating people.*

Maybe she'd go with the stomach flu instead.

But before she could call, Marc said, "I'm not sure that's a good idea. Because of what happened this morning, I'm extremely late to meet with a client. An important one. My boss will hand me my ass if I miss the appointment altogether."

Sierra stared at him, unable to believe what he'd said. Right now, Jeffrey was out there somewhere, maybe killing more people, and Marc couldn't go looking for him because of *work*? Marc went on before Sierra could challenge him.

"Besides, if you're right and Jeffrey's memory is returning, wouldn't he be just as likely to seek you out at the college as anywhere else? He's already made contact with you once today. Maybe he'll try again. You *are* his sister, after all. It might be better if you teach your class. That way, you'll be on campus if he goes there."

"So essentially you're suggesting we do nothing."

"No." Marc didn't meet Sierra's gaze as he said this. "I'm just saying that it might be more effective to let him come to us. But for that to happen, we need to go about our regular routines."

She supposed there was a certain logic to what Marc proposed, but she knew logic was far from his sole motivator.

"You're afraid to find him, aren't you?"

"Fuck yes, I'm afraid!"

He took a long drink of his coffee.

"You didn't see what I saw," he said. "If you had...."

She wanted to tell him that no matter what Jeffrey had become or what he'd done, he was still her brother, and how could she be afraid of him? But in truth, she *was* afraid. She wanted to see her brother again, but she was also terrified of doing so.

Marc sighed, seeming to deflate as he did.

"I know you think I'm a coward, and maybe I am. But I can't face him again. Not now. I need some time to come to terms with what I saw, you know?"

She did know.

"All right. I'll teach my class and you meet your client. I'll be done around one thirty. I'll call you then and we can figure out what to do. Sound good?"

Marc gave her an almost pathetically grateful smile.

"Yes. Thank you."

He tossed a couple dollars onto the table to pay for his coffee, said goodbye, rose, and headed for the door. He walked at a deliberate pace, as if having to force himself not to run.

She wondered if he'd answer when she called later, or if this was the last she'd see of him. Then again, he'd called her to tell her about seeing Jeffrey. He could've kept his mouth shut and tried to avoid getting further tangled up in all this if he'd wanted. Maybe he was telling her the truth when he said he just needed some time to process what had happened. But what if, after he'd had that time, he decided he wanted nothing more to do with Jeffrey?

She'd go it alone, then. What other choice did she have? As scared as she might be, she wouldn't abandon Jeffrey. She'd lost him once. No way would she lose him again.

CHAPTER SIX

Stuart was parked across the street from Temptations. He'd come here with Sierra a couple times, but he'd never liked the place. He'd rather go to a good burger joint any day.

So far, Krista had proven herself a most useful companion. In many ways, she was the perfect woman: she lived to serve him and did as she was told. Too bad she didn't have a body with big tits and a tight cunt, but he supposed you couldn't have everything. She *did* have a wicked tracking app, however, which allowed him to pinpoint Sierra's location. After he'd tracked her here and parked, Krista informed him that she had another app that would ensure he could listen in on her conversation with whoever she was meeting without leaving the car. And that Sierra *was* meeting someone, Stuart had no doubt. A teasing whore like her always had a man or two on the line.

"Would you like me to activate the listening app?" Krista asked.

"Damn straight."

An instant later he regretted his words. The swollen conglomeration of flesh where his Bluetooth receiver had merged with his ear began to change, skin, cartilage, plastic, and metal shifting, twisting, reforming. The resultant pain was so intense that for a moment he blacked out, but then his vision cleared, almost as if he were a machine that had temporarily gone offline and was being rebooted. Soon after, the pain eased and then disappeared entirely. He reached up and gingerly touched the object that now protruded from the right side of his head. It felt like a small dish of some kind, and then he realized what it was: a miniature parabolic microphone, a device for picking up sound from a distance, the sort of thing spies used.

Awesome. He'd always wanted one.

The driver's side window hummed as it lowered.

"Please give me a moment to lock in on Sierra."

A second later, Stuart heard Sierra telling a server she'd like a Caesar salad and an iced tea. The sound was so clear and crisp, it was as if he were seated next to her.

"Krista, you are the shit!"

"Thank you, Stuart."

He settled back into his seat, closed his eyes, and listened.

For a while, it was pretty dull. Sierra sat quietly while she waited for her food, thanked the server when it arrived, and then started eating it. Stuart was beginning to think he'd wasted his time following her here, but then Marc Naranjo came in and joined her.

Stuart didn't know Marc. He'd met the guy a couple times, but they hadn't interacted much. Stuart didn't have anything against gays so long as they left him the hell alone and didn't do any gay shit in public. Did Sierra have a thing for gay guys? He'd heard of women like that, who hung around with gay men, hoping they'd eventually turn straight for them because they were so *special*. He'd thought Sierra was smarter than that, but then she *was* a woman, and for women, emotions – no matter how stupid – trumped brains every time. On the other hand, maybe Marc was bisexual, and he'd come here because he wanted to make a play for Sierra. How kinky would that be, fucking the brother and, a year after he died, fucking the sister? But Sierra *loathed* Marc. She blamed him for Jeffrey's death.

He listened as they began talking.

"I'm glad you went ahead and ordered. I have absolutely no appetite myself."

"I don't have much of one either."

"Thank you for coming here. I was sure when I called you'd think I'd lost my mind."

"The jury's still out on that. For both of us."

Their voices were drowned out by a sudden staticky crackling, so loud it made Stuart wince in pain. He reflexively reached up to pull the parabolic mike from his ear, forgetting it was part of him. He grabbed hold of it and yanked, but all he succeeded in doing was adding to his pain. Then, as quickly as it had come, the static faded away to silence. He waited to hear Sierra's and Marc's voices again, but they didn't return. He was about to ask Krista what had happened to the mike, but a bone-deep weariness overtook him then, and he found it a struggle to keep his eyes open. He was so tired, he felt as if he could nod off right here and sleep for a month. It took an effort, but he managed to speak, his voice little more than a whisper, his speech slurred.

"What's…wrong?"

"Your power level has fallen dangerously low. You need to recharge before you lose power entirely."

His thoughts were fuzzy, sluggish, and it took fierce concentration for him to make sense of them.

"What happens when…power gone?"

"You'll shut down, of course. However, I advise against allowing that to happen. Humans – even augmented ones such as yourself – aren't as easy to restart as machines. Sometimes they can't be restarted at all."

She said this with a tone of mild bemusement, as if she couldn't understand how humans could be so limited.

"Shut…down?"

It sounded to him like another way to say *die.*

He pictured himself sitting in the Camaro, window down, eyes closed, body still. How long would he remain like that until someone realized he was dead? Hours? Days? Would someone only think to check on him when they passed by his car and smelled the rank odor of decay wafting from inside the vehicle?

"What do I do?" He sounded like a weak, frightened child, and although he hated himself for it, he couldn't stop himself from pleading. "Please, Krista. Help me!"

Krista had guided him since the moment he'd first heard her voice. But instead of answering his question this time, she said, *"You know what to do."*

She sounded cold, much different than her normally pleasant tone.

He felt the weariness even more intensely than before, and he knew he was going to be in deep shit if he didn't do something soon. *Think, you dumbass!* And then, just like that, the answer came to him.

"Need to...recharge."

"There you go! Now, was that so hard?"

It made sense. He was partially machine now, a goddamned cyborg. But he had no idea how to recharge himself.

Krista let out an exasperated sigh. *"Look in your pocket."*

Feeling like he was moving through cold molasses, Stuart reached into his right pants pocket. His hands found a coiled metallic cable, and he withdrew it. The object hadn't been in his pocket earlier, he was certain of that. He'd never seen it before. But here it was, another gift from Krista. At first the object looked like any other charger – outlet plug on one end, device plug on the other. But it shifted in his hand, coils rippling as if the charger was alive and was stretching itself after a period of confinement. The unexpected movement startled him, and he almost dropped the charger, but it settled down and grew still. He started to ask Krista how he was supposed to use the charger, but instead he closed his hand around it, opened the Camaro's door, and stepped outside.

He was so weak his knees buckled, and he had to grab hold of the open door to keep himself standing. His head swam with vertigo, and he closed his eyes and waited for it to pass. The dizziness didn't go away entirely, but it receded enough that he risked opening his eyes again. His vision was blurry around the edges, but he could see well enough, and while his knees still felt weak, they continued to keep him upright. Figuring that this was the best he was going to get, he closed the car door and moved to the rear of the vehicle, keeping his left hand on it to support himself as he shuffled forward, barely able to lift his feet off the ground.

He made it to the sidewalk – nearly tripping in the process – and began walking east, choosing the direction at random. He wasn't sure what he was looking for exactly. Should he go into a shop and search for a power outlet? That didn't feel right, but what else—

He stumbled then and would've gone down if a man walking in the opposite direction hadn't reached out and caught him.

"Easy there, fella. You all right?"

The man was in his forties, and while not exactly fat, he was what some would politely describe as beefy. He had a round face with puffy jowls, a thatch of brown hair, and a thin mustache that looked like it belonged more on the lip of an adolescent than a middle-aged man. He wore an ugly shit-brown suit with an equally ugly yellow tie. His brown shoes had tassels on them, which Stuart regarded as a major fashion mistake. The man reminded Stuart a bit of Alton, his late and not particularly lamented manager. This was the sort of man Alton might've become in several years' time, and Stuart decided he'd done Alton a favor by frying his ass.

The man gave Stuart a smile, and when he spoke, there was no mockery or irritation in his voice, only kindness.

"Did you have one too many last night? Or maybe this morning?"

They were close enough to the college for the man to be a professor who'd stopped for lunch between classes. The guy's breath smelled like onions, and Stuart wondered what the fucker had eaten for breakfast. Whatever it had been, the man's breath turned his stomach.

The man frowned as he got a closer look at Stuart's face. "What's wrong with your eyes? They're silver. Are you wearing contacts or something? And your *ear*...."

Stuart didn't respond to the man's words. He felt a pinch of pain behind the front teeth in his lower jaw, and when he probed the area with his tongue, he encountered a small hard object embedded in the soft flesh of his mouth. In his ear, Krista said, *"It's a port."*

Stuart now knew where one end of the charger went, but as for the other....

The device had remained motionless since he'd left the car, but now it began to move again. It swiftly uncoiled and the plug end shot out of his hand toward the man in the shit-brown suit. The metal prongs on the plug grew sharp, like the fangs of a striking snake, and embedded themselves in the man's forehead. Blood ran from the wounds, and the man's eyes went wide with pain and shock. He let go of Stuart and reached trembling hands toward the plug. His fingers found it and tried to pull it loose, but it was dug in too deep.

The other end of the plug leaped out of Stuart's hand and shot toward his mouth. It wriggled its way between his lips, past his teeth, and found the newly installed port. It inserted itself with a small *click*, and white light exploded behind Stuart's retinas. He felt strength flooding back into his limbs, felt his mind become clear once more, his thoughts sharp and nimble as every cell of his body filled with dancing electric flame. He felt strong, powerful, invincible.

He felt the cable in his mouth jerk taut, and this sensation was followed by the sound of something heavy thudding to the sidewalk. His vision cleared and he found himself looking down at the man in the shit-brown suit. He lay on the sidewalk in a fetal position, curled in on himself like a dead spider. His hands were contorted claws, and his face was twisted into a rictus of pain. His eyes were gone, and wisps of steam rose from the empty blackened sockets.

The plug was still stuck in the man's forehead, but now it wriggled itself loose and flew toward Stuart, trailing drops of blood behind it. The cable retracted as it came, and just as the plug was about to collide with his teeth, he opened his mouth and the plug went inside. He felt it compressing as it burrowed beneath his tongue, and while this process hurt, he was getting used to the pain his new body modifications caused, and he endured it. The pain ebbed, and when he ran the tip of his tongue over the area where the port and charger had been, he felt only a small lump covered by newly healed flesh.

"The charger will remain in storage until you need it again," Krista said. *"By the way, recharge successful. Power level at maximum."*

There was a sense of approval in her voice, as if she were proud of him.

He gazed one last time at the man whose life he'd stolen, and then he turned and headed into the street. Drivers braked to avoid hitting him, cursed and sounded their horns. Stuart ignored them, was barely aware of their existence. The entirety of his attention was focused on the café across the street. His nerves were on fire, and his heart thrummed like a finely tuned engine. Screw listening in on Sierra's conversation with Marc. He'd rather speak to them in person. Halfway across the street, he began running, arms and legs pistoning with machinelike precision. Dark anticipation filled him as he thought of what he'd do to Sierra and her fag boyfriend when he confronted them.

A small part of his mind wondered if anyone had seen what he'd done to the man in the shit-brown suit. No one had been close by on the sidewalk when Stuart killed him, but traffic had been flowing in the street. Had a driver witnessed what he'd done and called 911? Were police already on their way? But even if he hadn't been completely absorbed in fantasies of retribution, he wouldn't have cared about the cops. Let them come. He was fully charged and ready to rumble.

He burst into Temptations, flinging the door open so hard that it tore halfway off its hinges. Everyone in the café turned to look at him, eyes widening, mouths dropping open. Stuart ignored them all. He only cared about Sierra and Marc.

⋆ ⋆ ⋆

Wendy Morgan had worked at Temptations for eighteen months. She was taking acting classes in Riverbank's theater department, and she'd had some small roles in a couple campus productions. Nothing spectacular, but they were, as one of her teachers put it, résumé-builders. Classes at Riverbank weren't expensive, but they weren't free either, and Wendy could only afford to be a part-time student. Her two-year degree would most likely take her four years, or longer, to complete, but that was okay. By the time she was finished, she'd be ready to start auditioning for real acting jobs, although this would necessitate moving somewhere with a more vibrant theater scene than Bishop Hill. Aside from the college, there was a dinner theater in Ash Creek, and that was it. Chicago had a strong theater scene, and it might be more doable financially. Cleveland, Cincinnati, and Columbus were possibilities too.

One of the reasons she was taking her time to complete her theater degree – one she'd never told anyone about – was that she had a suspicion that she wasn't a very good actor. That she sucked, in fact. She might be adequate enough to be in a crowd scene, maybe even have a line or two, but no more than that. No small parts, only small players. She truly believed that. But the idea of being relegated to bit parts throughout her career – and maybe not even being able to land those outside Riverbank – terrified her. People always said to follow your dreams, but what if those dreams never went anywhere?

She'd started working at Temptations right out of high school, and it was an okay job. The work wasn't too hard, and the café's owner was nice enough to her employees. The pay wasn't great, but it covered her rent and tuition. Mostly. The tips left something to be desired. A lot of students ate here, and they were just as poor as she was. But whenever she closed, she got to take home any baked goods that were on the verge of going stale, and that was a nice – if fattening – perk. Sometimes she worried that she'd end up working at a server, either here or somewhere else, her entire life, while continuing to audition for parts she was never going to get. It was a big reason why she felt anxious and depressed most of the time, although she did her best to hide it, especially when she was at work. Nobody wanted to be served by someone who looked like they were contemplating suicide all the time, and they sure as hell didn't want to tip them.

Wendy was having an especially bad Monday. On Friday, she'd auditioned for a part in the theater department's fall production of *Cat on a Hot Tin Roof.* She knew it was a long shot, but she *really* wanted to play the part of Maggie, the female lead. The cast list had been posted on the department's call board this morning, and she'd stopped by to check it out. She'd been so nervous when she stepped up to the call board, moving past other students who were talking excitedly about who was and wasn't cast. When she didn't see her name on the list, she immediately reread it to make sure she hadn't somehow overlooked it. But no matter how many times she read the list, her name remained absent.

She'd already been working for a couple hours by the time the brunette woman with the funky Egyptian-themed bag walked in. She thought she was older than her by a few years, but she was cute, and she was pleased when she sat at one of her stations. Maybe the day was starting to look up.

But she soon discovered the woman was preoccupied, and

she ignored Wendy's attempts at small talk. *Another rejection*, she thought, but she forced herself to continue smiling as she took the woman's order and brought her food. Before long, an older man joined the woman, but all he wanted was coffee. At first Wendy wondered if the guy was the woman's boyfriend or something. She kept an eye on them while she served other customers, and after a bit she decided that not only weren't they lovers, they weren't even friends. Their body language indicated how uncomfortable they were in each other's presence.

Eventually the man left, and Wendy returned to the table to ask the woman if she'd like any dessert, but she was even less responsive than she had been before. She paid her bill and left, and Wendy felt depressed once more.

I can't act, and I can't get cute women to talk to me.

She was bussing the woman's table when the café door flung open, and a guy in a black polo shirt and jeans entered. At first Wendy thought the man was injured. A lump of swollen, sore flesh protruded from the side of his head where his ear should've been, and there was a piece of electronic equipment kind of like a mini satellite dish stuck in the mass, as if someone had jammed it there. The sight of it caused Wendy's stomach to lurch. But then she saw the man's eyes – his *silver* eyes that had no iris or pupil – and she felt a watery sensation of fear in addition to her nausea.

Everyone in the café fell silent and turned to look at the man. Wendy stood frozen, bent over the table, holding the bowl containing the remains of the woman's Caesar salad. The man with the disfigured ear and metallic eyes took a quick look around the café, body motionless as his head swiveled from right to left then back again. His gaze fixed on Wendy, and he walked straight toward her.

"Where is she?" he demanded.

He stopped in front of Wendy and thrust his head forward until their noses almost touched. Wendy thought of the way two dogs would get in each other's faces when they were angry, practically nose to nose as they growled and barked. She felt heat emanating from the man's body, as if he were running a fever, and Wendy wasn't certain, but she thought she could detect a soft thrumming sound, as if a large piece of electrical equipment were running nearby.

"The woman who was sitting here." The man pointed to the empty seat as if to clarify his statement. "What happened to her?"

Initially, Wendy was too frightened by this strange man to answer him, but her actor's mind took over, and she found herself giving him a crooked smile. She put the salad bowl back down on the table, straightened, and met the stranger's silver-eyed gaze without flinching.

"Who wants to know?" she said, her voice a laconic drawl.

The stranger blinked several times, as if he were having trouble believing what he'd heard.

"Are you shitting me?" The man's brow furrowed in anger, and tiny bolts of electricity flashed across his eyes. Inside, Wendy cringed in fear, but outwardly her expression remained unchanged.

"No, I'm not," Wendy said, voice calm but firm. "I can't just give out information on customers to anyone who asks. It's unprofessional."

Out of the corner of her eye, Wendy noticed the guy working the bakery counter bring his phone to his face, then turn his back in order to conceal what he was doing. She hoped he was calling the police. She had no idea how much longer she could keep up her act.

Wendy had never seen anyone actually grind their teeth in frustration before, but that's exactly what the man did now. His teeth were the same silver color as his eyes, and as they ground together sparks shot forth. Wendy might've thought the sparks to be an illusion of some kind, but they struck her on the face and neck, causing pinpricks of hot pain.

"I'm only going to ask this one more time, bitch." The silver-eyed man's voice was low and dangerous now. "Where. Did. She. Go?"

Wendy's façade – which hadn't been all that strong to begin with – was on the verge of collapse. She wanted to say something cool and cutting, the kind of line that a movie hero would say to a bad guy to bring him down a couple pegs and let him know what kind of woman he was dealing with. But nothing came to mind, so

Wendy reluctantly, and with no small measure of disappointment in herself, fell back on the truth.

This time when she spoke, her voice was toneless and weak, without a hint of bravado. "She paid her bill and left a couple minutes before you came in."

The silver-eyed man looked at her for several moments, and Wendy tried and failed to read the emotion in those inhuman eyes. But finally the man smiled, displaying his silver teeth.

"There, was that so hard?"

For an instant, Wendy felt a wave of relief. Maybe now that she'd answered the man's question, he'd leave without hurting anyone – especially her.

But then the man spoke again. "I'm already at full charge, but you know what they say. You can never have too much of a good thing."

The man opened his mouth and something shot forth. At first she thought it was his tongue, but it was a plug of some kind with sharp prongs and a thin metal cable played out behind it. The plug struck her forehead with such force that the prongs sliced through the skin and dug into the bone beneath. The pain was worse than anything Wendy had imagined possible. She felt a draining sensation then, as if she were a giant bottle of water that had sprung a leak. She felt her thoughts become thinner, smaller, and she heard people screaming, but the sound came from so very far away.

She had time for a final thought before the last vestiges of her consciousness disappeared forever.

All the world's a stage....

* * *

Stuart jogged across the street toward his Camaro. He saw that a group of people had gathered around the body of the man in the shit-brown suit, but none of them looked his way. He heard sirens approaching, and he knew someone had called 911 about the waitress, the man in the shit-brown suit, or both.

He climbed into the Camaro and the engine roared to life, the car anticipating his need. The door shut on its own and the seat belt snaked across his chest and buckled him in. He felt the car in a way he'd never been able to before. He was connected to it, and it to him. They were part of each other now, the same way Krista was part of him. The seat was molded to his body, accepting him, holding him, *caressing* him.

"Do you wish me to locate Sierra?" Krista asked.

Stuart was tempted, but he'd just killed two people in the area, and the police would be all over the place soon. He wasn't afraid of being caught, but he didn't want the hassle of dealing with the cops if he didn't have to.

"Not now, Krista. We can catch up to her later."

Thanks to Krista's tracking app, he could find Sierra any time he wished. But for now, he thought it would be a good idea to put some distance between himself and the approaching authorities. He put his hands on the steering wheel, and his mind and nervous system connected to the car as smoothly as if he were one machine attaching itself to another. He felt the steering wheel give under his fingers, and he watched as his hands fused with the leather and plastic. There was some pain, of course. A certain amount always accompanied change, but in the end it was worth it.

Stuart grinned. "Better living through technology," he said.

The gearshift slid into drive by itself, and Stuart pulled into traffic and drove away.

⋆ ⋆ ⋆

As Sierra drove away from Temptations, she had a horrible realization. If Jeffrey did start to seek out familiar places, there was one he'd be drawn to more strongly than any other. She grabbed her phone and called her mother.

"Sierra, is that you?"

"Yes, Mom."

For some reason, her mother didn't seem to trust her phone's display screen when it indicated who was calling, and she always checked to confirm the caller's identity.

"Hello, sweetie. How are you today?"

Her mother sounded normal, but she placed a slight emphasis on the word *today* that spoke volumes. Sierra felt guilty for not having checked in with her parents earlier. She was hurting today, but it had to be so much worse for them. Jeffrey had been her brother, but he'd been their firstborn.

"I'm all right."

A lie, and a damned big one, but there was no way she could tell her mother the truth. Assuming that Jeffrey hadn't paid a visit to her and Dad. But now that she had her mother on the phone, she had no idea how to broach the subject.

"How are you and Dad? Has anything, uh, *happened* today?"

As soon as the words were out of her mouth, she wanted to take them back. *Real subtle, Sierra.*

Her mother was silent for a moment, and Sierra imagined her trying to figure out what the hell her daughter had meant by this odd question.

"Well, your father and I didn't sleep too well last night. And there were some tears this morning from both of us. But we're doing a little better now."

Sierra let out a sigh of relief. If Jeffrey had gone to her parents' house, her mother would be freaking the fuck out right now. But she sounded normal. Sad, but normal.

"How are *you* doing?" her mother asked.

"Pretty much the same."

Sierra had reached campus and she slowed as she approached the faculty parking lot. Riverbank had been built in the early Seventies, and the buildings looked like three-story blocks of dull concrete, which made it seem more like a prison than a place of education.

"Are you still planning on coming over for dinner tonight?"

To anyone else, her mother's question would've sounded casual, but Sierra could detect the plea in her voice.

"Of course. I'll be over after my afternoon class at ArtWorks."

She had no idea if she'd be able to keep this promise. It all depended on whether or not she and Marc could find Jeffrey, and if they succeeded, what happened after that.

"Good. I'm making meat loaf."

Sierra felt herself choke up. Their mother's meat loaf – which

Sierra had always found a little dry – had been Jeffrey's favorite meal. It took an effort for Sierra to get words out.

"Sounds good."

They were both silent for a moment, neither knowing what more to say, but neither wanting to end the call just yet.

Sierra pulled into the faculty lot, found a space, and parked.

"Do me a favor, Mom?"

"Of course, dear. Anything."

"If something strange happens, call me right away. Okay?"

She could feel her mother trying to figure out what she meant by *strange*, but her mom promised she would. Sierra told her she loved her and asked her to give her love to Dad, and then she ended the call.

Her parents lived on the other side of town, and assuming Jeffrey remained on foot it would take him a couple hours to walk there. And he would only be able to manage that if his mind cleared enough for him to remember the route. With any luck, her parents would remain safe and blissfully unaware of their son's resurrection while she and Marc tracked Jeffrey down. At least she hoped so.

She grabbed her bag, got out of her Beetle, and started walking toward the anonymous gray building where her noon class was held.

⋆ ⋆ ⋆

Grace stood before shelves filled with beautiful bottles of amber liquor, and unlike the last bottle she'd had, these all had labels. Woodford Reserve, Maker's Mark, Buffalo Trace, Knob Creek, Blanton's, Four Roses, Old Forester, Basil Hayden's, Breckenridge, Low Gap, Widow Jane, Crown Royal....

There was no way she could choose, so she closed her eyes – sandpapery lids descending over hard, dry orbs – reached out, and fumbled until her fingers closed around the neck of a bottle. She pulled it off the shelf then opened her eyes. Angel's Envy, $50.99. She brought the bottle close to get a better look at its contents. The Happy Hours liquor store was lit by fluorescent lights, but despite the garish illumination, the bourbon in the bottle seemed to glow with its own warm fire. She felt an unpleasant tightening in her mouth, and she realized her body was attempting to drool, but didn't have the moisture to do so.

She'd come here to purchase a bottle with the ten dollars she'd found in her apartment, something cheap like Old Crow or Early Times. But now that she held the Angel's Envy – which was considerably more than ten dollars – an overpowering thirst took hold of her. It went beyond the merely physical. It felt as if all of her – mind, body, and soul – was dry as the fucking Sahara and that she would crumble to dust and drift away on the wind if she didn't get this glorious ambrosia into her belly now, and fuck how much it cost.

She broke the foil seal and tossed it aside. She eyed the cork with frustration, and was about to break off the neck of the bottle by smashing it against the edge of one of the shelves, when the index finger of her left hand twitched. This was followed by a burst of pain so intense it made her gasp and nearly caused her to drop the bottle. She looked at her hand and saw a small length of bone had pierced through her fingertip – no blood; she was too dry inside. As she watched, the bone twisted and curled, reshaping itself into—

—a corkscrew.

She attempted a smile, but her dry, tight lips – already cracked and split – didn't have enough elasticity left to get the job done.

She held the bottle with her right and pressed the pointed tip of her – she supposed it was a *bonescrew* – to the cork. She wasn't sure whether she should turn the hand with the bonescrew or turn the bottle to extricate the cork, but she didn't need to do either. The bonescrew began twirling on its own, digging into the cork, sinking deeper with each revolution. When the top of her finger came in contact with the cork, she yanked and it came free with a satisfying *pop*. She'd never heard a more beautiful sound. The bonescrew spun in the opposite direction as it retracted into her finger, and when it had withdrawn completely, the cork dropped to the floor to join the discarded cap.

Her hand trembled as she brought the bottle to her mouth, as much from psychological as physical need, if not more. She tilted back her head, lifted the bottle, and drank.

She didn't swallow so much as open her throat to create a clear channel to her stomach, and poured the bourbon into herself. In her haste to get the whiskey into her, some of it spilled onto her lips and chin, but it didn't go to waste. Her thirsty body absorbed the bourbon directly into the skin. She finished the bottle in the time it would take her to draw in a breath and release it. It was gone so fast. Too fast.

Her tongue tingled, and a pleasant warmth spread through her midsection. Her headache – which she'd become so used to by now that she paid it little mind – receded. She drew the back of her hand across her mouth to wipe it, although it wasn't necessary. Her parchment skin rasped as it moved across her leathery lips.

"That's the stuff."

A general sense of well-being came over her, and for one bright, shining moment, all was right with the world. She didn't hate her ex, didn't resent her children, wasn't angry at Sierra, and most importantly of all, she didn't hate herself. Unfortunately, this didn't last. The warmth dissipated rapidly, along with its emotional counterpart. She felt thirstier, *emptier* than ever. It wasn't fair! She just wanted to feel good, just for a little while. Was that too much to ask of the world?

Snarling, she hurled the bottle at the floor. It exploded into dozens of glass shards, which skittered across the tile like sharp-edged insects.

"What the hell do you think you're doing?"

She turned before her clawlike fingers could encircle the neck of another bottle and saw a woman in her thirties standing in the aisle gawking at her. The woman was shaped like a pear and sported a bright green faux hawk. She wore a flannel shirt untucked, the sleeves rolled up to display the interlocking tattoos covering her forearms. An employee nametag was pinned to the left breast of her shirt, and it said *Velda*.

"What the fuck kind of name is that?" Grace demanded.

Velda didn't answer. Her eyes were frightened-deer wide, and the color had drained from her face. Grace began to grow angry. So she was older than this woman by a decade or two. Or three. Just because she was old(ish), didn't make her some kind of monster.

Velda found her voice then.

"P-please leave. I don't care about the booze you drank. Just go. *Please.*"

The woman's reaction disgusted Grace. She'd thought the younger generation was supposed to be so tolerant, so 'woke'. But Velda was obviously an ageist of epic proportions. Grace started toward the bitch, intending to give her a piece of her mind. Velda took a step back as Grace approached and raised her hands as if to fend her off. For Christ's sake, what the hell was wrong with her? Was she mentally ill or—

Grace's thought was interrupted by a painful cramping in her gut, accompanied by an intense burning sensation. She felt hot liquid gush upward and sear the back of her throat, and she barely managed to open her mouth in time as a stream of brown liquid shot forth. It struck Velda in the face, and she gasped and choked as the substance ran into her eyes, up her nose, into her mouth. She slapped frantically at her face, attempting to wipe it clean, but all she succeeded in doing was smearing it around. As soon as the stream of liquid vomit ceased, Grace felt better. That'd teach her to guzzle an entire bottle at once.

Velda stopped smacking her face then. Her features went slack and her arms flopped to her sides.

"How can I help you?" Velda asked, voice toneless and devoid of inflection.

Grace looked at her, unclear what was happening.

"Go fuck yourself," Grace said.

Velda didn't speak as she undid the snap on her jeans, pulled down the zipper, and slipped her hand inside her underwear. A second later she began vigorously masturbating. Her face remained expressionless as she did this, as if she were sleepwalking or in some kind of trance.

"That's disgusting," Grace said. "Stop it."

Velda immediately withdrew her hand from her pants, but she made no move to zip up her jeans.

Interesting....

"Touch your nose," Grace said.

Velda did so.

"Bite your tongue."

Velda did this too, biting down hard enough to draw blood. Her expression didn't change, though. It was as if she no longer felt pain. Or if she did, she didn't care about it.

Grace attempted a smile again, but with no more success than she'd had before.

"I think I know how you can help me, Velda dear. Wait right here while I pull my car up to the front, okay?"

Velda didn't respond. She simply stood there, motionless, barely breathing, a thin line of blood from her wounded tongue running from one corner of her mouth.

Grace grabbed a bottle of Blanton's, and this time she did break it open on a shelf. She drank it down as she walked toward the front of the store, swallowing several shards of glass that had fallen into the bourbon. As dry and painful as her throat was, she barely noticed.

CHAPTER SEVEN

Al Mills had worked as a law officer in Bishop Hill since he was twenty-five. He was forty-four now, which meant that next year he'd have twenty years in and could retire at half pay. His wife wanted to move somewhere warmer, like Florida or California. Al liked the desert climate better and was hoping to talk her into moving to Phoenix. He wanted to start his own security business, and he was looking forward to being his own boss.

Not that being a cop in Bishop Hill was a bad gig. It was a nice enough place to live, and crime was relatively low. Mostly speeders, drunk drivers, petty theft, vandalism, bar fights, and domestic violence. Murder was rare, and when it happened, it was usually during an argument between people who knew each other. You hardly needed the deductive skills of Sherlock Holmes to work here. In fact, he'd never drawn his service weapon once in the line of duty in the last nineteen years.

Although retirement was never far from his mind these days, he liked to think he didn't suffer from short-timer's syndrome. He tried to approach his shifts with the same work ethic as he had on the day he'd started. But when he heard over the radio that some psycho had killed a couple by the college using some kind of weapon that burned out their *eyes*, for fuck's sake, he couldn't help feeling grateful that he hadn't gotten the call. The last thing he wanted was to get killed shortly before he retired. His wife would never forgive him.

He was driving through the parking lot of a shopping center on the east side of town – which people called the 'Least Side' because of how rundown it was – when something strange caught his eye. An extremely thin, almost skeletal woman wearing what appeared to be a pink robe along with a matching pair of fuzzy slippers stood next to a Lexus. The vehicle was parked alongside the curb in front of Happy Hours liquor store, one of its rear doors open, and a younger woman stood close by, holding a dolly loaded with four large cardboard boxes. The top box was open, and the older woman was pulling bottles of liquor from it and putting them in the vehicle's back seat. That wasn't the only dolly either. There were two more, each holding four boxes, all of which presumably also contained liquor. There was no law against buying booze in bulk, but it was certainly odd. What bothered Al most was the way the older woman was loading her car. Instead of having the other woman – who Al assumed was an employee of Happy Hours – load the boxes into the trunk, the older woman was loading the bottles one at a time into the back seat. Maybe she needed to do it that way for some reason, had some kind of physical condition that prevented her from lifting full boxes. She did look frail. But then again, she could've driven the liquor home in the boxes, opened them when she arrived, and carried them in a couple at a time – assuming she didn't have anyone to help her. He couldn't escape the suspicion that the only reason anyone would want the bottles loose in their car was for easy access, meaning there was a damn good chance they intended to drink while they drove.

If he had short-timer's syndrome, he would've said fuck it and driven on by. Whatever was happening here was hardly the crime of the century. But he was determined to do his job to the absolute best of his ability until the day he handed in his badge and weapon.

He pulled up behind the Lexus and parked. He didn't hit the cruiser's lights, though. Right now he was just checking out the situation. If it turned out to be nothing, he'd be on his way. If not, these two women would have some explaining to do. He turned off the cruiser's engine and climbed out of the vehicle. He didn't undo the snap that secured his weapon in its holster. Neither of the women looked particularly dangerous, and he didn't want to come across as a hard-ass right off the bat. A large part of police work was communicating with people, and it was hard to get them to talk – and even harder to get them to listen – if they thought you might pull a gun on them any second.

"Good afternoon, ladies."

The woman standing behind the dolly didn't look at him, which set off alarm bells for him right away. *Everybody* looked at a cop approaching, regardless of whether they were innocent or not. People responded like they were small animals sensing the presence of a much larger predator approaching. They froze and fixed their gazes on what they saw as a potential threat, waiting to see what was going to happen next and hoping the predator would pass them by. But not this woman. She stared straight ahead without expression, as if he didn't exist. Was she on something? It sure as hell looked like it.

He turned his attention to the older woman then. She'd been putting a pair of bottles in her car as he walked up, but now she withdrew and turned in his direction, giving him his first good look at her. His earlier impression of the woman as skeletal had been more on the mark than he'd realized. She looked like a cancer victim in the last debilitating stage of the disease, her body devoured from the inside out. Only a few wisps of hair clung to her otherwise bald scalp, and her skin looked as tough and dry as old boot leather. Her face was a skull covered by a paper-thin layer of flesh, and her hands were twisted, bony claws. She exuded a harsh astringent odor, as if she'd recently taken a bath in one hundred proof alcohol. The sight of her was so disturbing that Al undid the snap on his holster and kept his hand close to his weapon. His instincts told him to turn around without saying a word, get back in his cruiser, and drive away without looking back. But he was a sworn officer of the law, and he remained where he was. When he spoke, his voice was calm, but firm.

"Would you mind telling me what—"

The skeleton woman opened her mouth wide, wider than should've been possible, and a stream of brown fluid jetted out. Al tried to bring up his hands to shield his face, but he was too slow. The liquid splashed into his face, and he took a step backward, spitting and gasping.

"What the *fuck*?"

He took hold of his weapon but didn't draw it. He stood motionless, all thought and feeling gone. In that moment, the consciousness that called itself Al Mills ceased to exist, and in its place was an empty vessel, ready to serve its new master. Al was never going to retire, never going to start a business and be his own boss. All because he was too damned conscientious. Not much of an epitaph, perhaps, but it would have to do.

* * *

Grace looked over her new servant. He was tall and fit. Not bad-looking either. His black hair had more than a little gray in it, but she thought it made him look distinguished. She'd always found a man in uniform sexy, but the fact that his uniform was currently wet with her vomit dulled the effect quite a bit.

"Help her load the car," she ordered.

The officer's face showed no expression as he stepped forward. Grace moved out of the way and watched as he took over the task of emptying boxes and placing bottles in the back seat of her Lexus. He was able to work faster than she had, and in no time at all the job was done. After placing the last bottle in the car, he stepped back and stood next to Velda, both of them motionless and expressionless as they awaited her next command.

Empty cardboard boxes lay on the sidewalk where the officer had tossed them, and Grace kicked one aside as she walked up to the man. Up close, he was even more good-looking than she'd thought, and she reached out and stroked his cheek with her claw fingers. If he was truly hers to command, she could make him do whatever she wanted to her – and she could think of a lot of delightful activities they could engage in. But the thought did nothing for her. Sexual desire was a distant memory now. She had only one need, and the back seat of her Lexus was filled with it. Still, a police officer could come in handy in many other ways, so she decided to keep him. First, though, she wanted to test his loyalty.

"Shoot her."

The officer showed no hesitation. He drew his weapon, turned toward Velda, pointed the barrel at her head, and fired. The gunshot was much louder than Grace expected – she'd never been around guns before – and it startled her. Velda's head snapped back as the rear of her skull exploded in a spray of blood and brains. She collapsed, falling onto one of the cardboard boxes and crumpling it. The officer holstered his weapon, turned back to Grace, and awaited her next order.

She was pleased with his performance. "Good boy," she said, and had to resist an urge to pat him on the head. She hooked a thumb toward the Lexus. "You're driving. Get in."

The officer opened the driver's side door of the car, slid into the seat, then closed the door after him. He put on the seat belt and Grace laughed, a hollow, brittle sound, like bones tumbling down a flight of stairs.

"Safety first," she said.

She went around to the vehicle's passenger side, got in, and selected a bottle from her back seat supply at random. She opened it, removed the cork, and took a healthy swig.

"Do you know where Gold Medal Bank is, over on Kennard Road?"

"Yes."

"That's where we're going."

She'd worked there as a loan officer for thirteen years until they'd thrown her ass out on the street. She wanted to pay the old gang a visit and let them know how she felt about being unceremoniously kicked to the curb. And when she was done there, she'd have her new friend drive her to the Historic District so she could drop in on Sierra at ArtWorks. She still wanted her goddamned purse back.

The officer started the engine, put the car in gear, and pulled away from the curb. Grace liked having a chauffeur. It made her feel important. Better yet, it left her hands free so she could drink all she liked as they drove. She finished the bottle she held, rolled down her window, tossed the empty out, then turned around to get another.

She smiled. This was turning out to be a pretty goddamned great day after all.

* * *

Getting through class was tougher than Sierra had anticipated. It was an introductory drawing class, and the students were working on drawing various small objects they'd brought from home – keys, silverware, flashlights, kids' meal toys, pill bottles, mini-staplers, and such. The catch was they had to swap objects with another student and draw the new one. Sierra didn't have to lecture, which was good since she didn't think she'd be able to string together two coherent thoughts today. But she had to walk around and give feedback to students as they worked, and she had difficulty concentrating on their drawings. In a lot of ways, delivering a canned lecture would've been easier. She was mentally exhausted by the time class ended, and she was more than ready to leave campus and go in search of Jeffrey. She hoped Marc had had enough time to get used to the idea of hunting down his dead boyfriend, but if she had to go it alone, she would.

Normally she had an office hour after class, but she intended to skip it today, hoping the department chair wouldn't notice. But she had to walk by her office – really a space she shared with other part-time faculty – on her way out of the building, and when she did, she groaned inwardly. A student from one of her summer classes was standing in the hall outside her office, waiting.

The girl – Sierra couldn't recall her name at first – smiled as she approached. The student was a petite African-American girl with large owl-eye glasses who always wore oversized sweaters to class, even when it was warm out.

"Hi, Ms. Sowell! I was hoping that I could pick up my portfolio from last semester?"

Sierra remembered the girl now. Her name was Jennifer Greer, and she had an annoying habit of bending her sentences as if they were questions. Sierra did her best to smile back at Jennifer.

"No problem," she said.

As she fished around in her bag for her keys, she saw the office next to hers was open and a light was on inside. Fantastic. The last thing she needed today was to have an encounter with Mandy Porterfield. If she could get Jennifer's portfolio to her quickly, maybe she'd be able to sneak past Mandy's office without the woman noticing.

Fat chance of that, she thought.

She unlocked her office, turned on the light, and went to her cubicle, Jennifer trailing along behind. There were six cubicles crammed into the office, and Sierra's was all the way in the back. None of the others were in use at the moment, which suited her just fine. She didn't feel like saying hi to any of her fellow teachers right now. The portfolio cases from the summer's advanced drawing class were lined up on the floor next to her chair.

"See yours?" Sierra asked.

Jennifer stepped forward, flipped through the cases until she found hers, then picked it up.

"Thanks, Ms. Sowell. See you later!"

Jennifer left and Sierra followed her out. She locked the door as Jennifer headed down the hallway, and she was beginning to think she was going to escape without having to deal with Mandy when she heard, "Good afternoon, Sierra."

She turned and saw Mandy Porterfield standing in the open doorway of her office.

"Hi, Mandy." She didn't bother trying to conceal the disappointment in her voice.

Mandy taught in the mathematics department, but she didn't fit the bookish, nerdy stereotype of a math professor. She looked more like a headmistress at an elite – and extremely strict – private school. She wore her auburn hair up in a tight bun and dressed in conservative business attire: suit jacket, knee-length skirt, blouse buttoned all the way to the top. She preferred subdued colors – blues and grays, mostly – and never wore patterns. No jewelry of any sort, and her makeup was so understated it was almost impossible to tell she wore any at all. She was almost six feet tall and always stood ramrod-straight, which only served to accentuate breasts so large they must've caused her constant back pain. Tall women often wore flats to keep from drawing more attention to their height, but not Mandy. She wore heels, every damn day, even in wintertime when she might have to walk through snow.

People thought of mathematicians, when they thought of them at all, as logical, methodical, emotionally restrained beings, fleshly incarnations of calculating machines. Mandy, however, was a woman of strong passions, but those passions had nothing to do with math, teaching, or her students, and everything to do with the campus organization she was lead advisor of: the Traditional Values Club. If there was a socially conservative cause – especially if it was related in any way to sex – Mandy wasn't just for it; she thought everyone else should be too. And if they didn't agree, she thought there should be laws to force them to. Right was right, as far as she was concerned, and when it came to what was right, the end justified the means – always.

Sierra hated walking by Mandy's office. She displayed graphic pictures of aborted fetuses on her door, along with printouts of messages like *Homosexuality is a Choice: Choose God Instead* and *Chastity is Sexy. Save Yourself for Marriage.* Sierra didn't share Mandy's beliefs, but that wasn't why she loathed the woman's door display. She thought Mandy's signs – especially the ones with the dead bloody fetuses on them – were unprofessional and created a threatening environment for students. Sierra had complained to human resources about Mandy's pictures before, and while she was always promised the matter would be 'looked into', nothing ever happened. She'd heard that Mandy had a lawyer on speed dial and was ready to sue the college the instant anyone in the administration so much as suggested she remove the pictures from her door.

As far as Sierra was concerned, Mandy Porterfield was a bully – most likely a sexually repressed one – and having office space next to her was the worst thing about teaching at Riverbank.

Mandy gave Sierra a thin, bloodless smile.

"Will I see you at today's meeting? Everyone's welcome, you know. I'd love to see you come." Her smile widened almost imperceptibly.

Sierra hated it when Mandy did this. She'd say things that sounded like double entendres, speaking them in a honeyed purr that was almost but not quite vulgar. As near as Sierra could tell, Mandy said these things without any conscious awareness, but that only made them creepier.

Sierra glanced at a flyer taped to the wall beside Mandy's door.

Traditional Values Club Meeting Today.

1:30–2:30. Library Meeting Room C.

Today's Discussion: Homosexuality, the Bible, and You.

She faced Mandy once more.

"My brother was gay, and there was absolutely nothing wrong with him."

"You're such a good sister, Sierra. So loyal. It must have been difficult to lose him."

He might not be as lost as you think, Sierra thought.

"I have something I really need to do right now, Mandy, so if you'll excuse me...."

She started to go, but Mandy took hold of her arm and stopped her. The woman's hand felt moist, almost as if she were sweating, and she could've sworn that Mandy moved her thumb back and forth the merest fraction, as if caressing her skin.

"Today's the anniversary of the accident, isn't it?" Mandy said. "It might make you feel better to come to the meeting. You could tell us about Jeffrey. What he was like, how you've dealt with his loss." She paused, then added, "How he died."

Sierra pulled her arm free from Mandy's grip and scowled.

"What do you mean 'How he died'?"

"The accident happened after a fight with his boyfriend, didn't it?"

Sierra had been so grief-stricken in those first days after her brother's death that when Mandy had approached her and asked if there was anything she could to do help, Sierra told her the details of what had happened, all of them. Now she regretted letting her guard down around the woman.

"Your brother is in a sinful relationship with another man, has an argument with him, and drives off just as a powerful storm is gathering.... Some might see that as a sign."

Sierra was getting angry now.

"Are you suggesting that god killed my brother to punish him for being gay?"

Mandy shrugged. "I'm not *suggesting* anything, but I do find it interesting that—"

Sierra grabbed hold of Mandy's shoulders and slammed her against her office door. Mandy didn't look surprised at all by

Sierra's reaction. On the contrary, Sierra thought she detected a flicker of a smile cross the woman's face. But it was gone before she could tell if it had been real or just her imagination.

"I don't give a shit what you believe," Sierra said. "You want to hate gays? Fine, go ahead. But when you try to spread your hatred to other people under the guise of championing 'Traditional Values', that's when I have a problem."

She glanced at Mandy, but the woman looked back at her smugly, as if by shoving her against the door, Sierra had proven something Mandy had always suspected about her.

Some of the anger left Sierra then, and she let go of Mandy and stepped back.

"Just leave me alone from now on. Please."

Then she turned and hurried off down the hallway. There was a water fountain at the end of the hall, and a man was bent over it drinking. He wore a black suit – a very *deep* black, like a starless night sky that went on forever. He had to hold his long blond hair back to keep it from getting wet as he drank. For a moment, Sierra thought she recognized him, but she couldn't place where she might've seen him before. As she passed the man, he glanced in her direction and gave her a wink.

Jesus, she thought. *What the hell is it with all the weirdos today?*

* * *

Mandy stood in her office doorway and watched Sierra walk away. She was a pretty girl, even if she did tend to dress on the frumpy side, and she had an interesting way of swaying her hips as she walked, the motion somehow demure and provocative at the same time. Mandy wondered if it was something she did on purpose, or if it was completely unconscious. She suspected the latter. Sierra didn't strike her as the overtly sexual type. Even so, a temptress was a temptress, whether or not she intended to be one, and Mandy didn't approve. *She* was careful about the way she walked, was always aware of roving eyes upon her. Men, women, it didn't matter. Their hearts overflowed with lust, and they sized up everyone they saw in terms of how attractive they were and whether or not they wanted to fuck them. Mandy made sure to comport herself in public in such a way as to not fuel their wickedness any further. Her manner of dress, her almost complete lack of makeup, the asexual way she moved.... They were all part of her camouflage, a way of rendering herself sexually invisible.

And for the most part, it worked. Oh, there were some men – and women – who were attracted to her ice queen persona. They viewed it as a public cover for a secret sexual inferno blazing inside her. Or they saw her as a challenge: could they manage to break through her passionless exterior and awaken the real woman inside? Mandy always rebuffed advances from these people, and while she knew it probably wasn't charitable of her, she enjoyed seeing their disappointment and frustration when she denied them.

Despite the Traditional Values Club's focus on combatting homosexuality, Mandy had nothing against gays specifically. She was against *all* forms of immoral sexual activity. Sex before marriage, sex outside of marriage, promiscuity, masturbation, polyamory.... Basically, if it involved genitals and didn't have anything to do with procreation, she considered it wicked and sinful. But she wasn't a fool. She knew that an overall anti-sex message would fall on deaf ears in this culture, where sex was celebrated and encouraged in all aspects of life. She viewed her crusade against homosexuality as a starting point, a loose thread to tug on that would hopefully lead to the entire sweater unraveling eventually. Turn people against gay sex, and then you could turn them against other types of immoral sexual behavior. It was like working a complex math problem. It had to be accomplished one step at a time.

Mandy had come to understand the evils of sexuality when she was in junior high. She'd developed breasts earlier than most of the other girls, and her new boobs drew everyone's attention. The boys, who even at the beginning of adolescence were little more than sex-obsessed animals, couldn't keep their eyes off her. Sometimes in class they'd rub their crotches while looking at her. Teachers were fixated on her tits as well. The male teachers' gazes always fell to her breasts whenever she passed, and the female teachers gave her sympathetic looks, as if they understood what she was going through. Most of the female teachers, that is. Some of them looked at her with disapproval, and she could guess what they were thinking: *There goes a slut in training.*

The situation only got worse in high school. Her breasts grew even larger, and she developed an hourglass figure that drove boys wild and made the other girls resent her. She did her best to ignore the stares and the glares, to pretend she didn't hear the crude comments as she walked through the halls.

How can you stand up straight with those things?

Man, what I wouldn't give to jugfuck her!

I could suck on those titties for days!

Somehow she made it through her freshman year. She hoped her sophomore year might be better, that maybe the other kids would be a little more mature this year. But it was just as bad as ever. Worse, because now boys were hitting on her all the time. They acted as if they liked her, but the entire time they spoke to her, their gazes kept dropping to her chest.

But then one day Ronnie Neal, a junior who played on the school's baseball team, approached her. He was good-looking and nice, and he didn't look at her boobs the entire time he spoke to her. He asked her out to a movie, she accepted, and he was a gentleman the entire time. Eventually, they had sex, and while it was scary and awkward, it was also loving and wonderful, and for the first time she was glad she had a woman's body, grateful for the pleasures she could give and receive.

She fell in love with Ronnie – or, at least, what a fifteen-year-old who's beginning to explore her sexuality thinks of as love – and they had sex several more times. She thought she was living in the best of all possible worlds, and she no longer cared if people stared at her breasts. Let them look. She loved Ronnie, and she was pretty sure he loved her, and to hell with everyone else.

And then came the day when Ronnie said he had a surprise for her. His parents had gone out of town for the weekend, and they had the house to themselves. He wanted to have sex in his parents' bed, an idea she found a little icky but also a little sexy. More than a little. He told her to get naked and slide under the sheets, and she did, him standing there fully clothed and watching her. Then he told her to wait right there while he got the surprise ready. He left the bedroom, closing the door quietly behind him.

The sheets were invigoratingly cool on her bare skin, and she wiggled on the mattress, enjoying the sensation. Her nipples were hard as rocks and throbbed with a delicious ache, and she was so wet between her legs that she could feel the fluid moistening her thighs and dampening the sheet beneath her. She wondered what sort of surprise Ronnie had for her. Was he putting on some sexy underwear that he'd bought without her knowing? Was he bringing something from the kitchen, like chocolate sauce or whipped cream that they would smear over each other's bodies and lick off while they screwed?

The door opened and Ronnie – naked, full erection bobbing as he walked – came into the bedroom. But he wasn't alone. Four other boys followed, friends of his from the baseball team, all of them just as naked and hard as he was. None of the boys said a word as they took up positions around the bed, two on each side, Ronnie at the foot. Ronnie pulled the sheet off her, wadded it up, and tossed it in a corner. He was smiling. The other boys were smiling. Then all five of them crawled onto the bed and onto her.

She didn't remember much after that. She remembered hands and mouths and cocks and pain and cum, but no faces. Thank Christ, no faces.

Afterward, Ronnie's friends left without a word, and when they were gone, Mandy started crying. Ronnie told her he was sorry, that he'd thought she'd enjoy it, that he never would've invited his friends over if he'd known she'd react like this. He got into bed and tried to hold her, but she pushed him away so violently he rolled off and fell on the floor. He got pissed then and told her if she was going to be a whiny little cunt then she should get dressed and get her whore ass the hell out.

She did so, crying the entire time. She cried a lot more during the rest of the weekend, and on Monday she feigned illness so she could stay home. Her parents made her go back to school on Tuesday and as she walked through the hallway to her locker, she saw the smirks and the disapproving looks, and the sheer loathing that was in so many of the students' eyes, and she felt a deep shame. She knew what had happened hadn't been her fault, but that didn't change the way she felt.

She never spoke to Ronnie again, and he soon moved on to a new girl. She didn't date again in high school, but when she got to college – where no one knew about her past – she'd tried to have relationships, but they always ended badly, if they managed to get off the ground in the first place. By the time she started her doctoral program, she'd not only given up on sex, she'd begun to see society's obsession with it as a pernicious defect of the human animal, one which needed to be corrected. She'd found a purpose in life, a higher calling, and for the first time since the moment Ronnie had led his friends into his parents' bedroom, she was happy.

Mandy was so lost in her memories that she wasn't aware anyone had approached her until she heard a man speak.

"Ready for the meeting?"

Startled, she turned to see Conrad Haskell standing next to her. Conrad was shorter than she was, almost fifteen years older, and he had what was euphemistically referred to as a dad bod, but she still thought he was a good-looking man. He had a full head of thick brown hair, and he always wore bow ties that he tied himself. No clip-ons for him. She liked his smile too, found it warm and genuine. But what she liked most about him was that he was a complete beta male, easily led. Compliance was an extremely attractive quality in a person, Mandy thought.

She suspected Conrad might have a crush on her, but he wasn't the kind of man who'd come out and admit it. He was the type who'd wait until she approached him romantically, convinced that some day she would. The poor fool.

Conrad was co-advisor on the Traditional Values Club with her, and he was dedicated to the cause of promoting a higher moral standard on campus. But while Mandy was primarily concerned with sexual matters, Conrad – who taught political science – was a proponent of every hard-right conservative stance there was, both social and economic. He had a tendency to lecture people on politics, which quickly became tiresome, but he was an effective ally in her work, and she appreciated his assistance.

She gave him a smile.

"Central Duplicating delivered some new flyers. They came out looking pretty good, I think."

She walked into her office, and Conrad remained outside, always the perfect gentleman. She was disappointed. She found the idea of being alone with him in the confined space of her office – where they would be forced to stand close to each other – to be a pleasant one. But she shouldn't think such things, and she banished the thought from her mind. She picked up the stack of flyers, turned out her office light, and closed the door. She handed Conrad a flyer from the top of the stack and he examined it.

"Looks great." He handed it back. "I especially like the title. It's catchy *and* thought-provoking."

The topic for today's discussion was *Who's in Charge – You or Your Sex Organs?* Beneath the title was information on joining the Traditional Values Club, along with the web addresses for sites dealing with abstinence and how to combat homosexual urges.

"But don't you think the phrase –" he lowered his voice, " – *sex organs* is a little graphic?"

"That's the point. If we used *genitals* it wouldn't have the same impact."

"I, ah, suppose so."

She enjoyed watching him squirm. The word *sex* alone was enough to make him uncomfortable, but with *organs* attached to it, she thought he might come down with a case of the vapors and fall back onto his fainting couch.

"How about I head on down to the library and make sure everything's ready?" he asked.

There was no need. The meeting room had a lectern for a speaker to stand at and a half dozen round tables with plastic chairs arranged around them. It was always the same every time they used it. But Conrad was an anxious person, and one way he managed his anxiety was by over-preparing.

"Sounds good," she said. *As if I could stop you*, she thought.

Conrad smiled with more than a little relief. "Okay. See you in a bit."

He still had the flyers, and he took them with him as he left. She had no doubt that when she arrived at the meeting room, he'd have neatly placed the flyers on each table, one per chair, with the rest left on the lectern in case they received a larger crowd than they expected and needed to distribute extras. They'd never had that large a crowd yet, but she admired Conrad's optimism.

She went back inside her office to answer a couple emails and respond to a voicemail, and then she turned off the light and closed the door. As she locked it, a powerful thirst came over her. It felt as if she hadn't had anything to drink in days. Her throat felt as if it were swelling shut and she found it hard to breathe. What in the world was happening to her? Was she having some kind of allergic reaction? She'd eaten a salad in the cafeteria for lunch, but she hadn't put anything on it that she hadn't had before.

She hurried toward the drinking fountain at the end of the hallway. She wanted to run, but she didn't want to draw attention to herself, so she settled for a fast walk. When she reached the fountain, she abandoned any pretense of normal behavior. She lowered her head to the nozzle, pressed the push button, and water streamed into her mouth. She slurped and gulped like an animal, water spilling over her chin and dripping into the basin. But no matter how much she drank, her throat remained swollen. More, it seemed to be getting worse. If she couldn't get some relief soon, she was afraid her airway would be cut off entirely. She'd pass out then, and if she didn't receive prompt medical attention, there was a good chance she'd die. She felt herself start to panic, and she was about to lift her head from the fountain and go seek help when she caught movement out of the corner of her eye. A man was walking past, one she'd seen before, when she was speaking with Sierra. She'd never seen him before then but given his suit – which was such an *odd* black – and his long hair, she thought he might be a new, somewhat eccentric, faculty member.

Thank god, she thought. *He'll see I'm in distress and help me. I'll be okay. I'll—*

She turned her head to look at him, tried to say something,

but she couldn't get any words past her swollen throat. He kept walking, not bothering to spare even a short glance in her direction. She thought she would have to reach out and grab his arm as he passed, shake him and force him to pay attention. But before she could, his hand strayed toward the water nozzle, and his index finger tapped it. Just once, but his fingernail made the metal ring, as if he'd struck a bell. And then something else began coming out of the nozzle, a thick viscous substance that splattered into the basin as it fell, collecting in thick globs that refused to go down the drain. Her face remained close to the fountain, although she'd raised her head enough when she tried to speak that the muck didn't strike her. Revulsion filled her, and she was about to draw back and step away from the fountain when the smell hit her.

It was a foul salty musk that she couldn't name, but which she nevertheless recognized on a primal level. She breathed it in, unable to stop herself, and as she did her revulsion fell away to be replaced by *need*. So strong, so overwhelming, that she couldn't have stopped herself if she wanted to, and she most definitely did *not* want to.

She leaned her face to the thick stream and drank greedily. If she'd drank like an animal before, now she did so like a frenzied beast, vigorously lapping at the stream, reaching into the basin with her hands to gather the globs of muck and jam them into her face. She moaned and snarled as she swallowed, shaking her head rapidly back and forth as if trying to force the gooey substance down faster to make room for more. The swelling in her throat eased, as did her breathing, but she barely noticed. All she cared about right then was getting as much of this glorious stuff into her belly as she could. A memory came to her as she swallowed mouthful after mouthful. Ronnie and her lying in bed after having sex, the air filled with the mingled scents of their lovemaking. His semen, her vaginal fluid blending together into a heady perfume of lust. That's what she was drinking now, that scent given physical form.

And with this realization, the muck turned to water once more, and when she looked at the basin, the globby bits of the stuff were gone. All she saw was clear liquid swirling around and down into the drain.

The tasteless water now filling her mouth disgusted her, and she spit it out violently. Then she stood and looked around to see if anyone had been watching her. Students and faculty passed by, but no one looked in her direction. Despite the scene she'd made, no one seemed to have noticed, and she was relieved. She looked for the man in the black suit, but she saw no sign of him. The…a term drifted into her mind: *aqua sexus,* the water of sex. Yes, that was perfect. The *aqua sexus* had started flowing the instant after the man in the black suit had touched the fountain's nozzle. It was crazy, but she couldn't escape the feeling that the man had caused the *aqua sexus* to flow. She wanted to find him—

—and thank him.

She felt deliciously warm inside, her muscles relaxed and loose, not an ounce of tension to be found in them. For the first time since that awful day with Ronnie and his friends, she felt completely at ease in her body. She felt *free.* She could take off her clothes right here and stride down the hallway naked without the least hint of self-consciousness. The thought of doing so, of everyone's eyes on her as she walked past, excited her, and she felt her sex grow instantly wet.

She let out a languorous sigh and stretched, reveling in the sensation of her body moving. She felt as if she'd awakened from a years-long dream, a butterfly finally emerged from its chrysalis. She felt so good, so *right.* She'd been reborn, and she wanted to share this magnificent feeling with others, help them experience the great gift of carnal liberation. And she knew where a group of people in dire need of hearing her message were gathered, and brother, did they need what she now had to give them.

As she started walking down the hall she removed her suit jacket and dropped it to the floor. She undid the first few buttons on her blouse to display her cleavage, then reached up to undo her bun. She shook her hair loose and ran her fingers through it to straighten it out. The sensation felt so goddamned good, a small orgasm shivered between her thighs. She smiled. That had been nice, but it was only the beginning.

There's more where that came from, girl, she thought. *A lot more.*

"I'm going to fuck the world!" she shouted, then she laughed when startled faculty and students turned to look at her, not believing what they'd heard.

She continued on, her hips swaying in a way they never had before. *Better than Sierra's, I bet.* This afternoon's meeting of the Traditional Values Club was going to be something special.

CHAPTER EIGHT

Corliss emerged from an empty classroom after Mandy walked past. It had been a busy day for him up to this point, but now that all the pieces were in place, he could sit back, relax, and watch as the events he'd set in motion played out. If he'd wished, he could've peeked into the future and glimpsed all the possible outcomes of his efforts, but he refused to give in to the temptation. Where would be the fun in that?

He had one last errand to attend to first, though.

He stepped back into the classroom, opened a rift, stepped through, and sealed it behind him. The next three people who walked through the space where the invisible rift scar was would begin hearing voices whispering the most obscene and blasphemous things in their ears. The voices would continue their awful litany day and night without cease, driving these people to jam sharp objects into their ears in an attempt to find relief. They'd succeed in destroying their hearing, of course, but the voices would continue uninterrupted, whispering filth in their minds until the day they died.

* * *

Randall pulled his Lincoln Town Car into his driveway and parked. He didn't bother putting the vehicle in the garage since he planned to return to the Historic District soon. He had more work to do there – a *lot* more.

He got out of the car and paused to look across the street at the Sowells' house. Most of the homes in the neighborhood were of a type, and theirs – his too, for that matter – was no exception. Two stories, white siding, black roof and black shutters, short driveway, small yard, one tree in front (oak) and another in back (elm). Dana Sowell wasn't much of a landscaper, unlike his Erika, who planted flowers every spring and tended them lovingly. Hedges surrounded the Sowells' house, and they always needed trimming. Their roof was missing a number of shingles, their cement driveway had several large cracks in it, and their grass was always too high. Randall believed a family's house was the face they chose to present to the world, and that face told you everything you needed to know about them. The Sowells' face said they were lazy, inconsiderate people. Lazy because they didn't maintain their property the way they should, and inconsiderate because their house was a blight on the rest of the neighborhood.

No wonder Sierra had turned out the way she had.

As he walked toward the front door of his house – which had green shutters, a green roof, and yellow siding – he clutched his special Chuck in his hand. Except it no longer felt right. He looked down at his hand and didn't see the coppery blade or the handle with the three-dimensional Chuck on the end protruding from his grip. He opened his hand and saw that all he held was a normal Chuck – a penny with a smiley face on one side. He frowned. He could've sworn that he'd grabbed the knife off the passenger seat when he'd gotten out of the car. But this obviously wasn't it.

He returned to the car, opened the door, and slid into the driver's seat, not bothering to close the door behind him. He didn't see the knife sitting on the passenger seat, and he spent several minutes searching for it, checking to see if he'd placed it in the glove compartment or if it had fallen between the seats. But he couldn't find it. He ran his hand over his head in a gesture of frustration and was surprised to find hair on the back of his head. He angled the rearview mirror so he could look at himself and saw he appeared as he always did these days: a tired, middle-aged man. His skin wasn't yellow and his features were normal.

That couldn't be right. He'd *changed*. Not only had he felt it, he'd seen his yellow hands, had reached up and touched his oversized round head, the line of his mouth, the smooth place where his nose had been. He'd become a living Chuck, and he couldn't have been happier. Had it been some kind of delusion? A bizarre imagining produced by his aging mind? But it had seemed so *real.*

He'd thought he'd come home to share the wondrous transformation that had befallen him with his wife, to show her that his making and handing out Chucks all these years hadn't been a *foolish and annoying hobby*, as she'd once told him. But he had nothing to show her now.

Depressed and more than a little worried about his mental health, he got out of the car, closed the door, and headed up the walkway to the front door. It wasn't locked – they never locked it during the day – and he went inside. He immediately heard his wife puttering around in the kitchen, humming happily to herself. Erika was constitutionally incapable of being quiet for more than a few seconds at a time, and he could always locate her by listening for the sounds of cupboard doors being shut loudly, the refrigerator door being slammed, or one appliance or another running.

He entered the kitchen and found Erika standing in front of a counter, chopping vegetables on a wooden cutting board. A large pot rested on the stove beside her. He assumed she intended to make her famous vegetable soup for dinner tonight. She thought it was one of his favorite meals, and he'd never had the heart to tell her that he thought the soup was just okay. She hadn't started cooking anything yet, and the kitchen smelled only of the lavender perfume she wore. She always put some on in the morning, regardless of whether she planned to leave the house or not. He didn't recognize the tune she was humming, but that was no surprise. She loved music, but she couldn't carry a tune to save her soul.

She glanced over her shoulder as he came in and smiled.

"You're back early."

Erika was a short woman, just under five foot, and she used a small stool to stand on when she worked in the kitchen. She'd been a tiny slip of a thing with fiery red hair when they'd married, but her hair had long ago become gray, and her body was matronly plump. She wore makeup and jewelry every day, even if he was the only one who would see her. *A girl likes to look her best,* she'd say whenever he told her she didn't have to fuss about her appearance, not at her age, which was a long way from when she could've been considered a girl.

She didn't dress up at home, though, opting for comfort over fashion. Today she wore a white sweatshirt decorated with pictures of autumn leaves, a pair of jeans, and house slippers. She couldn't abide walking barefoot in the house or going about in socks. She made him wear slippers too when he took off his shoes, and he suspected she had some kind of aversion to seeing bare feet, kind of the opposite of a foot fetish.

He expected her to put down her knife, step down from her stool, walk over to him, stand on her tiptoes, and give him a peck on the cheek. It was what she always did when he came home, a ritual so often performed that by now it was as immediate and unthinking as a reflex. But she didn't do that. Instead, she stared at him, eyes widening.

"What in the world happened to you? Are you all right?"

"I have no idea what you're talking about."

She still stood on her stool at the counter, but now she turned around to face him.

"Your *clothes*," she said.

He frowned. "What's wrong with—" He broke off as he looked down and saw dark splotches on his sweatshirt and slacks. At first he couldn't figure out what the stains were or how he'd gotten them, but then it came back. He remembered the young mother with the tattoos and piercings, remembered what he'd done to her and her squalling bastard child.

He grinned. It hadn't been a delusion! It *had* happened! He didn't know why he'd changed back to his normal self, but that wasn't important now. All that mattered was for a time he had been a Chuck, had been *the* Chuck.

"Don't worry about it. I'm sure it'll come off in the wash." He said this even though he had no idea if the stains would come out or not.

"But it looks like *blood*. Are you sure you haven't been hurt?" She stepped off the stool and came toward him, obviously intending to examine the stains more closely, as if she didn't trust his self-assessment.

He held out his hand and opened it to display the Chuck that had until recently been a copper knife.

Erika stopped dead when she saw the Chuck and scowled.

"You're not trying to give me one of those damn things, are you? You know how much I hate them."

He bristled at the derisive tone in her voice.

"No. I want to tell you about something that happened to me today in the Historic District. Something *wonderful*."

"You told me you were going to go walking down by the river. You said you haven't been getting enough exercise and that a walk in the fresh air was just what the doctor ordered. Are you telling me you didn't go walking?"

Erika was the sweetest woman he'd ever met – until it came to the subject of Chucks. She'd never understood his hobby, and his numerous attempts to explain it to her over the years hadn't helped. She told him it was weird, that it made people uncomfortable when he approached them, that not only were Chucks creepy, there was something almost indecent about giving them to children.

It's like you're a pedophile using your goddamn Chucks as a way to get close to kids, she'd once said.

That one had really hurt. Randall loved children, and he'd never do anything to make them feel the least bit afraid and unsafe. And to insinuate that he had sexual urges regarding children wasn't only disgusting, it was also insulting. He suspected the true reason Erika hated him passing out Chucks was that it embarrassed her, just as it had embarrassed their son and daughter while they'd been growing up. Erika couldn't bear the thought of other women looking at her and whispering, *That poor thing. You know she's married to that freak who passes out the smiley-face pennies? I'd just* die *if my husband did anything like that.*

He was tempted to make up another lie rather than tell her the truth, but he was sick of hiding the part of him that wanted to make the world a better place from his wife. It was the best part of him, damn it, and he was proud of it, regardless of what Erika thought.

"It's true. I didn't go walking by the river. I went to the Historic

District so I could pass out Chucks. I lied because I didn't want to deal with you giving me grief about it."

"Oh my god," she said. "You promised me you weren't going to do this anymore."

"I said I wouldn't pass them out at the mall over in Ash Creek anymore. I never said I planned to stop altogether."

"Jesus Christ."

Randall flinched at her casual blasphemy. Erika only swore when she was nail-spitting mad, and nothing got her worked up like the subject of Chucks.

"I did pass some out today. I ran into Sierra Sowell and tried to give her one, but she refused it."

"Good for her," Erika said.

Up to this point, Randall had worked to maintain a positive attitude, but Erika's negativity was making it difficult. He felt anger rising in response to her, and he knew that if he let it take hold of him, they would end up in a shouting match. And that went against everything the Chucks stood for. They were about happiness and togetherness, about *Have a nice day,* not *Fuck you, bitch.*

The Chuck he was holding twitched in his hand, and it felt heavier now. Not much, but a little. Its shape had changed too, oval now instead of round.

Despite Erika's attitude, he continued on, determined to tell his story. Once he began in earnest, the words tumbled out of him, and he went on until he was finished. Erika didn't interrupt him further, but as she listened her expression changed from angry to disbelieving to horrified.

"You've finally lost your mind," she said. "I've been worried for years that you'd go crazy one day, but I always told myself I was letting my imagination get the best of me. I never thought it would really happen." Her gaze focused on his clothes then, or more accurately, the stains *on* his clothes. "Did you really… hurt someone?" Her voice was tentative as she asked this, as if she wasn't sure she wanted him to answer.

He frowned. Hurt? He'd taught the woman and her brat a little respect, sure, but he hadn't hurt them. Had he?

A mélange of sights and sounds tumbled through his mind

then. The child screaming, the woman begging him to stop, the copper Chuck blade rising and falling, blood arcing through the air. So much blood....

The Chucks in his pocket rustled against one another with soft metallic whispers.

"We need to get you to a hospital." Erika's eyes shone with tears, and her voice was close to a sob. "They'll be able to help you there."

She took hold of his sleeve and started to walk away, obviously intending to lead him to the car. Instead of going along with her, he wrapped his left arm around her chest and pulled her against him. She let out a choked squeak and tried to pull away, but he held her too tight. The Chuck in his right hand lengthened and grew heavier as it once more assumed the form of a copper knife. He closed his fingers around it, and it felt so right in his hand, as if it were a long-lost part of himself that he hadn't realized was missing until it returned. He felt his head swell, his hair fall out, his features simplify and became exaggerated, cartoonish. He looked at the hand that held the knife and was gratified to see his flesh had become yellow once again.

"Randall! Let me go! Please!"

She struggled to turn her head to look at him, and when she finally managed to catch a glimpse of his visage, she screamed.

"Call me Chuck," he said.

* * *

When he was finished, Erika lay on the kitchen floor. Her mouth and throat were jammed full to overflowing with Chucks, and her sweatshirt was riddled with slash marks and the white cloth was soaked dark red. Blood pooled on the floor around her body, splattered the cupboards nearby. The ceiling was stippled crimson, and Randall thought it made an interesting Jackson Pollock-type pattern. He'd never been a fan of modern art, but he liked this. Oh yes, he did.

He thought Erika might've liked it too, but her dead eyes stared sightlessly up at the ceiling, her days of appreciating art over.

He was glad to be back to his smiley-faced self, what he was beginning to think of as his *true* self. Maybe he only became Chuck when there was Chuck's work for him to do, when his blade was needed to excise a piece of negativity from the world and make it a better place. That's what Chucks were for, after all. To make everything better. So if he wanted to stay Chuck, he needed to keep busy. That would be easy enough. The world was full of negative people who needed a permanent attitude adjustment.

Like Sierra.

He thought of their encounter earlier, of how she'd not only spurned his offer to give Chucks to her students, she'd told him how she *really* felt about his modest attempts to make the world a better, nicer place.

You're not making people feel better. You're not brightening their day. All you do is creep them out and make them feel sorry for you!

How long had she felt like that? Had she been lying to him ever since she was a child? It didn't seem possible, but after today, his notions about what was and wasn't possible had become considerably more flexible. He supposed Sierra couldn't be blamed for her attitude, not entirely. Children learned from their parents.

Maybe it's time I went across the street and had a talk with the Sowells, let them know what sort of daughter they raised.

And while he was at it, he could have a discussion with them about the length of their grass.

Plus, they should know Sierra's work schedule and could tell him where she'd be this afternoon. He'd like to pay her a visit too, and introduce her to the very special Chuck he now carried.

Gripping his blood-slick knife tightly in a banana-yellow hand, he headed for the front door.

★ ★ ★

Conrad stood next to the lectern, doing his best to keep smiling. It was 1:35 and Mandy still wasn't there. She was the most punctual person he'd ever met, and he'd never known her to be late for anything. In fact, she was usually early. It was one of the qualities he admired most in her. It was a sign not only of a well-ordered mind but a considerate one as well. Mandy did not believe in wasting anyone's time, least of all her own. He wondered if something had happened to her, if she was sick or hurt. Should he return to her office and check? But if she arrived while he was gone, she'd be furious at him. Better to remain here, wait, and try to keep his anxiety from building.

The Traditional Values Club wasn't one of the more popular campus organizations. There were six round tables with six chairs apiece – the numbers bothered him, were too close to 666 for his comfort – and only half of them were occupied. The group was a mix of students, staff, and faculty, all of them more or less regular attendees. Conrad was disappointed that there weren't any newcomers, but at least the number of attendees hadn't dropped since the last meeting, so that was something.

The people waited patiently enough. A few looked over the flyers Conrad had placed on the tables, some stared down at their phones, some spoke in soft tones, and some looked at Conrad, their eyes shining with the fervor of true believers. Conrad knew he should appreciate those who were so devoted to the club's cause, but privately, they made him uncomfortable. They were too unthinking in their devotion, and it creeped him out a little. He would never express this aloud, though, especially not to Mandy. She'd consider it a weakness on his part, and he didn't want her to think less of him.

Conrad was attracted to Mandy, but he made sure to play it cool whenever he was around her, and he was certain she had no idea how he felt. His attraction to her wasn't carnal, though. Sure, she was a beautiful woman with a great body. Whether she was teaching class or walking down the hall, people's eyes were drawn to her and followed her every move. Conrad wasn't entirely immune to her physical charms, but what he liked most about her was her strength of character and her willingness – no, her eagerness – to champion a cause that was deeply unpopular in this corrupt culture. And her attitude toward casual pleasure-focused sex mirrored his own. He was divorced from his first wife – an elementary school teacher who lived in Akron – because they hadn't been sexually compatible. Gail had been willing to wait until they were married to consummate their relationship, but once the ink was dry on their marriage license and the vows were spoken, she'd become a different person. The stereotype was that women provided sex to men in order to get them to the altar, and after that, they were no longer interested in lovemaking. It had been the opposite in his marriage, though. Not only did Gail want to have sex all the time – two, sometimes three times a week – but she also wanted to try different positions and other stuff that made him uncomfortable and even revolted him. Over the first year of their marriage, he'd tried to be a good husband to Gail and take care of her needs, but he couldn't make his body perform when it didn't wish to, and eventually their marriage fell apart. Gail had made it out to be his fault, had even called him a *limp-dick motherfucker* at one point, but Conrad didn't see it that way. Gail was the one with the problem, the one focused so entirely on her own pleasure that she was willing to sacrifice what was otherwise a perfectly good marriage. Their divorce saddened him, but he would've been lying if he didn't admit it had come as a relief to him as well. He'd refrained from dating after that, unwilling to enter into another relationship that was ultimately doomed to fail.

But then he'd met Mandy, and he thought he might've found his match at last, someone who was more interested in relating on an intellectual level than a sexual one, someone who not only wouldn't demand sex from him but was repulsed by the very idea. In short, Mandy was his dream girl.

He'd been working with her advising the Traditional Values Club for the last few years, but in all that time, he'd never been able to get up the courage to tell her how he felt. If she rejected him, he didn't think he could take it. Where would he ever find someone who matched him as well as her? He kept telling himself that someday he'd work up the nerve to confess his love for her, but deep down he knew he probably never would.

It was 1:42 by the time Mandy entered the library meeting room, and when she did, Conrad's jaw literally dropped open. She'd removed her suit jacket, undone several of the buttons on her blouse to display an alarming amount of cleavage, and let her hair down. It was wild and mussed, as if she'd just risen from bed –

or perhaps had been engaging in activities far more vigorous than sleep. But while all of these changes were disturbing, the biggest change was in the way she carried herself. She didn't so much walk as she did glide, seeming to luxuriate in her body's every movement. Her hips swayed provocatively, and her breasts were thrust forward. He'd never realized just how big they were, and he wondered how she managed to keep them contained within a simple garment made out of thin cloth and a few small buttons.

There was something else different about her too, something that Conrad felt but which he couldn't put words to. She exuded an aura of sexuality, almost a scent, musky and dangerous, the smell of a lion enclosure in a zoo, of an apex predator on the hunt. A word for it came to him then.

Pheromones. She was pumping the chemicals out like an industrial factory that disregarded every environmental regulation ever written. The air suddenly felt heavy – hotter and more humid – and Conrad found himself beginning to sweat. He wasn't the only one affected. Everyone in the room watched Mandy, transfixed, eyes aflame with desire. Conrad's penis stiffened, becoming so hard that it hurt. He couldn't recall the last time he'd had an erection, but he'd never had one like *this* before.

He clasped his hands in front of his crotch to hide his rock-hard dick. Mandy glanced down at his hands as she approached the lectern, then she looked up and gave him a knowing smile that made him feel deliciously dirty inside. Part of him was alarmed by Mandy's transformation, shouted at him to leave before whatever was happening went any further. But most of him wanted to remain right where he was and bask in Mandy's aura of sex. He thought he finally understood how Gail had felt, and if he could've gone back in time right then to the early days of their marriage, he would've fucked her so hard neither of them would've been able to walk for days.

Mandy took her place behind the podium. She nodded to Conrad, this time giving him a smile that was closer to a leer, then she faced this afternoon's audience.

"Sorry I'm late, everyone. My pussy was so hot it felt like the goddamned thing was filled with fire ants, and I had to stop at a restroom and masturbate to take the edge off. I came so hard, I think I broke the fucking stall."

A few people looked shocked, as if she'd slapped them across the face, but most chuckled, Conrad included. He didn't want to, but the sound came out of him all by itself, as if made by someone else who had taken over his body.

"I know you're all here today to listen to a talk about how homosexuality is unhealthy at best, and evil at worst. But I thought we could dispense with that bullshit and fuck instead. Who's with me?"

Without waiting for replies, Mandy began unbuttoning her blouse. Conrad watched, fascinated, as her breasts were revealed. Not all of them, of course. She was wearing a peach-colored bra, but her tits were so large the cups could barely contain them, and it looked as if they might spill out any second. Her erect nipples pushed against the fabric. They were so hard Conrad wouldn't have been surprised if they tore a pair of holes in the bra and popped right through. When she had the last button undone, she tossed the blouse aside. She then kicked off her shoes, unzipped her skirt, and shimmied out of it, revealing panties that Conrad at first thought were a darker peach than her bra, but then he realized the panties were the same color. They only looked darker because they were soaked from her arousal. She stepped out of her skirt and let it lie on the floor. She undid her bra, and her breasts spilled forward, free at last.

Mandy threw the bra into the small audience, and a male staff member – who worked in the maintenance department if Conrad remembered correctly – caught it, brought it to his nose, and inhaled deeply. On one level, Conrad was appalled by the man's behavior, but on another he was jealous as hell. Mandy slipped out of her panties and tossed them into the audience as well. A young girl, presumably a student, caught them. She jammed the wet area into her mouth, closed her eyes, and made *mmmmmmm* sounds as she began to suck Mandy's juice from the cloth. Conrad was even more jealous this time.

Mandy put her hands on her hips and turned halfway to the

side to display herself. Conrad thought she was magnificent. She was perfectly proportioned, skin flawless, muscles toned, not an ounce of fat on her. Now that her vagina was exposed to the air, it exuded a powerful musky odor that Conrad found quite literally intoxicating. It was like a drug in aerosol form, and as he breathed it in, the last of his inhibitions faded. He started tearing off his clothes, not caring if he damaged them. All that mattered was getting the damn things off as swiftly as possible. The rest of the attendees began disrobing just as frantically, and within seconds everyone in the meeting room was naked. An array of body types was represented – tall and short, thin and fat, athletic and sedentary. Small breasts, large breasts, firm ones, saggy ones. Huge penises, smaller ones, circumcised and not, thin and thick, straight and curved. But regardless of the differences, the bodies had one thing in common: they could all fuck and be fucked, and that made them almost unbearably beautiful.

Everyone stood motionless for several seconds, admiring the naked bodies that surrounded them. And then, as if some invisible signal had been given, they grabbed whoever was closest and began kissing, touching, fondling, gripping, pinching, twisting, sucking, biting, and penetrating. Some lay atop tables or sat on chairs as others explored their bodies, but most fell to the floor in groups of twos, threes, and more. Soon Conrad couldn't tell where one person began and another ended. It was as if they'd become a single mass of flesh, and he ached to join them. He stroked his stiff cock as he stepped forward, but a hand gripped his shoulder, stopping him.

He turned to see Mandy smile at him lasciviously.

"Oh no you don't, mister. You're *mine*." Her gaze lowered to take in his erect cock, and her eyebrows lifted. "Conrad! I had no idea!"

Now it was his turn to smile. "My ex-wife used to say that it was wasted on a man like me."

"Well, I intend to put it to good use."

She stepped forward, her breasts pressing against his chest, and they kissed. For Conrad, it was the culmination of a desire that he'd never dared acknowledge, not even to himself, and he gave himself over to her completely.

What happened next was an ever-shifting kaleidoscope of physical sensation. Conrad no longer thought on a conscious level. He became a being comprised entirely of nerve endings and pleasure points whose only purpose was to feel. He'd always pictured heaven as a realm of eternal spring – warm sun, green grass, stately trees, pleasant breezes, all enjoyed in the company of the righteous and the faithful. But now he knew that heaven was surrendering to one's deepest urges, to free from its cage the animal that lay at the core of every human, so it could feast.

Gail, if you could see me now!

After several minutes of fucking Mandy and being fucked by her in return, Conrad found himself on his knees behind Mandy, who was on all fours, pounding himself into her. He gripped her hips so tightly his fingernails drew blood, and his pelvis slapped against her ass so hard, it sounded as if he were striking her with a wooden paddle. Conrad was drenched in sweat, and his pulse thrummed in his ears, a rapid trip-hammer beat. The moans of pleasure and cries of ecstasy produced by their fellow revelers created a carnal chorus for their lovemaking, although love had absolutely nothing to do with their exertions.

"That's it!" Mandy cried out. "Don't slow down – it's about to happen!"

Somewhere in the recesses of his mind, a part that was still a person named Conrad Haskell, and not just a cock with a body attached to it, thought that was an odd way to communicate the approach of an orgasm. *It's about to happen*. But the thought never made it to the forefront of his mind, and he increased the speed and intensity of his thrusts, hoping to help Mandy get to where she so desperately wanted to be.

It had been a long while since he'd had sex with anyone, but while he'd been far from a skilled lover in the past, he was no stranger to what it felt like when a woman came around his cock. With a penis like his, all he had to do was lie back and let his partner do all the work. Gail had almost always come when they'd made love, even if he didn't. He sometimes wondered if he had let her continue to use his body whenever she wanted if they'd still be married. So when he felt his dick being pulled forward, as if by some internal suction within Mandy, he knew something was wrong.

"Don't stop!" she cried. "Goddamn you, do not *stop*!"

The suction increased, and sharp pain shot through his penis and into his groin muscles. He wanted to stop, to pull out and scrabble away from Mandy, put as much distance between the two of them as he could because something was wrong inside her, very, very wrong. But his body was no longer his to command. He belonged to Mandy now, utterly and completely, and he would do as she commanded. He had no choice. He thrust faster and faster, barely able to breathe now, his heart beating so fast that he could no longer detect the pause between its beats. He wondered if his middle-aged heart would give out from the stress, and he almost wished it would. At least that would put an end to this mindless fucking. Had he thought this was heaven? What a joke. This was hell. *His* hell, endless sexual slavery to a woman who only wanted one thing from him, a woman he could never truly satisfy, no matter how hard he tried.

The suction increased to the point where he thought his dick was going to be torn out by the roots, but then his body began to feel strange. Rubbery, less solid, almost as if he were liquefying inside. He thought of the way a spider injects a fly with a chemical that turns its inside to goo, which it can more easily slurp up. And then he felt a great pulling, and his body rushed toward a darkness that engulfed and consumed him. He didn't have time for a last thought, but if he had, it might've been, *At least I'll never have to grade any student exams again.*

★ ★ ★

Mandy's climax was the most intense sensation that she'd ever experienced. Every nerve ending in her body exploded with so much pleasure that for an instant she lost consciousness. But she felt something more, a satisfied fullness inside her, as if she'd just eaten a meal comprised of all her favorite foods. She felt energized, strong, *alive*.... But there was one thing she didn't feel, and that was Conrad's monster cock sliding in and out of her. Still on her hands and knees, she looked back and saw Conrad wasn't there. She glanced around the room, and while she saw a number of writhing naked bodies, none of them was his.

It came to her then, whispered by instincts she hadn't known she possessed, and she couldn't stop herself from laughing. Conrad had come inside her – *literally* – and she had absorbed him, taken his life, his energy for her own.

Satisfied, at least for the moment, she stood and quickly dressed. She didn't bother putting her bra back on, though, or her panties. She'd never wear either of the damn things again. When she was clothed, she gazed upon the men and women who'd come to the meeting and ended up indulging in one of the oldest traditional values the human race had ever known. She hated to leave them while they were still having so much fun, and for an instant she was tempted to disrobe once more and wade into the action. But there was someone else that she'd prefer to get her hands on. Someone she'd love to possess in the same way she now possessed Conrad.

Sierra.

"It's been fun, kittens, but Momma has to be going now. Don't stop on my account." She thought for a moment. "In fact, why don't you keep fucking until you die? You'll never know any greater pleasure than what you're experiencing right now, so you might as well go out while you're on top. Or bottom."

They didn't acknowledge her command, didn't so much as look at her, but their actions became more frenzied and violent, and Mandy knew they would do as they were told.

She made her way through the mass of copulating bodies, breathing in traces of sexual energy that they'd shed. This didn't feed her as fully as Conrad's life force had. It was like eating a small handful of peanuts instead of a full-course meal, but it was tasty nonetheless.

"Waste not, want not," she said, and smiled as she left the meeting room.

★ ★ ★

She didn't expect Sierra to be in her office. She'd seen her leave earlier, after all. But she needed to get inside. Why, she wasn't sure, but she knew she had to if she intended to claim Sierra's life force. She considered calling campus security and making up some story about why she needed them to let her into Sierra's office. She could tell them she'd left something important in there, something she needed badly, and since Sierra wasn't on campus, could they send someone to help her? Yes, that would work, but she didn't want to wait for a security officer to arrive. From past experience, she knew it could take anywhere from five minutes to forty-five. She wanted to enter Sierra's office *now*.

Without thinking about it, she took hold of the knob, pressed her shoulder to the door, and shoved. There was a groan of metal as the lock began to give, and then a *snap* as it broke. The door swung open and Mandy grinned. Evidently, she was stronger now. Much.

She turned on the light, stepped into the empty office, and closed the door behind her. Now that the lock was broken, the door didn't close fully, but that was all right. She didn't need to be in here very long. She'd been in the office before and knew which cubicle was Sierra's. It looked exactly as you'd expect from an art teacher. A poster of Monet's *Water Lilies* tacked to one wall, a poster of Norman Rockwell's famous self-portrait in which he sat at an easel looking into a mirror as he painted an image of himself, a wall calendar that displayed paintings by Georgia O'Keefe. She had a Bob Ross Funko Pop! figure on her desk next to the computer, along with a ceramic pencil-and-pen holder she'd made in college as an undergrad. It wasn't very good, and Mandy thought Sierra had made a wise decision in deciding to devote herself to watercolors as her chosen medium. There were a number of portfolio cases stored next to the chair, but those belonged to students and didn't concern her.

Acting on instinct once more, she bent her face to the computer keyboard and sniffed, drinking in the scent of Sierra's fingers. She then lifted the phone receiver and smelled it. She replaced it, then got down on her knees in front of Sierra's office chair and pressed her nose against the fabric. She inhaled deeply this time, pulling in every bit of Sierra's scent that clung to the seat. The combined smell of Sierra's cunt and ass was like the aroma of fine wine to her, and she could've remained here for hours, breathing it in and becoming increasingly intoxicated. But that's not why she'd come here. She understood that now. When she was finished, she stood, closed her eyes, and once more inhaled through her nostrils. In her mind, she envisioned a golden thread that wound through the cubicles to the office door. She followed this trail, still keeping her eyes closed. When she reached the door, she opened it and stepped into the hall, eyes still shut. The golden thread continued on down the hall to the stairs, where she could no longer see it. She then opened her eyes. The golden thread that indicated Sierra's scent trail was no longer visible to her, but she could *feel* it, and she knew she could find Sierra wherever she went.

Mandy smiled.

"I'm coming for you, sweet thing. And when I find you, *you'll* come for *me.*"

She started down the hallway, following the golden thread of Sierra's scent and imagining all the things she'd command the woman to do to her once she had her in thrall.

Afternoon delight, indeed.

CHAPTER NINE

Jeffrey was enjoying himself. He couldn't feel the sun or the breeze on his skin, which admittedly was disappointing, but from all appearances, it was a thoroughly pleasant fall day. He'd been walking for a while now, he wasn't sure how long, but he'd covered a lot of ground and wasn't tired in the slightest. He felt as if he could keep on wandering like this forever, stopping only to greet people and bestow upon them the great gift he had to offer. He wished his thoughts weren't so jumbled, though. He had difficulty focusing on one thing for more than a few seconds before his brain moved on to something else. It was like he had a world-class case of ADD, his thoughts sliding away from him like quicksilver. His memory wasn't any better. He couldn't recall what he'd been doing this morning before walking into town. Worse, he couldn't remember anything farther back than that. Whenever he tried, his head hurt, and if he persisted, the pain intensified to the point where it became unbearable. So naturally, he'd stopped trying.

Flashes of memory came to him unbidden at times, though, scraps of sights and sounds that made little sense. Kissing a man he loved. Laughing with a woman who he also loved, but in a different way, deeper, as if she were part of him. There were moments when his memories became clearer – like when he'd seen the woman – Sierra? – through the window at the art place and left her a message etched in brick, and when the man – Marc? – approached him as he was giving his gift to the woman and her dog. These moments didn't last, though, and his thoughts devolved into a disordered mess once more. It was frustrating, but it was also nice in a Zen kind of way. It kept him living in the now, and if he just relaxed and went with it, it was as if he existed in a state of grace, a peacefulness that he hadn't known since his time in the womb.

He hadn't consciously chosen his route all morning, had been content to wander and allow impulse and circumstance to choose for him. But that didn't mean his subconscious didn't give him a nudge in one direction or another at times. That was how he'd come to pass by ArtWorks, and why'd he'd ended up walking around shopping centers where he and Marc used to go. And it was also why he now found himself standing outside the three-story office building that housed Reliant Financial, the place where he'd worked. He didn't recognize it as such, of course, but he felt compelled to stop and stare at it.

There were no signs outside to say what businesses leased space inside the building. The only identifier was the street number – 683 – indicated by large metal numerals bolted to the brick above the glass-door entrance. It was a professional building, a place where physicians, lawyers, psychologists, accountants, and financial advisors like Jeffrey once was plied their trades. The parking lot was testament to this, as it was filled with new – or relatively new – vehicles that were quite expensive. Jeffrey's pickup, nice as it was, had been seriously out of place here, and he'd gotten a kick out of that. He'd never been the kind of person to put much stock in appearances.

If he remembered any of these details now, they were like faint, distant echoes spoken in a language he only half understood. Still, he felt compelled to enter the building, so that's what he did.

Once inside the lobby, he turned to look at the directory attached to the wall near the building's sole elevator. He gazed upon the names without recognition until he came to Reliant Financial, second floor. The words didn't mean much to him in and of themselves. His reading comprehension skills were spotty at best now. But a word did enter his mind then, a simple concept that brought with it a strong sense of belonging.

Work.

Jeffrey stepped to the elevator, pushed the button to summon the car, and waited. He wasn't sure how long he'd been gone, but it felt like it had been a while. He was going to have a lot of catching up to do, but that was okay. He'd never been afraid of a little hard work, and it would be good to see everyone again, even if he couldn't quite remember who *everyone* was.

The elevator *ding*ed as it arrived, and the door slid open. Smiling, Jeffrey stepped inside and pushed the button for the second floor. As the door slid shut, he thought, *I wonder if they'll be glad to see me.*

⋆ ⋆ ⋆

"I saw him with my own eyes this morning, and I still can't believe it," Sierra said.

"Right? It's insane!"

Marc drove while Sierra held his phone and watched a video a friend had sent him. The friend worked at Reliant Financial, and was in fact the guy who'd thrown the barbecue party where Jeffrey and Marc had met. The video wasn't very long, less than thirty seconds, and it showed Jeffrey standing in the office, looking around, his mouth set in a dreamy smile, as if he was drunk or high on some really good shit. On the video, the friend said, *"That looks like Jeffrey, doesn't it? I mean* exactly *like him. But that's impossible!"*

Yes, it is, Sierra thought. But just because something was impossible, didn't mean it couldn't happen.

She played the video three times. The image was often blurry and the phone shook in the man's hand, but the picture was clear enough for her to be sure it was Jeffrey she was looking at. When she was finished watching the video, she put Marc's phone down between them on the seat.

Marc had called her after her encounter with Mandy, before she could call him. He'd received the video in the middle of the meeting with his client, and he'd been so freaked out that he cut the meeting short, got in his car, and called her while he was hauling ass toward the college. He picked her up outside the faculty parking lot, and now they were heading for Reliant Financial where, it seemed, her brother had returned to work after having been dead for a year.

"Do you think he's hurt anyone?" Marc asked. He was driving too fast and too recklessly, especially for an insurance professional, but Sierra wasn't about to tell him to slow down.

"Not before the video was taken. If Jeffrey had hurt anyone, there'd be screaming and running."

Of course, that didn't mean Jeffrey hadn't decided to give his 'gift' to someone after the video had been recorded, but she didn't say this aloud. She didn't need to. Marc was as aware of the possibility as she was.

"I texted him immediately and told him everyone needed to evacuate the office. He didn't text me back, though, so I don't know if he got the message. Or if he did...."

"It was too late," Sierra finished.

"Yeah."

They continued driving in silence after that. Sierra had no idea what Marc was thinking, but she was desperately trying to come up with some way they could help Jeffrey and prevent him from hurting anyone else. She was glad that seeing the video had motivated Marc to get past his initial shock at seeing Jeffrey alive – or maybe a better word would be *not-dead*. They might not like each other, but she thought it would take both of them to get through to Jeffrey. If that was even possible. So far, her plan consisted of Marc and her confronting Jeffrey, talking to him, and hoping they could reason with him. But if they couldn't, if his mind was too far gone, what could they do to stop a living ghost who could kill with a single touch? What could anyone do?

She hadn't come up with anything better by the time they reached the building that housed Reliant, and she decided Marc and she would have to pray that Jeffrey responded to them. And if he didn't, they'd have to improvise. She didn't think much of her plan when it came to their prospects for long-term survival, but it was the best she had.

Marc pulled into the building's lot, found an empty space, and parked. Sierra looked at Marc and he at her, as if each was hoping to borrow a measure of courage from the other. But neither had any to spare, so they got out of the car and started walking toward the building's entrance. Sierra experienced an impulse to reach out and take Marc's hand for support, but she resisted the urge. Just because they were temporarily allies, didn't make them friends. She kept her eyes on the entrance, expecting a mass of people to come running out of the building any second, shouting and screaming. But no one did.

Not a good sign, she thought.

There was a dreamlike quality to their short trip across the parking lot. Everything seemed to take longer than it should, like time had slowed, and she felt disconnected from her own body, an outside observer watching a pair of morons marching to their deaths.

They entered the lobby and found it empty and silent. The quiet was eerie, as disturbing in its own way as a chorus of throat-tearing screams. Maybe more so. A sweet-rank odor of rot hung in the air, telling Sierra that her brother had passed this way.

Marc pushed the button for the elevator, and they stepped back as it descended, instinctively giving themselves room in case someone should rush out at them when the door opened. But the car was empty. They stepped inside, Marc pressed the button for the second floor, the door closed, and with a slight judder they began to ascend. Jeffrey's rank scent filled the elevator car, so thick Sierra had to breathe through her mouth, as did Marc. She didn't like the idea of drawing the stench into her lungs, feared some portion of Jeffrey's deathtouch might cling to his stink and infect them. She imagined her lungs decaying until she could no longer breathe, imagined the rot sweeping through her body like a virulent fire, devouring her from the inside out as it spread. Her heart sped up and sweat broke out on her brow, but otherwise, nothing happened. It seemed however the deathtouch worked, whether Jeffrey controlled it or not, his flesh had to be in contact with another's for it to activate.

The elevator *ding*ed when it reached the second floor, and even though Sierra was expecting it, the sound made her jump. The door opened, and after a moment's hesitation, the two of them stepped out. The hallway was as quiet and empty as the lobby, but if anything, the silence was more disturbing. It felt heavier somehow, more oppressive. And the smell of rot filled the air, so thick it almost felt like something solid. Reliant Financial's offices were located to the left of the elevator, and Sierra and Marc started toward them. They passed a periodontist's office and a bankruptcy lawyer's before coming to Reliant. There were no windows in the hall, just heavy wooden doors with the names of businesses displayed on the wall next to them. So Sierra and Marc would get no advance warning about what waited for them inside.

"I have an absurd impulse to knock first," Marc whispered.

Sierra ignored him. She took hold of the doorknob, turned it, and slowly pushed the door open. She entered the office, Marc following close behind.

It had been a long time since Sierra had last visited Jeffrey at work, but the office layout was the same as she remembered. There was a large open space in the middle with four desks pushed up against one another, two on each side. There were three individual offices with their own desks and chairs sitting in front of them. The desks in the middle were where the financial advisors did their work, and the individual offices were where they met with clients. A lot of the advisors' work was done online or over the phone, so a larger overall space wasn't necessary. Even so, Reliant's owner kept promising her employees that they'd move to nicer digs, but it hadn't happened yet. Sierra wished it had, because Jeffrey wouldn't have been able to find them then.

There was no one in the outer office. Computers were booted up and running. Coffee mugs and a soft drink bottle sat on desks, alongside a half-empty snack bag of peanuts and a candy bar wrapper no one had gotten around to throwing away yet. Piles of gray dust rested on the carpeted floor near the desks – four of them. A cell phone lay next to one of the piles, which Sierra guessed were the remains of the man who'd sent Marc the video of Jeffrey. The stink of rot suffused the room, so thick it made her eyes water.

She heard the sound of typing and saw that Jeffrey was seated at a desk in one of the individual offices, fingers moving across a computer keyboard, as if he was pretending to work. He looked worse than he had when she'd seen him earlier at ArtWorks. His skin was gray and shot through with thin black veins. His eyes were covered with a milky cast, and Sierra wondered how he could see through them.

He noticed Sierra and Marc watching him, looked up, and smiled.

"It had been a long time since I'd seen them," he said, "so I just had to give them all hugs."

Her stomach lurched, and she swayed, suddenly dizzy. They were too late.

"It's also been a while since I've seen you two, hasn't it?" Jeffrey frowned. "I'm sorry, but I don't quite remember...." He trailed off, eyes widening in recognition. "Sierra! Marc!"

At that moment, Sierra forgot four people had recently died here. She felt a flush of emotion upon hearing Jeffrey say her name, so strong she felt like laughing and crying at the same time. But then Jeffrey stood and came walking toward them, arms outstretched.

Sierra held up her hand to stop him.

"Don't come any closer," she said.

Jeffrey looked confused and more than a little hurt, but he halted and dropped his arms to his sides.

"Are you mad that I didn't go into ArtWorks to talk to you this morning? My memory's been messed up lately. I recognized you as someone I knew, someone I thought was named Sis, but that was all." He smiled. "It sounds dumb now that I've said it, but it's true." He looked at Marc. "My memory was working better when I saw you, hon. Not perfectly, but enough so that I knew who you were and what we meant to each other." His expression softened, and sorrow came into his eyes. "I'm sorry if I scared you. I didn't mean to."

"You're doing a damn good job of it now too." Marc gestured to the nearest pile of gray dust. "Did you *have* to kill them?"

Jeffrey looked shocked.

"I didn't *kill* them. I *freed* them!"

"They don't look very free to me," Marc said. "Unless your idea of freedom is to end up stored in an urn on somebody's mantle and getting dusted once a week."

"What you're looking at is only the residue of their physical bodies. The people aren't there. As I said, they've been released."

"Released to what?" Sierra asked. "To where?"

Jeffrey opened his mouth to answer, but then he frowned. After a moment, he continued, but with less confidence than before.

"I'm not sure," he admitted. "I just know that it's somewhere better than here."

"Just about any place is better than Bishop Hill," Marc said, "although I'm partial to Hawaii. I've always wanted to learn to surf. Or maybe parasail. That looks like it would be fun too."

The man was babbling, and Sierra wondered if it was a nervous habit or if Marc had experienced his fill of weirdness for one day and was on the verge of mentally shutting down. She couldn't afford to lose him now, so she punched his arm as hard as she could.

"Ow!" Marc turned toward her. "Why did you do that?"

"To help you stay focused, dumbass." She turned her attention back to Jeffrey. "Do you know what happened, how you... came back?"

Jeffrey cocked his head to the side, clearly puzzled. "Back? Was I gone?"

She didn't want to tell him. How could you inform your only sibling that he was supposed to be several miles from here, buried in Woodlawn Cemetery? But as it turned out, she didn't have to.

"You were in an accident," Marc said. "On this day one year ago. You didn't make it."

Jeffrey looked from Marc to Sierra then back to Marc again.

"You mean I died?"

"Yes," Sierra said. "It was the hardest thing that I—" She glanced at Marc. "That we've ever been through."

Marc looked at her in surprise, but he nodded. Sierra continued.

"I dreamed you would come back. I saw the whole thing – the accident and the weird guy in the black suit who resurrected you. Part of the dream came true – here you are. But what about the other part? Is that man real? Is he responsible for you being... like this?"

Jeffrey looked at her, his expression blank. She didn't know if he hadn't understood what she'd said or if he had and simply didn't want to answer.

"Even if you don't remember the accident, you have to know it's not normal to be able to reduce people to piles of dust just by touching them," she said.

"It's like you brought something of the grave back with you," Marc added.

"We love you, Jeffrey, and more than anything else, we want to help you. But you can't keep killing people. It's wrong."

She wondered if such concepts as right and wrong made sense to Jeffrey anymore. He sounded focused right now. He remembered both of them and was able to express himself clearly. But who knew just how many of his memories were still missing? He saw nothing wrong with what he'd done to his former coworkers, and that alone argued against him being completely sane.

"I already told you, I freed them!"

Jeffrey sounded on the verge of anger. Sierra and Marc exchanged worried glances. This was not going the way either of them had hoped.

"Come with us," Sierra said. "We'll go somewhere we can talk. Together, maybe the three of us will be able to figure out what happened to you."

"And how to fix it," Marc added.

Jeffrey's expression had eased as Sierra spoke, but when Marc tacked on his addendum, Jeffrey scowled darkly.

"I don't need to be fixed. There's nothing wrong with me!" He shouted the last few words, and the carpet under his feet blackened then crumbled to gray dust, leaving him standing on a patch of tile.

So he doesn't need to use his hands to make things decay, Sierra thought. *Good to know.*

"Of course there's nothing wrong with you, love," Marc said. His face was pale, and his words came out in a nervous rush. "It's more like you're sick, and we want to help you get better."

Marc's latest tactic didn't play any better with Jeffrey than the first. If anything, he reacted more strongly.

"What I have – what I am – is not a disease," he said, voice smoldering with fury. "I have a gift to give people, the greatest gift of all, and it's…it's beautiful!"

Sierra wasn't sure, but for a moment she thought she detected a hint of doubt in her brother's voice. But if he did have any doubts, they quickly vanished, and his face became a mask of resolve.

"You two, always harping at me about one thing or another.

Sierra thinks Marc's not good enough for me, Marc thinks I have an unhealthy relationship with my sister.... You're right, Marc, I am sick. Sick of both of you! Neither of you are worthy of my touch. You don't deserve to be free. But you don't deserve to walk out of here either."

Keeping his gaze fixed on them, Jeffrey got down on one knee and placed a hand palm-down on the carpet. A black blight spread outward from his hand, similar to what had happened earlier when he'd gotten angry, only much faster. The black patch grew irregularly, and when an edge of it touched the leg of one of the desks, the rot transferred to it and all its contents. As the blackness permeated the desk, it rapidly decayed and collapsed into dust. The blight caused by Jeffrey's deathtouch continued to spread through the office, picking up speed as it went. The other desks caught it and fell apart, then their chairs. The black rot reached one wall and began to travel upward, chunks of paint and plaster falling and bursting into puffs of dust as they struck the floor.

Jeffrey had said they didn't deserve his gift, but he didn't need to touch them directly to kill them. He could cause the building to collapse around them, and they would end up just as dead as if he'd turned them to dust.

There wasn't time to say anything. Sierra grabbed hold of Marc's hand and ran toward the door. They plunged into the hall and Marc tried to pull her in the direction of the elevator, but she feared it wouldn't be fast enough. The door to Reliant's office blackened and disintegrated, as did chunks of the wall around it. Sierra heard muffled shouts and screams, and she knew the rot was spreading throughout the entire building.

Stairwells were located at each end of the hall, and Sierra pulled Marc toward the closest one. She felt the floor shudder beneath her feet, and a large chunk of ceiling fell behind them with a hiss like sand sliding through an hourglass. When they reached the stairwell, Sierra grabbed for the door, but it fell away to dust before she could grip the knob. They moved into the stairwell and started down the stairs, taking them two at a time. Sierra had to release Marc's hand so they could navigate the stairs, but he no longer needed her encouragement to keep going. Gray dust rained down on them as they descended, and at one point the handrail collapsed, nearly causing both of them to fall. If they had started on the third floor, they probably wouldn't have made it, but as it was, they came out the emergency side exit just as the entire building came down.

They were engulfed by a cloud of dust, the material still solid enough that it knocked them off their feet and onto hard asphalt. Sierra felt sharp pains in her left elbow and knee, and she drew in a breath to cry out, but she took in lungfuls of dust and began coughing violently instead. She tried not to think about how some of this dust used to be people, but she failed miserably. The world was a solid smear of gray, and her eyes watered and stung as she looked for Marc, but she didn't see him, couldn't see anything. She tried to call out to him, but she couldn't stop coughing long enough to shout his name. She got to her feet, unsure whether her injured knee would bear her weight, but it did, although it definitely complained about it. She squinted her eyes to keep as much dust out as she could, and she stepped forward, hands held out before her as if she were blind. She supposed for the moment she was.

When the building had come down, the mass of descending dust had sounded like falling water, like the rainstorm that had contributed to her brother's death. But now it was silent, the dust-choked air muffling all sound in the vicinity. Her coughing fit didn't help either. How could she hope to hear anything over her own noise? Surely Marc could hear her, though. He must be searching for her even now, trying to hone in on her coughing, using it as a beacon to guide him through the gray. Unless something had happened to him. Maybe the blast of dust that shot outward when the building collapsed had struck him harder than her. Maybe he'd hit his head on the asphalt and was unconscious, maybe even dead if he'd hit hard enough.

A terrible possibility occurred to her then. What if Jeffrey had survived the building's disintegration? He would've only fallen a single story, with plenty of dust to soften his landing. And it wasn't as if he was human anymore. She did know what he was, but there was a damn good chance that he wasn't easy to kill. After all, he'd returned from the dead once, hadn't he? What would stop him from doing so a second time? Or a third?

So Jeffrey was close by, wandering through the dust-fog, quite probably searching for her so he could finish the job he'd started. She pictured his arms outstretched like hers, his deadly fingers moving tentatively in the air, feeling for something to grab hold of. Something like her. Maybe he'd changed his mind about bestowing his 'gift' upon her, and any moment she'd feel his touch, and within seconds she'd become part of the dust-fog, drifting, drifting....

When the hand took hold of her elbow – the uninjured one, thankfully – she screamed. Or rather tried to. All she managed to do was suck in more dust and cough even more violently than before. She tried to pull away from Jeffrey's grip, knowing that it was likely too late, that she was already in the process of being unmade and just didn't know it yet.

"Sierra, it's me!"

Marc's voice was as rough and dry as a two-pack-a-day smoker's, but right then she thought she'd never heard anything more beautiful. She stopped resisting and allowed Marc to lead her. The dust-fog grew thinner the farther they walked, and soon Sierra was able to make out dim shapes in the gray. Cars, she realized. Marc had led her to the parking lot. The vehicles were covered with a fine layer of dust, almost as if it was lightly snowing.

Marc took her to his Civic, unlocked it, and they both got in. When they shut the doors, Marc locked them, activated the engine, and turned the car's air on recirculate full blast. Now that they were out of the dust, Sierra realized Marc was coughing too, only not as hard as she was. But the clean air inside the car was already helping, and their coughing began to ease. Her eyes weren't so teary either, and when Marc hit the wipers to clear off the windshield, she saw the huge dust cloud outside was beginning to settle. Nothing remained of the building except for a small section of the foundation and uneven lengths of pipe jutting up from the ground. She saw the shadowy form of a person walking toward them, and she knew who it was before the air around him cleared enough to reveal it was Jeffrey. He was covered in gray dust, making him look like the ghost he was.

She tried to shout *Go!* but the word came out as a harsh croak. She had no idea if Marc had understood her or not, but he threw the Civic into reverse and backed out of the space so fast that he hit the car parked directly behind them. There was a jolt, then he put the car in drive and hit the gas. At first the Civic didn't go anywhere, its tires spinning on the dust-covered asphalt. But they managed to get a grip at last, and the car shot forward.

Sierra looked out the passenger window as they flew past Jeffrey. His expression was a strange mixture of anger and sadness, and he stretched a hand toward them as they drove off. She didn't know if he was still trying to kill them or if he simply wanted human contact. Maybe both, she thought.

⋆ ⋆ ⋆

Jeffrey watched as Marc and Sierra flew out of the parking lot onto the road, tires screeching, and raced off. His anger drained away, and all he felt was a deep longing to be with the two people he loved. He looked down at himself and saw he was covered with what looked like gray ash. Had there been a fire? He couldn't remember. Damn it, what the hell was wrong with him? Why couldn't he think straight for more than a few minutes at a time? Why did he have such trouble remembering things? He had a vague memory that he'd been talking to Sierra and Marc. But after that, nothing.

"I'm a man of many talents, but brain surgery isn't among them."

Jeffrey turned to see a man standing next to him. There were footprints in the gray dust behind him, showing where he'd walked, but they stopped a few feet away, as if he'd appeared out of thin air at that point. Long blond hair, weird black suit. The man seemed familiar, but Jeffrey didn't recognize him.

Jeffrey frowned. "Do I know you?"

"That's a very good question. When it comes down to it, can any of us say we truly know anyone else, at least in the ways that matter most?'

Jeffrey stared at the man as he chewed on his words, trying to make sense of them.

The man smiled apologetically. "Sorry. Your brain was damaged in the accident that killed you, and I was only able to repair it partially when I resurrected you. As much as I'd like to believe I'm omnipotent, I must admit to falling a bit short of that designation."

"I was…dead?"

Snippets of memory swirled in his mind, all of them unconnected and lacking context. Driving on a rainy night. Making love to Marc in a tent during a camping trip. Arguing with Sierra on the phone. Killing the woman and her dog. Having dinner with his mother and father. Standing in a cornfield looking at the man in the black suit. Greeting his coworkers after a long absence, seeing their confused and frightened faces, moving toward them, arms outstretched, ready to hug the friends he hadn't seen in so very long.

To make things even more confusing, he kept hearing voices, speaking so softly he couldn't make out what they were saying – or in one case, barking. Maybe they weren't saying anything, speaking only nonsensical syllables, a mad gibberish that held no more meaning than the drone of insects. But he sensed intent behind the voices, a desire to communicate, to be truly heard. But he could no more grasp meaning from the voices than he could make sense of his own chaotic memories.

He looked over his shoulder at a great mound of gray dust, the air filled with drifting particles of the stuff.

"It wasn't a fire," Jeffrey said.

"No," the man in the black suit confirmed.

"I did that."

"Yes."

Jeffrey could almost remember Sierra and Marc confronting him in the Reliant office. They were the only ones there because everyone else…everyone else….

"Was dead," the man in the black suit said. "You killed them."

Jeffrey frowned. "I gave them a gift."

The man in the black suit shrugged.

"Tomato, tamahto. I stopped by to see if you'd like a lift. The show's about to begin, and if you try to hoof it, you'll never get there in time."

"The show?"

"That's right. And it's going to star two of your favorites: your sister and your boyfriend." He smiled, but his eyes remained cold as distant stars. "You might even have a part to play yourself."

Jeffrey could make almost no sense of what the man was telling him, but he understood the most important part.

"You can take me to Marc and Sierra?"

"That I can, my undead friend."

That was all Jeffrey needed to hear.

"Okay. Let's go."

The man in the black suit looked him over.

"You're a mess, aren't you?"

He leaned forward, pursed his lips, and blew out a puff of air. A powerful wind kicked up and wafted across Jeffrey, blowing most of the gray dust off him.

The man in the black suit eyed him critically.

"It's not perfect, but I suppose it'll have to do."

He turned then, his fingers lengthening into ebon claws, and he slashed the air, creating a rift through which Jeffrey could see.... He squinted. Was that the Historic District?

The man in the black suit gestured to the rift.

"After you."

Jeffrey looked at the man for a moment. He had a strong feeling that going along with anything he suggested was a bad idea. But he needed to be with the people he loved, so he stepped forward into the rift.

The voices inside his head cheered.

CHAPTER TEN

Marc drove back to campus so Sierra could get her Ladybug, and they both headed to the Historic District. Sierra drove in a daze, not really thinking, operating on automatic pilot. Both Marc and she had done their best to brush the gray dust off their clothes and out of their hair, but they could only do so much, and quite a bit of dust still clung to her clothes and body. It smelled faintly chalklike, but the odor wasn't too strong, and she was grateful for that much at least.

She had no idea what to do next, so she headed for ArtWorks, and Marc followed. Ordinarily, she taught an afternoon class there on Mondays, Wednesdays, and Fridays, and since she had nowhere else to go, she decided to stick to her schedule. Besides, Karolyn was a calm, steadying influence, and that was something Sierra desperately needed right then.

She found a place to park, as did Marc, and she waited for him on the sidewalk. When he caught up to her, they headed to ArtWorks, neither of them speaking. It was as if both of them wanted to pretend, at least for the next few moments, that they hadn't witnessed a building – and everyone within it – being reduced to a mound of gray particles.

As they walked, Marc reached out to take her hand, and she let him, in need of human contact as badly as he was. They were still holding hands when they entered ArtWorks.

* * *

Stuart's Camaro was parked down the block from ArtWorks, but thanks to his enhanced vision – another augmentation courtesy of Krista – he had no trouble seeing Marc take Sierra's hand. More infuriatingly, he saw she didn't pull her hand away.

"Goddamned cheating bitch," he muttered, his voice accompanied by a burst of angry static that came from somewhere deep inside him.

"It certainly appears that way," Krista said.

"And didn't I say Marc was bi?"

"You did."

"This is so *sick*. It's like she's not only cheating on me, but both she and Marc are betraying Jeffrey."

"Disgusting."

Krista had continued upgrading Stuart after he'd left Temptations, and now he was as much machine as man. Maybe more. His hands – now as silver as his eyes and teeth – were still melded with the steering wheel, and with a thought, he separated them.

"Open the door, Krista. It's time I taught her a lesson about showing respect for people." He smiled. "Namely me."

The door didn't open, though, and when he tried to open it himself, it refused to budge.

"Open the goddamned door, Krista!"

"My apologies, but it's not quite time for you to get out of the vehicle. We need to wait."

"Wait? What the hell for?"

He was furious. Krista was a digital assistant, a fucking *program*. She had to do what he said.

She's a lot more than that, a part of him that was still human thought. *You think a simple program could do what she's done to you?*

"We must wait for the others," she said.

"What others?" he demanded, but she didn't answer. He asked again, shouting the question, but she remained silent. Frustrated beyond all measure, he raised a fist, intending to bring it down hard on the dashboard. But when he tried, he discovered his arm was locked in place, and he was unable to move it, not even a fraction.

"Behave," Krista said.

Stuart realized then that the relationship he thought he had with Krista – that of tool and user – was accurate, but he'd been mistaken about his role in the equation.

Arm still raised, he sat back in his seat, gaze fixed on ArtWorks' entrance, and waited for Krista's next command.

* * *

Just like Stuart, Randall had parked his car down the block from ArtWorks, only on the other side of the street. He had yanked the rearview mirror off the windshield because he'd returned to his normal form after leaving the Sowells' house, and he couldn't wait until he could be his true self again.

His sweatshirt, slacks, and shoes were all covered with blood, and although he'd tried to be careful, he'd gotten some on his car's upholstery. He wished he'd thought to put on some fresh clothes when he'd been home, but he'd been too eager to go across the street and have his little 'talk' with Sierra's parents, and after that, he'd been too excited to find Sierra and teach her the importance of respecting the Chuck. His clothes were so sodden with blood that they were wet and tacky against his skin, and he found the sensation most unpleasant. But there was nothing he could do about it at the moment, so he would have to endure.

He held his special Chuck, the one that sometimes was a copper blade, clenched tight in his right hand. He knew when the time came, it would return to its true form, just as he would, and until then he'd keep it closed in his fist, where it would be safe. Despite how many Chucks he'd used today, his right pants pocket bulged with more. He hadn't resupplied when he'd been home. They were just *there*, one more bit of Chucky magic.

While he waited for Sierra to arrive – as he knew she would; he'd gotten her work schedule from her parents before they died – he found his thoughts returning to Erika. In his mind, he once again saw her lying on their kitchen floor, surrounded by blood, eyes wide and staring, mouth and throat crammed to overflowing with Chucks. At the time, he'd felt immense satisfaction for giving Erika what she had so richly deserved. But now he began to question what he'd done. Maybe, just maybe, he'd gone a little too far. Sure, Erika had never liked or understood his Chucks, but she'd been supportive in every other way, and she'd been a good mother to their children.

The kids. He'd almost forgotten about them. What were they going to think when they found out not only that their mother had been murdered, but their own father was responsible? What would his grandchildren think when they were old enough to learn the truth about how their grandmother had died?

He felt as if he were starting to wake up from a horrible nightmare only to discover that the awful events which had occurred in his dream had actually happened. He'd killed his dear wife, and four others as well. The Sowells, the tattooed mother, and her child. God, the *child*! He could see the boy's face, features contorted in agony, hear the shrill scream as Randall ravaged his tiny body with his copper blade.

He thought he was going to be sick.

The Chuck felt heavy in his hand now, far heavier than a mere penny. It was weighted with the guilt he now felt for the lives he'd taken, crimes that before today he would've never imagined, let alone committed. The Town Car's windows were down, and he brought his right hand up and pulled it back, intending to hurl the Chuck out the window.

You don't want to do this.

He heard the voice in his mind, but it wasn't his. It was as if his brain were a receiver picking up a transmission from somewhere else. He didn't recognize the voice – which possessed a tinny quality, as if someone was speaking into a can – but it felt familiar somehow, like a voice you knew you'd heard before but couldn't immediately place.

"Yes, I do," Randall said. But there wasn't as much conviction in his tone as he would've liked.

You want to go back to being mocked and ridiculed? Do you want people to go on laughing behind your back, to keep pointing and saying, "There goes that weird old creep who passes out those stupid-ass pennies with the smiley faces on them. What the fuck is wrong with him? He should be locked up in the nuthouse where he can't bother anyone anymore." Is that what you want?

As the voice spoke, Randall felt his guilt melt away to be replaced with burning anger.

"No. No, I do not. All I've ever done was try to make the world a better place in my own small way. What's wrong with that?"

Nothing, the voice said.

Randall felt the Chuck in his hand twitch as if in response to his anger, felt his skin tighten, become smoother, and take on a yellowish hue. His head swelled like a lemon-colored balloon, and his grin became an upward-curving lipless line. The Chuck had changed as well, and it was once again a copper dagger. Randall now understood where the voice in his head had originated.

"Thanks," he said.

No problem. Us Chucks have to stick together.

Randall saw Sierra drive by in her red VW Beetle then. He watched as she parked, got out of her vehicle, and was met by a man he didn't recognize. When they began holding hands, he wondered if the man was a new boyfriend. Just about anyone would be better than that Stuart character.

Randall reached for the driver's side door handle, intending to get out of his car and confront Sierra.

Hold off, the blade said.

Randall's finger rested on the button to unlock the car door, but he didn't press it.

"Why?"

Revenge is a dish best served cold.

Randall had never heard that phrase before, but it made perfect sense. He'd wait until his anger cooled a bit, and then, when he was once more able to think clearly and logically, he'd go into ArtWorks and slice the bitch into ribbons.

Now you're talking! the knife said.

Randall ran his thumb along the blade's edge, the sharp metal peeling open the skin, causing it to bleed, but he didn't care. What was a little more blood to him? Besides, there would be more than enough blood for him soon, an ocean of the damn stuff, and he would dive in, explore its depths, and never again come up for air.

That's my Chuck! the dagger said.

* * *

"See anything yet?" Grace asked.

"Nothing yet, ma'am," Officer Al said. He sat behind the wheel of her Lexus, gaze fastened on the entrance to ArtWorks. At least, she assumed that's what he was doing. She couldn't tell from the back seat, but he hadn't failed to obey one of her commands yet, and she felt confident he wouldn't do so now. She would've kept watch herself, but she was too busy celebrating what had been an altogether satisfying reunion with her former coworkers at Gold Medal Bank. And for Grace, celebrating meant drinking. She'd polished off two-thirds of the bourbon supply she'd gotten from Happy Hours, and she was currently working on another bottle. She'd lost count of how much she'd polished off since leaving the liquor store, and really, why bother counting? Who cared how much she'd had, just so long as there was *more*?

When they'd arrived at the bank, Grace had commanded Officer Al to accompany her. There was a security officer inside, and she wanted Al – and his gun – there in case the guard grew suspicious. Her caution turned out to be unnecessary. Grace shot a stream of vomit into the man's face, and she then had two armed servants. She ordered both of them to draw their guns and keep the staff and customers quiet and still. They did so, and she went from person to person, vomiting on each one until they all belonged to her. She wasn't certain she'd managed to get everyone before one of them pushed an alarm button to summon the police. She thought she had, but she decided not to waste time in case she was wrong.

She ordered everyone – with the exception of Officer Al – to engage in hand-to-hand combat until every last one of them was dead. Customers and staff fell upon one another like wild animals, biting and clawing, punching and kicking. The security officer used his gun to take out three people, but a loan officer jammed a pair of scissors into the base of his skull, killing him instantly.

Grace watched the fun for another minute before turning to leave, Officer Al following obediently behind, like a faithful dog. There was a security camera mounted over the door, and she blew it a kiss on her way out.

That'll teach you to fire me, assholes.

Now Grace poured the last few ounces of bourbon down her throat, killing another bottle.

Revenge had turned out to be even more delicious than she'd anticipated, and confronting Sierra about her stolen purse was going to be the cherry on top.

Grace dropped the empty onto the Lexus's floor, which was already covered by a collection of bottles. It clinked when it struck the others, but it didn't break. Too bad. She'd become quite fond of the sound of shattering glass.

She grabbed a fresh bottle from her dwindling supply – a return visit to Happy Hours might soon be in order – and opened it. Before she could bring it to her dry, cracked lips, Officer Al said, "Based on the description you gave me, I think that's her."

Grace leaned over the back of the seat and peered through the windshield. It was Sierra, all right, and she was holding hands with some man Grace didn't recognize. She wondered if he was a new boyfriend and Sierra was taking him to ArtWorks to show him Grace's stolen purse, and then they'd laugh and laugh.

"Do you want me to apprehend her?" Officer Al asked.

Grace giggled. Al sometimes spoke as if he were a TV cop, and it amused her.

"In a minute. Let me finish this bottle first." She eyed the few full bottles sitting on the seat beside her. "And maybe these others too. I want to make sure I'm well-fortified when I confront that thieving bitch."

"Fortify away," Officer Al said.

And that's exactly what she did.

⋆ ⋆ ⋆

Mandy drove her Ford Mustang convertible with the top down so she could more easily follow Sierra's scent. She didn't need to visualize the golden thread that represented the woman's trail. By now, following it was a matter of instinct, as natural and unthinking as the beating of her heart. Normally she listened to a classical music station while driving, but now she had her radio turned to hard rock. She wasn't familiar with any of the tunes, but she loved the pounding beat and the snarled lyrics, and she blasted the music as loud as the car's speakers could handle. She enjoyed the feeling of wind in her face, her hair trailing behind her. The world was filled with incredible sensations like this – existence itself was orgasmic – and she couldn't believe she'd never allowed herself to experience them for so long. In many ways, she could barely remember being that woman, closed off from her body, so deeply fucked up about sex that she'd become obsessed with preventing others from enjoying themselves. She felt as if she'd had a conversion experience, that she'd been led out of darkness into light. Warm, wet, throbbing light.

Her thoughts turned back to the meeting – the final one, she supposed – of the Traditional Values Club. Her memories weren't so much focused on sight and sound as they were the physical pleasures she'd experienced. Those memories were so richly detailed that recalling them was like experiencing them all over again. And the most vivid and intense of them all was the moment Conrad had become hers. This was a memory she would revisit often, she thought. She would feed on others, of course. Many, many others. But Conrad had been her first, and you never forgot your first time.

A thought came to her then. It was comprised partly of the memory of the awful day when Ronnie had brought his friends into his parents' bedroom to do as they would with her, and partly of images from the orgy in the library. There was a connection between them, and it took her a second to realize what it was. She had taken control of Conrad and the others at the meeting with her new powers and forced them to behave in ways they never would have on their own. She'd *used* them, Conrad most of all. She'd killed him for her own pleasure and to increase her strength. And so, a question: how was the creature she had become any different from Ronnie and his friends?

For a moment, she considered the terrible implications of this question. But then she figured, fuck it. She *liked* what she was now, and she wouldn't return to her old self regardless of how many people she had to suck into her snatch to stay like this. She was free, she was strong, and she could do whatever the hell she wanted. And right now, she wanted Sierra.

She soon entered the Historic District, and she recalled Sierra once telling her that she also taught at a combination art gallery/school here. She spotted it at once – it was rather hard to miss with the murals painted on the outside walls – and she peeked through the windows as she drove by. Her eyesight was much sharper now, and she was able to make out tables and chairs, along with artwork displayed in various places. She saw two women, both working with students, but neither of the teachers was Sierra. Then she was past the building. Sierra's scent was all over the gallery, but it wasn't fresh. She'd tracked her here, so....

She saw Sierra standing on the sidewalk, waiting as a cute guy approached her, and Mandy shut off the radio as she drew closer. She knew the man was gay the instant she saw him. She could now read a person's sexuality with preternatural skill, and this man didn't have a heterosexual bone in his body. If anyone had asked Mandy this morning what her sexual preference was, she would've said *none*. Now she would answer *more*. She wondered if her newfound power would be able to convince Sierra's friend to make an exception for her. She'd seen what it could do in the library meeting room, but she was unsure what its limitations were. She would enjoy finding out, though. Field research could be so much fun.

She glanced at Sierra and her friend as she drove past them. She was tempted to throw them a wink and a knowing smile, but she didn't want to give Sierra any advance warning that she was coming for her. She wanted it to be a surprise. But Sierra didn't so much as look in her direction. She kept her gaze fixed straight ahead, an almost shell-shocked look on her face. And she had bits of gray schmutz clinging to her clothes and hair. Most unattractive. Mandy didn't know what she'd gotten up to since leaving campus, but whatever it was, it looked like it had taken a toll on her. She hoped Sierra wasn't completely wrung out. She was going to need every ounce of energy she possessed for what Mandy had planned for her.

Conrad might've been her first, but Sierra would be her second.

She continued down the block, looking for a place to park.

* * *

Jeffrey stepped out of the rift and onto the sidewalk directly across the street from ArtWorks. The man in the black suit followed, and when he was through, he pinched the rift shut with his hands. Jeffrey thought he could still see a faint shimmer in the air where it had been, like the distortion caused by heat waves rising from hot asphalt. A sense of wrongness emanated from the shimmer, which made him uncomfortable, so he looked away.

He saw Sierra and Marc walking on the opposite sidewalk.

Sister, he told himself. *Lover.* He was determined not to forget them again. *Sister. Lover. Sister. Lover.*

He watched as they began to hold hands, and continued like that until they entered the building with the paintings on the walls outside.

Work. Sierra's work. Work, work, work.

The sight of them holding hands both warmed and saddened him. He was glad to see them close like that. They hadn't gotten along when he was alive, might've even hated each other. He wasn't sure. But it saddened him because he knew the reason they needed one another's emotional support was because of what had happened at Reliant Financial. He had killed everyone else in the building, dozens of people, reduced to dust in a matter of moments, unmade as if they'd never existed at all. What would Sierra (*Sister*) and Marc (*Lover*) think of him now? How could they ever trust him again?

"Perhaps if you tried to explain it to them?" the man in the black suit said. "They love you. They'll listen."

Jeffrey didn't reply as he continued watching the building (*Sierra's work*). Up and down the block, car doors opened and four very strange people got out of their vehicles and began converging on ArtWorks.

He turned to look at the man in the black suit.

"Do you really think so?" he asked.

The man smiled, displaying teeth that were too sharp to be human.

"Only one way to find out."

Jeffrey thought about this a moment, decided it was true, and started walking across the street.

* * *

Karolyn was at a table working with Sierra's afternoon students, a group of AP high-schoolers who got out of their last class of the day to attend ArtWorks. In the back, Gloria Morales, a local ceramicist who taught art classes to make extra money, was helping a group of adults – mostly moms and senior citizens – make clay sculptures. She was a big woman with a shaved head who always wore sandals, jeans, and tentlike T-shirts with cartoon characters on them. Today's shirt featured Daffy Duck. Gloria looked over at Sierra and waved as she entered, but Sierra didn't possess the presence of mind to wave back. The high-schoolers were working with pastels, and when Karolyn saw Sierra and Marc enter, she told the students to keep working and walked over to the two of them.

Sierra was worried Karolyn would be angry with her for arriving late to class a second time in the same day, but there was only concern on the woman's face as she approached.

She smiled at Marc. "I haven't seen you for a long time. How are you?" She made a face then, as if regretting her words. "Sorry! I forgot this must be a hard day for you too."

"You have no idea," Marc said.

"I'm so sorry I'm late again," Sierra said. She wanted to add more, but she was at a loss for words. How could she tell Karolyn that her dead brother had come back to life as some kind of monster whose touch could disintegrate an entire fucking building and everyone within it? Karolyn would think that she'd lost her mind, and Sierra wasn't certain she'd be wrong.

Marc came to her rescue.

"We met for lunch to talk about Jeffrey, and it turned out to be harder than we anticipated. I don't think she's in any shape to teach this afternoon."

"Of *course* she isn't," Karolyn said. She took Sierra's hands in hers and gave them a squeeze. "I'll continue with your class. Why don't you and Marc go sit in the break room for a bit? You can continue talking back there and no one will bother you."

Sierra managed a grateful smile. "Thanks."

Karolyn smiled back, but then her gaze focused on Sierra's hair, and she frowned.

"You've got—"

"We walked past a construction site," Marc said. "We got a little dusty."

Karolyn looked at Sierra as if she was waiting for her to confirm this. But when Sierra said nothing, Karolyn evidently decided to abandon the subject.

"Let me know if either of you need anything," she said. And with a last sympathetic look, she returned to the AP high-schoolers and their pastel drawings.

As if by unspoken agreement, Sierra and Marc had let go of each other's hand when they entered ArtWorks, and now there was an awkwardness between them, as if they'd crossed a line into uncharted territory and weren't sure how to behave. They were supposed to hate each other, deeply and passionately, and people who hated each other generally, as a rule, didn't hold hands. Sierra thought they'd both been filling in for Jeffrey – or rather, Jeffrey as he'd been before the accident. That version of her brother would've been there to support both his sister and his boyfriend after they'd experienced a traumatic event like the destruction of Reliant's office building. And since that Jeffrey couldn't be there for them, they had to be there for each other. It was almost as weird as Jeffrey returning from the grave.

Sierra led Marc to the break room, which was located in the back not far from where Gloria worked with the adult students. Gloria didn't know Marc, but she gave Sierra a sad, understanding look as they passed. Sierra was beginning to find people's sympathy irritating, and she wished she hadn't confided in so many people about the emotional toll her brother's death had taken on her. Still, she forced herself to smile and nod at Gloria as they went by.

There wasn't much to ArtWorks' break room: a small round table with a couple chairs, an old couch, an equally old easy chair, a refrigerator, and a counter on which rested a microwave and the most important piece of equipment the gallery possessed – the coffee maker. A fresh pot had been brewed, and Sierra took a couple foam cups from a cupboard and poured coffee for each of them. She didn't bother doctoring either of them. She figured they could both use the hi-octane stuff right now. She gave Marc his coffee, and they sat at the table. Neither of them spoke right away. Instead they sat quietly, waiting for their coffees to cool.

Now that Sierra had a chance to catch her breath, the unreality of their situation hit her full force. How was it possible for someone to return from the dead? More than that, *why* had it happened, and more specifically, why had it happened to Jeffrey? And was the man in her dream, the mysterious figure with the long blond hair and strange black suit, responsible? Yesterday, she would've said the idea that someone could step out of a dream and into reality was ridiculous, but now she believed anything was possible. And that thought was terrifying. If *anything* could happen, if there were no real rules to existence, then the universe was a madhouse, and all its inhabitants inmates.

Both of her parents were religious to a certain extent. They were hardly fanatics like Mandy, but they did believe in god and in Christianity as the best way for them to know god. If their mom knew about Jeffrey's miraculous resurrection – which seemed about as far from being Christlike as you could get – she might've said that when bad things happen, it's god's way of testing his children. Not to make them prove their faith in him, that would be cruel. But so they might discover the true strength within them. Sierra had always thought that idea, like pretty much everything about organized religion, was a crock of shit. But now she supposed it was as good a theory as any.

Now that she'd seen how dangerous Jeffrey was, she knew she had to warn her parents. They wouldn't believe her and would think she needed serious psychiatric help, but at least they wouldn't be taken by surprise if Jeffrey showed up on their doorstep to give them a couple of his deadly hugs. She took her phone from her bag and called her mother. After several rings it went to voicemail, and Sierra disconnected without leaving a message. She got the same result when she tried her dad's phone, but this time she did leave a message.

"Dad, if you or Mom see…someone who looks like Jeffrey today, it's *not* him. Whoever it is tried to contact me today, and he's dangerous. Don't let him get near you. If you see him, call the police. I know this sounds crazy, but I'll explain more later." As if she could ever come up with a satisfactory explanation for this madness.

She disconnected and put her phone on the table, in case either of her parents called her back.

"Think they'll listen to your warning?" Marc asked.

"I don't know. I hope so."

Marc nodded, as if to say he hoped so too.

"I think I know why Jeffrey came back," he said.

"You do?"

"Yeah. What do ghosts always want from the living? Revenge. Or justice, depending on how you look at it. It was my irrational jealousy that drove Jeffrey out into the storm that night, and you were arguing with him on the phone not long before the accident. We're responsible for his death, the two of us, and he's come back to make us pay for our sins against him."

If Marc had told her this earlier, Sierra would've become furious and said things like, *How dare you blame me when it was your crazy jealousy that upset him that night* and *I was his sister! I always supported him, no matter what!* But now, after everything that had happened today, she knew she couldn't lay this all at Marc's feet. She shared at least equal blame in Jeffrey's death, if not more because she was his sister. They had both done Jeffrey wrong, and maybe he had come back to make them pay for what they'd done.

She was about to tell Marc this when she heard Karolyn scream.

* * *

Karolyn was circling slowly around the table, inspecting the high-schoolers' work, when the front door opened and a scarecrow of a woman walked in on stick-thin legs. She held a nearly empty bottle of liquor in one hand, and her bloodshot eyes darted back and forth, as if she was searching for something. Or someone. A middle-aged and not particularly fit police officer followed behind her, his expression blank and his eyes glazed over. His gun was unholstered, and he held it down at his side. The woman resembled a skeleton wrapped in ancient parchment instead of skin, and she reeked of alcohol. But as disturbing as the woman's visage was, what alarmed Karolyn most was the sight of the gun in the officer's hand. Dozens of news stories raced through her mind, accounts of crazy people walking into schools and businesses with guns and opening fire. This guy might be wearing a cop's uniform, but that didn't mean he was the real thing. Karolyn might have been more willing to give him the benefit of the doubt if he hadn't been accompanying the skeleton woman. Karolyn didn't consider herself psychic in the least bit, but you didn't need special perceptions to know that there was something unnatural about the woman. Unnatural and dangerous.

As the owner of a school, Karolyn had read up on how to deal with an active shooter situation, but now that it looked like one might be happening, she couldn't remember a damn thing she'd read. She started walking toward the pair, not having any idea what she was going to say or do, only knowing that she had to do *something.*

She tried to put on a smile, but all she succeeded in doing was drawing her lips back from her teeth, almost as if she was snarling at them.

"Can I help you?"

Her voice was strained and tight, but she was surprised she managed to get the words out at all.

The woman's bloodshot eyes fixed on Karolyn, and she couldn't believe how dry they looked. *Like a mannequin's eyes*, she thought.

"I wish to speak with Sierra. Can you get her for me, please?'

The woman's voice sounded rough as two pieces of sandpaper being rubbed together, and her breath was *deadly*. It stank of liquor and vomit, and Karolyn thought the smell of it might make her throw up as well.

Karolyn had no idea who this woman was – hell, she didn't know *what* she was – but she wasn't about to produce Sierra for her.

"I'm sorry, but she's not working this afternoon." Technically, this wasn't a lie.

The police officer, who'd been staring into the distance while the women talked, now turned toward Karolyn, awareness coming into his gaze.

"Don't give us that shit," he said, his voice curiously monotone. "We saw her come in here."

He raised his gun partway as he said this, and while he didn't directly threaten Karolyn with it, the implication was clear: talk or else.

"I really *am* sorry," Karolyn began, "but—"

She broke off as the door opened once more to admit a man with a large round yellow smiley face for a head, wearing a bloodstained sweatshirt and holding a copper knife.

"Hi!" he said in a cheerful voice. "Is Sierra here?"

Karolyn found the skeleton woman disturbing, no doubt, and the cop's gun scared her. But the smiley-face man was too much for her to deal with, and she screamed.

CHAPTER ELEVEN

Sierra and Marc did not move immediately. They looked at each other, and Sierra thought they were each considering the same thing: leaving by the rear entrance and getting as far away from there as possible. The animal part of Sierra – the shivering, furry little creature that lives at the core of all humans – wanted to find a safe place to hide until the danger, whatever it was, passed. But Karolyn and Gloria were still out there, not to mention the students. Sierra couldn't abandon them just to save her own ass, as tempting as that might be.

She stood and hurried toward the break room's door. After another moment of hesitation, Marc followed, although he did not look happy about it.

When they entered the main part of the building, Sierra expected to see Jeffrey standing in front of Karolyn. But her brother wasn't there. Instead, three other people had come into ArtWorks: a cadaverously thin older woman, an overweight middle-aged cop, and a man wearing a smiley-face mask. The cop had drawn his gun and held it pointed at the smiley-face man's head.

"Don't move," the skeletal woman said to the smiley-face man, "or Officer Al will put a bullet into your giant yellow head. Isn't that right, dear?"

"Bang-bang," Officer Al said and grinned.

Sierra had never seen the police officer before, she was sure of that, but there was something familiar about the other two. She thought she recognized the thin woman's voice, but she couldn't quite place it. And while she'd never seen anyone wear a big round smiley-face mask like that – especially one that had a moveable mouth – the man's clothes were familiar. And then it hit her, all at once.

Grace.

Randall.

Something had happened to change them, just as Jeffrey had been changed. From where she stood, she could see through one of the front windows, and she caught a glimpse of a man standing on the other side of the street. A man with long blond hair, wearing a suit of the deepest black she'd ever seen. It was the man from last night's dream, the one who'd brought Jeremy back. He was real. There was no way he should've been able to see her from so far away, not with the afternoon sunlight reflecting off the windows. Nevertheless, he grinned and gave her a quick wave.

She was about to ask Marc if he also saw the man in the black suit, but before she could say anything, Grace and Randall – who as far as Sierra knew didn't know each other – began arguing.

"Whatever you want with Sierra, it's not more important than what *I* want, and I was here first."

Randall's smile – which Sierra was beginning to think wasn't on a mask but rather his actual face – fell.

"I've known Sierra since she was a child, practically from the day she was born. My claim long predates yours."

Oh my god. His face is a giant Chuck, Sierra realized.

Randall gripped his knife – which Sierra now saw had a Chuck on the end of its handle – more tightly, and for an instant, she thought he might bring it up and begin stabbing Grace with it. Officer Al must've had the same thought, for he said, "Take it easy, or instead of a nice day, you're going to have a very bad one."

If Randall was afraid of the man's gun, he didn't show it. Then again, it was impossible to read much emotion from his grotesquely minimal features.

Sierra had registered the blood on Randall's sweatshirt in passing, but now the implications of those stains hit her. Randall had used that knife to hurt people, maybe even kill them, just like Jeffrey had used his deathtouch. And Grace…had she killed as well?

Both sets of students had been staring at the strange newcomers since their arrival. The adults in back looked worried, as did the teenagers up front, but several of the high-schoolers had their phones out and were recording video. No one had panicked yet, but it was only a matter of moments before someone did. *Who knows?* Sierra thought. *Maybe it'll be me.*

"There's no need to get all huffy, darling," Grace said. "We're both reasonable adults. I'm sure we can come to some sort of understanding."

Before Randall could respond, Grace's mouth yawned wide, so much so she looked like a constrictor unhinging its jaw in preparation for feeding. Her head thrust forward, the motion reminding Sierra even more of a snake, and a stream of brown liquid blasted from her mouth to strike Randall's smiley yellow face. He turned his head away from the onslaught of vomit and raised his hands in an attempt to block the stream. Grace kept the vomit going for several more seconds, then the stream thinned, lost pressure, and finally cut off. She wiped the back of her hand across her mouth, dry skin rasping against dry skin.

"Feel any different?" she asked.

Randall's smiley face was now a frowny face. Brown liquid dripped from the yellow orb that was his head onto the floor, and his shirt now had vomit stains on it to go with all the blood.

"What in the *fuck* did you do that for?" Randall demanded. "Are you *insane*?"

Grace gave Randall an appraising look. "I guess it only works on normal people, and you look about as far from normal as it's possible to get."

"Says the vomit-spewing mummy," Randall muttered.

Sierra didn't know what was happening, but if Grace and Randall were even half as dangerous as Jeffrey, they needed to evacuate the building before anyone got hurt.

She turned to Gloria and spoke the woman's name in a loud whisper to get her attention. Gloria was so transfixed by the nightmarish drama taking place before her eyes that she didn't respond until Sierra said her name a second time. When Sierra had her attention, she gestured toward the rear of the building. At first Gloria didn't appear to understand, but then her face brightened and she nodded. She gestured for her students to follow her, and she got up and headed quietly toward the back. Her students went with her, all of them moving slow and silent. The rear entrance was located farther down the hall from the break room, and it let out onto an alley behind the building. Once everyone was outside, they could haul ass in any direction they liked. As they fled for their lives, Sierra hoped at least one of them would have the presence of mind to call 911 and report what was happening in ArtWorks.

While Sierra had been urging Gloria to get her students the hell out of the building, Marc had gestured to the high-schoolers to join the exodus. The kids got the message right away, but instead of trying to be sneaky about their departure, they let their fear get the better of them and started running.

Both Randall and Grace looked at the fleeing kids, but it was Officer Al who actually did something. He pointed his gun at the ceiling and fired. The gunshot sounded loud as cannon fire in the enclosed space, and everyone – including Gloria and her students, none of whom had made it to the hallway yet – froze.

"Everybody stay right where you are," Officer Al said. "Or the next bullet's going to go in one of you."

Someone made a soft keening sound and several people began crying, but no one moved.

Sierra wanted to shout, *Don't be idiots! He can't kill you all!* She didn't say this out loud, but she was shocked to find herself thinking such a thing. Did she seriously believe it was better for some of the students to die so others might live? Shouldn't she want *all* the students to survive?

Before she could pursue this thought any further, once again the door to ArtWorks opened, and this time it was Stuart who entered. At least, Sierra thought it was Stuart. Like Grace and Randall, he'd been transformed, only in his case, his flesh had been fused with machinery. His eyes, teeth, and hands were silver, and a small radar-like dish protruded from the left side of his head. He moved with fluid precision, his arms and legs bending strangely, as if they now had extra joints. His eyes locked onto Sierra as soon as he stepped inside, and they crackled with twin bursts of electricity. He smiled, cold and cruel.

Only then did he become aware of Randall and Grace.

"Who the fuck are you two?" he said. His voice sounded as if it was electronically synthesized, and there was angry static beneath his words.

Grace and Randall moved away from Stuart and each other, as if instinctively making room for themselves to fight. Sierra hoped that Karolyn would take advantage of the moment to get the hell out of there, but she didn't move a muscle.

She's too scared to move, Sierra thought. She didn't blame her.

Sierra started to walk forward, intending to go to Karolyn, take the woman's arm, and pull her away. Hopefully, the others would be too busy facing off against each other to notice what she was doing. But Marc took hold of her arm to stop her, and when she turned to look at him, he shook his head.

"Didn't you hear them?" he whispered. "They came for *you*. You can't get too close to them. Who knows what they'll do to you?"

She appreciated his concern, but that was the point. They *had* come for her. It was *her* fault they were here, and she couldn't let anything happen to Karolyn because she'd been stupid enough to return here after the Reliant building's collapse. If she'd known there were others pursuing her besides Jeffrey…she still might've come here. She hadn't been thinking clearly after the destruction of the building, but that was no excuse. Her friend was in danger – and so were Marc, Gloria, and all the students – and it was all because of her. She tried to pull free from Marc, but he tightened his grip on her arm. It seemed he was determined to prevent her from sacrificing herself.

She was about to turn and tell him to let her the fuck go, when Grace scowled at Stuart and said, "Who are you?"

"I'm Stuart. Sierra's boyfriend."

Grace laughed, a brittle-boned sound that made Sierra wince.

"*You're* the controlling little fuck with all the insecurities? Sierra's told me all about you. I really shouldn't do the thieving cunt any favors, but since you are *such* a douche…."

She gestured to Officer Al. The man aimed his weapon at Stuart and fired.

There was a loud *clang* and Stuart staggered back, but he didn't go down. Officer Al frowned and fired again, and he continued firing until his clip was empty. Each bullet struck Stuart, but they all clanged off his body as if it were armored. One of the bullets had hit his cheek and another his neck, blasting away flesh and revealing silver underneath.

"Thanks, Krista," Stuart said.

Sierra had no idea who he was speaking to, but then he opened his mouth and a cable shot forth. There were sharp prongs on the end, and they buried themselves in Officer Al's forehead. The man's eyes rolled white, and he dropped his empty gun as his body began spasming, as if he was having a seizure. His skin blackened, and his body shrank in on itself as a nauseating smell of burning flesh filled the air. And then Officer Al – who now resembled a man-shaped piece of charcoal with empty hollows where the eyes had been – stopped seizing. The cable detached from his forehead and flew back into Stuart's mouth. And then, as if the cable had been the only thing holding up Officer Al's corpse, the blackened husk of his body collapsed to the wooden floor, hitting with a soft crunching sound, like a pile of dead fallen leaves.

"That was a neat trick," Randall said.

Stuart acknowledged the compliment with a nod, but he didn't take his eyes off Grace. She stared at Officer Al's remains as if she couldn't believe what had happened. Then she glared at Stuart.

"You little bastard," she spat. "I'm going to tear your head off, vomit down your neck, and see if I can make your headless body my new servant. It'll be fun watching you bump into everything since you won't be able to see or hear. What do you think about that?"

Before Stuart could answer, the front door burst open and Mandy made her entrance. She looked at Grace, Randall, and Stuart, and her face wrinkled in disgust.

"My god, it's a fucking freak convention in here," she said.

Grace frowned, the desiccated skin on her brow cracking in several places.

"You're that bitch Sierra's always complaining about, the one that's got a hang-up about sex."

Mandy shot Sierra a glance before she answered Grace, her voice almost a purr.

"I may be a bitch, but I've recently reconsidered my attitude toward sex."

Sierra might've guessed as much from the woman's look. Her blouse was unbuttoned so far it was a miracle that her breasts hadn't spilled out, and her hair was not only down, it was wild and tousled. But more telling was the way she moved, with a leonine ease, a predator completely at home in her own skin and certain of her strength. She exuded a powerful musky scent that began to fill the building like an invisible fog of sexual energy, and when it hit Sierra with its full force, she became instantly wet, and she wondered why she'd never noticed how beautiful Mandy was before this. She wondered what it would be like to kiss her, to run her tongue over those velvet lips....

Mandy's pheromones affected everyone in the building, with the possible exception of Randall, who didn't appear to have a nose on his round smiley face. Stuart's eyes sparked with tiny bolts of electric current, and Grace, despite herself, licked her leathery lips with a lump of dried meat that served as her tongue. Of those standing near the entrance, Karolyn was affected the most. She forgot her fear of the monstrous beings who'd entered her school and sidled up to Mandy with a sly look on her face. She pressed herself against Mandy's body and kissed her long and deep, fondling one of her large breasts as she did so. In the back, Gloria grabbed a man old enough to be her father and kissed him so hard their teeth clacked together. The man kissed her enthusiastically back, and the other adults began touching each other, tentatively at first, but with increasing urgency. The high-schoolers, whose bodies were already experiencing the turmoil of adolescence, were hit strongest of all. Their skin flushed red, their breathing became heavy, and a couple began salivating so much drool spilled over their chins. Several began kneading their crotches while others turned to the student nearest them and began making out, and a few even dry-humped.

If it kept up like this, the afternoon students – teen and adult alike – would shuck their clothes and start rutting on the floor like animals in heat. And Sierra wasn't sure she wouldn't be down there getting it on with them. It had been a long time since she'd had sex, since she'd broken up with Stuart, in fact. She looked at him closely for the first time since he'd come in, and she realized his new cyborg look was actually kind of hot.

Christ, she thought. *Mandy's sex magic is even making Stuart look good to me.*

Marc grabbed hold of her shoulders and gave her a hard shake.

"Snap out of it!" he said. "She's casting some kind of sex spell. I'm halfway hard, and I've never been attracted to a woman in my life!"

Sierra still felt drawn to Mandy, but now that she knew the reason for it, she was able to resist her lure. So she'd been changed too. Another person from her life had been refashioned into some kind of distorted version of themselves. Randall had become the ultimate Chuck. Grace was a booze-spewing witch. Stuart had become one with his beloved technology, and Mandy had finally shed her inhibitions and self-loathing to become the apotheosis of sexual obsession. Sierra didn't know why they'd been chosen to undergo such transformations or what it had to do with her, which surely it did since she was the only connection between the four of them as far as she knew. But she felt confident of one thing: the man in the black suit, the one she'd seen resurrect Jeffrey in last night's dream, was responsible somehow.

And speaking of Jeffrey....

The door opened for a final time, and Sierra's brother entered.

"Looks like the gang's all here," Marc said.

Jeffrey looked worse than the last time Sierra had seen him. His gray skin was marred with patches of black in places, and it sagged, as if it was having trouble staying attached to his bones. Whatever power the man in the black suit had used to resurrect Jeffrey, it seemed to have its limits when it came to keeping his body fresh. He'd smelled bad in the Reliant office, but now he smelled worse, like a walking sewer, and his stench cut through Mandy's miasma of sex like a scalpel. Karolyn pulled away from Mandy, a look of horror on her face, as if she couldn't believe what she'd been doing. The students, both young and old, found their carnal urges deserting them as well, and they moved apart from one another, most looking embarrassed, but a few looked speculatively at the person they'd been kissing and touching, as if hoping they'd found themselves a special friend.

Even in a situation as fucked up at this, some people still let their genitals do their thinking for them, Sierra thought.

Mandy turned to Jeffrey and waved her hand in front of her nose.

"Honey, I don't know what your problem is, but your body odor is a real mood-killer."

Jeffrey ignored her, and he did the same to Randall, Stuart, and Grace. If he noticed anything odd about them, he didn't show it. But considering his current state, maybe they didn't look very strange to him. He glanced around, and when his gaze fell on Sierra and Marc, his face brightened.

"There you are! I want to tell you how sorry—"

He started walking forward as he said these words, but he hadn't gotten two steps before Randall interrupted him.

"You're supposed to be dead, son. Did you forget? Here, let me remind you." And with a single vicious swipe, he buried his copper dagger in Jeffrey's chest, all the way to the hilt. No blood emerged from the wound, but a thick clear liquid oozed slowly forth. Jeffrey didn't cry out in pain. He didn't so much as blink as the blade slid into his flesh. Randall still gripped the knife, and Jeffrey's gaze followed his hand to his arm and then his face.

He frowned.

"Mr. Kovach? Is that you?"

Randall – his smiley-face expression unvarying – gave his blade a twist when he withdrew it from Jeffrey's body. More clear fluid spurted from Jeffrey's chest onto his shirt, dampening the cloth.

Jeffrey's frown became a scowl.

"That wasn't very nice, Mr. Kovach."

Moving far faster than his decaying body seemed capable of, Jeffrey backhanded Randall across his orb of a face. The blow caused Randall to stagger to the side, and his yellow flesh turned black where Jeffrey's hand had struck him. The black patch swiftly turned gray and crumbled to dust, leaving behind a fist-sized divot in the right side of Randall's face.

"That *hurt*!" Randall shouted.

He swiped his blade toward Jeffrey again, but when Jeffrey tried to block the blow, the knife's edge sank into his right wrist and lopped the hand off as easily as if Randall had popped the head off a dandelion. The hand blackened on its way to the floor, and when it hit, it exploded in a puff of gray dust.

Clear ichor dripped from Jeffrey's newly made stump, but the loss of his hand didn't appear to hurt him. It did, however, make him angry. He started toward Randall, but the smiley-face man jumped back, stuck his free hand in his pants pocket, and brought out a number of Chucks that he then threw in Jeffrey's face. Sierra expected the pennies to hit and bounce off, but when they struck Jeffrey's skin, they sank in halfway and remained embedded.

It's like the edges are sharp, she thought. Chucks as *shuriken*.

Chucks protruded from Jeffrey's forehead, cheeks, chin, nose, and several had struck his eyes. Clear goo seeped from the wounds, especially from his eyes, making it look like he was weeping thick, gloppy tears. Jeffrey reached up to pull the Chucks off, but since he only had his left hand now, all he managed to do with the stump of his right was smear more goo onto his face.

Oh Jeffrey, Sierra thought. *Your eyes!*

Mandy, Stuart, and Grace stood by and watched Randall and Jeffrey fight with varying degrees of interest and amusement. Karolyn stood not far from them, once more paralyzed with fear. Her gaze was fixed on Jeffrey, who was working on removing the Chucks from his damaged eyes. When the others weren't looking, Grace turned her head toward Karolyn, pursed her lips, and spat a thin stream of brown liquid at Karolyn. The woman's aim was perfect, and the liquid struck Karolyn's mouth. Her lips were parted, and most of the brown stuff went right in. Only a few drops got on her face.

Karolyn stiffened and her features went slack. She no longer looked afraid. She looked like she didn't feel anything. Grace gave no command – at least not a verbal one – but Karolyn walked over to her desk, which also served as the school's reception area. She grabbed a pair of fabric scissors that she'd been using to cut cloth for a project yesterday, gripped them like a knife, and walked back to the others. Jeffrey and Randall still faced each other, but neither had made another move yet. Stuart and Mandy were still watching them as Karolyn stepped close to Mandy, raised the scissors, and plunged them down into Mandy's left tit. Mandy screamed and Karolyn – her face absolutely blank – yanked the scissors free in a spray of blood and raised them high once more in preparation for another strike. This time when she brought her hand down, Mandy was ready. She caught Karolyn's wrist and squeezed. Bones snapped like twigs and the scissors fell from Karolyn's hands to strike the floor. Despite her injury, Karolyn displayed no reaction. She merely stood there while Mandy, a bloodstain widening on the front of her white blouse, bent down to retrieve the scissors. While she was down there, she swept the scissors up between Karolyn's legs and buried them in her vagina.

Blood gushed down in a crimson waterfall, and while Karolyn again showed no reaction, this time her body shuddered once as if she experienced a severe shock. Witnessing this terrible act was too much for the students. Their paralysis broke and both high-schoolers and adults began running in a confused mass for the back entrance, shouting and screaming. Marc grabbed hold of Sierra's arm and pulled her to the side to get her out of the way of the stampede. Sierra barely noticed. She forgot to breathe. All she could do was watch as Mandy – her features twisted into a mask of savage delight – withdrew the scissors and rammed them in again. Karolyn shuddered once more and rocked back and forth, but she remained standing.

"Is that really necessary?" Grace said, her tone making her distaste clear.

"No," Mandy said. Blood stippled her face, and she grinned as she yanked out the scissors and stabbed Karolyn once more. "But it *is* a lot of fun."

Blood – so dark it was almost black – was leaving Karolyn's body in a torrent now, and her face paled. She remained standing for several more seconds, but when Mandy pulled out the scissors one last time, Karolyn's legs gave way and she went down. Her feet slid out from under her and she hit the floor hard.

Mandy stood, still gripping the fabric scissors, from which Karolyn's blood dripped, and she gazed down at the dead woman. Her smile was terrible to behold.

"Note to self: scissors do *not* make effective dildoes."

Stuart looked at her with disgust.

"I don't know what the fuck is wrong with you, lady, but you and the rest of these ugly bastards can fight each other all you want. I'm here for Sierra."

He moved past the others and started toward Sierra, but before he could get too far, Randall hurled his copper knife. It whistled through the air and struck Stuart between the shoulder blades. There was no blood, but a shower of sparks flew from the wound.

Sierra didn't know why the blade had penetrated Stuart's body when Officer Al's bullets hadn't. Maybe it was because Randall had attacked him from behind, surprising him. Or maybe Randall's knife, like Stuart's body, possessed otherworldly properties too. Whichever the case, Stuart's face contorted in pain, and he hunched over, teeth gritted, and tried to reach back to remove the knife. He couldn't quite get hold of it with his fingers, but five miniature silver tentacles emerged from his fingers, wrapped around the blade, and pulled. When the knife was free, the tentacles placed it in his hand. He closed his fingers around the blade and turned to Randall.

"Not cool," he said.

Stuart held the knife in his open palm. His finger tentacles touched their ends to the blade and the metal began to glow orange then red. The knife melted and Stuart turned his hand over and let the liquid copper splatter to the floor. The handle melted too, but the Chuck on the end came loose, fell, hit the floor, and bounced away like a smiley-faced ping-pong ball.

Gloria and the students were gone now, all of them having successfully escaped through the rear entrance. Only Sierra and Marc remained, and he was saying something in her ear. She was traumatized from witnessing Karolyn's death, and it took her a moment to understand what he was saying.

"We need to get out of here before we end up like Karolyn," he said. "Or worse!"

Sierra tried to imagine what could possibly be worse than what had happened to her friend, but she couldn't come up with anything – which she supposed was just as well, given how awful the reality had been.

She wanted to leave, she really did, but there was one thing she wanted more – to kill the bitch who had murdered Karolyn.

She started forward.

★ ★ ★

Sierra didn't have a specific plan. Her goal was clear: she wanted to hurt Mandy, hurt her *bad*. But the question was how to do it. All of them – Mandy, Jeffrey, Grace, Stuart, Randall – had been changed, but the last several minutes had shown they could be damaged. Mandy's injured breast was still bleeding, and Jeffrey's wounds continued to ooze clear fluid. Occasional sparks issued from the injury in Stuart's back, and the divot in Randall's face showed no sign of healing. She needed a weapon, something that could inflict more damage than a pair of scissors and do it quickly, before Mandy or any of the others could attack her. She might've made a try for the gun, which lay on the floor close to the blackened corpse of Officer Al, if the man hadn't fired all of its bullets. She mentally ran through a list of equipment and supplies in the building. Almost everything here was harmless, but she thought of two things that, if used in combination, might work.

She detoured toward a section of the floor where easels were set up. Some of them had paintings on them – simple works depicting houses, trees, and animals – but most were empty. There was a can of paint thinner on a nearby table, and she grabbed it. She quickly unscrewed the cap and discarded it. She then went to another work area, this one set up for small welding projects. Scraps of metal lay on a table, along with soldering wire, and what Sierra had come for: a handheld blowtorch. She picked it up, thumbed off the safety switch, and turned the flame setting as high as it would go. The torch had automatic ignition, so she wouldn't need to activate the flame until she was ready to use it. She then started for the front of the building once more.

By this point, the conflict between Mandy and the others had degenerated into an argument about who had the better claim to Sierra. Jeffrey hadn't joined in, though. He was still preoccupied with removing Chucks from his face. He'd cleared the ones from his eyes, but the sockets were filled with the thick goo he had in place of blood, and Sierra had no idea if either eye remained functional.

As she walked past Karolyn's body – careful to avoid stepping in her blood – she had to force herself not to look at it.

I'm sorry, she thought. And then she thrust her sorrow aside, leaving only a cold hatred for Mandy and a determination to make her pay for what she'd done. Sierra activated the torch as she drew near Mandy and visualized splashing paint thinner on her face and chest, then touching the torch flame to her and quickly stepping back as the woman became a big-titted bonfire.

But as Sierra approached, Grace smashed the mostly empty liquor bottle she'd been holding into the side of Mandy's head. The bottle broke and glass shards cut into Mandy's cheek, causing it to bleed heavily. Mandy growled, sounding more animal than human, and shoved Grace. The older woman stumbled backward just as Sierra came within striking distance of Mandy, and she collided with Sierra. Paint thinner sloshed onto Grace – not a lot, but some – and the torch's flame touched her. There was a loud *whumpf* as fire erupted on Grace, and Sierra jumped back, startled. She dropped both the paint thinner and the blowtorch, and they hit the floor. Without Sierra's finger depressing the ignition switch, the torch's flame cut off, and the paint thinner that spilled onto the floor from the fallen can didn't ignite. Sierra barely noticed. She was too transfixed by what was happening to Grace. Even though only a small portion of paint thinner had gotten on her, the fire spread rapidly across her body, and the woman shrieked in agony and flailed about, arms flapping wildly in a vain attempt to extinguish the flames that now engulfed her from head to toe.

At first Sierra didn't understand how so little paint thinner could cause such an intense blaze, but then she remembered what Grace's transformation had done to her. Her skin was dry as desert sand, and it had taken only a small spark to set her moisture-free body aflame. Sierra set aside her desire to get revenge on Mandy for Karolyn's death and decided to focus on keeping her own ass alive. She turned and ran toward Marc, who had already started running for ArtWorks' back entrance. *Smart boy*, she thought.

She heard a belching sound, and a gout of fire shot past her

on the left side. It was quickly followed by a second belch and another blast of flame, this one shooting over her head. Grace was vomiting that nasty brown liquid of hers, but like the rest of her, it had ignited and was coming out as jets of flame. In her peripheral vision, Sierra saw that the two flame streams that had missed her had already started a pair of fires – one in the painting area with the easels, and another on a wall where student self-portraits were displayed.

She's going to burn the whole fucking place down, Sierra thought.

When Grace wasn't vomiting, she screamed. For the most part her screams were incoherent, but at one point it sounded as if she shrieked words. Sierra wasn't certain, but they sounded like *I want my goddamned purse!*

And then Sierra was in the back hallway and running toward the rear door. Mark had already gotten out, and the door hung open, as if waiting for her to go through. She didn't keep it waiting long.

⋆ ⋆ ⋆

Jeffrey's vision hadn't been entirely destroyed. He could still see out of his right eye, a little, although the images were hazy and blurry. He first became aware that Grace was on fire when he saw a bright orange glow ahead of him. If his sense of smell had still functioned, he would've detected the stench of her burlap-like skin burning, and if his body could still register temperature, he would've been aware of the heat. So his first real clue that Grace was burning came from Stuart, who said, "Holy shit! The bitch is on fire!" then screamed in pain.

Jeffrey heard frantic movement then and sensed people passing him. He heard the front door knocked open so hard it tore half off its hinges, and he heard one of the front windows explode, as if something large and heavy had struck the glass. Grace's screams cut into his ears, and the orange glow in his vision began to move rapidly back and forth. Soon other orange glows blossomed, and he realized that Grace was running around, mindlessly spreading her flames in fear and agony. He guessed the sounds he'd heard a moment ago had been the others fleeing ArtWorks to avoid being devoured by flame, and he supposed he should do the same if he didn't want to become part of Grace's conflagration. The only problem was, he wasn't sure where the door was. He thought it was behind him, so he turned around, but all he saw was a brownish-black smudge. Was it a wall, or maybe smoke? He couldn't smell, and he didn't need to breathe, only inhale in order to speak, so if the building was filling up with smoke – which seemed likely – he couldn't detect it.

Since no other course of action presented itself, he started walking forward, hands – well, hand and stump – held out before him. As he searched for the door, he wondered if it might not be better to stay here and let the fire have him. He was supposed to be dead, he knew that now, and since the man in the black suit had brought him back, he'd killed people. He'd tried to kill Sierra and Marc, the people he loved more than anything in the world. He never should've been returned to life. It was a mistake, one he could rectify now, and by doing so he'd protect Sierra and Marc – not to mention everyone else in town – from him.

He stopped walking forward, dropped his arms to his side, then sat down cross-legged on the floor to wait.

Grace's screams cut out after that, and he knew she was gone, one less monster for the world to worry about. He hoped Sierra and Marc had made it out okay. He thought it likely they had. His sister was smart as hell, and she possessed an emotionally restrained calculating side to her that was useful in emergencies. One summer when he was thirteen and their parents were at work, he'd wiped out on his bike and cracked his head on the street in front of their house. Sierra had been playing with her Barbies in the yard, and when she saw him go down she calmly rose, went into the house, called 911, and then came back out to sit with him while she waited for help to arrive. She'd grabbed a clean washcloth on her way out and pressed it to his head to staunch the flow of blood. She'd felt nothing the entire time, she'd told him later. *I just did what needed to be done.*

Even in a situation as bizarre as this, he felt confident that Sierra would keep her head about her. Marc, however, wasn't so good at dealing with his emotions in a crisis, but Jeffrey knew Sierra would take care of him. They were safe, and once he was gone, they would stay that way. He wished he could say goodbye to them. He hated the thought that their last memory of him would be of a living corpse fighting other monsters in Sierra's workplace, but it couldn't be helped. He closed his eyes – not that it changed his vision much – and waited for death to claim him. Again.

"This is all very noble of you, but I'm afraid I still have need of your services."

It was the man in the black suit.

Jeffrey felt a hand take hold of his wrist – the one that still had a hand attached to it – and pull. He felt himself yanked onto a hard surface, and then the crackling roar of fire cut off. Someone, presumably the man in the black suit, helped him stand. He understood what must have happened. The man had opened a rift that opened onto ArtWorks, he'd pulled Jeffrey to safety, then sealed the rift once he was through.

"You're somewhat the worse for wear, aren't you?" the man in the black suit said. "If we had your hand, I could try to reattach it, but since you don't seem to have it on you, I assume it's been lost in the fire. I'm not sure I can do anything about your eyes, though. They've devilishly complex structures. Still, no harm in trying."

Jeffrey felt the man's fingers lightly touch his eyes. This was followed by a not unpleasant tingling sensation. After a moment, the man lowered his hands, and the tingling faded.

"How's that?" he asked.

Jeffrey turned to look across the street. His vision was still blurry but better than before, and he could see out of both eyes now.

"Improved," he said. "Not perfect, though."

He could see flames inside the building through the windows and open door, saw black smoke billowing through the openings as well. ArtWorks was lost.

"Good enough to help you get around?" the man in the black suit asked.

Jeffrey shrugged. "I suppose. You should've let me burn, though."

He turned and with a swift motion fastened his remaining hand around the man's throat. He concentrated the full force of his deathtouch on him, pictured his flesh turning black and shriveling as the life fled from his body. But after several seconds passed without anything happening, Jeffrey released his grip on the man's throat. When he took his hand away, he saw the skin on the man's neck remained smooth and healthy.

The man grinned.

"Did you honestly think I'd grant you a power that could harm me?'

"Figured it was worth a shot."

"I would've been disappointed if you hadn't made the attempt."

The sound of sirens filled the air.

"I believe the local fire department has been summoned," the man said. "They're going to have a difficult time battling this blaze. Its flames aren't exactly natural in origin."

Jeffrey couldn't see well enough to make out the man's features, but when he next spoke, his tone made Jeffrey think he was frowning.

"I didn't expect Grace to die this soon. Your sister is more resourceful than I gave her credit for. Still, I'm pleased with the way things are progressing. Quite pleased."

"Whoop-de-fucking-doo," Jeffrey said.

"I liked you better when your brains were scrambled. Hopefully, this period of lucidity will be as temporary as the others. Let us depart now. As much as I'd enjoy watching firefighters struggle to douse Grace's flames, we still have work to do."

"What work?" Jeffrey asked.

The sirens were louder now, and he knew the emergency vehicles would be here within moments.

"Phase One is complete," the man said. "Now it's time to begin Phase Two."

He locked his arm around Jeffrey's and began to lead him down the sidewalk. Jeffrey, seeing no other option, allowed himself to be led. He hoped the man was wrong about his mind and that his thoughts would remain clear. If so, he'd bide his time and wait for a chance to kill this black-suited motherfucker. He wasn't sure such a thing was possible, but if it was, he'd find a way to take the bastard out.

The man in the black suit whistled happily as they walked, and Jeffrey amused himself by imagining killing the man in ways that were extremely painful and messy.

CHAPTER TWELVE

Marc was waiting for Sierra in the back alley when she came out of the building.

"Thank god," he said.

"Thank butane," she countered.

Marc frowned, not understanding.

Sierra would explain later. "Come on, let's get out of here."

They hurried down the alley until they came to a cross alley. They took it, and eventually came out onto the street near where they'd parked. They were closer to Sierra's Ladybug than Marc's Civic, so they decided to take the Beetle. They climbed in as the sound of sirens filled the air. Sierra didn't think there was any way for firefighters or police to connect her and Marc to the blaze in ArtWorks, but she didn't want to stick around and end up being questioned by the cops. Plus, she had no way of knowing if Mandy, Randall, or Stuart had escaped the fire. It would be a relief if they all burned to death with Grace, but Sierra didn't think she'd be that lucky.

Then she remembered.

"Jeffrey."

Marc looked at her. "Is he…?"

"I don't know. Maybe."

Marc didn't say anything more, and she wondered if he was thinking the same thing she was, that it might be better if Jeffrey didn't make it out of ArtWorks.

She started Ladybug's engine and pulled away from the curb. As she drove away from the Historic District, a fire engine roared past them, siren wailing and lights flashing. It was soon followed by a paramedic vehicle and a pair of police cars. Considering all the mayhem that had taken place in Bishop Hill since sunrise, she thought the town's first responders had gotten themselves a real workout today.

She thought of Grace screaming as flames devoured what little flesh had remained on her bones. The woman had been troubled and too often was a pain in the ass, but she'd been a sympathetic ear when Sierra had badly needed one, and she regretted that Grace had gotten mixed up in all this, whatever *this* was.

"Where to now?" Marc asked. "I vote for the nearest bar. I could use a drink or twelve."

"As tempting as that sounds, I have another destination in mind."

She'd left her phone on the break room table when she'd heard Karolyn first scream, and she hadn't thought to retrieve it on her way out of the building. She'd been rather preoccupied with not burning to death at the time. She hadn't been able to get hold of her parents before all hell had broken loose in ArtWorks, and she needed to know if they were all right.

"I want to check on my mom and dad, make sure they're okay."

She thought Marc might object. Her parents didn't resent him as much as she did. *Had*. But he wasn't exactly their favorite person either. But he only nodded, laid his head back against the seat, and closed his eyes.

Sierra gripped the steering wheel tight, and tried not to think about black blood gushing from between Karolyn's legs as she drove.

* * *

Stuart had been standing close to Grace when she first burst into flame, and when she'd begun belching fire, he caught one of the streams on the left side of his head. Krista had attempted to augment him with a fire-suppressant attachment, but the flames were on the side of his head where the Bluetooth device had merged with his ear. The flames, which burned hotter and faster than ordinary fire, melted the dish jutting from his flesh and seared the skin around it. As badly as that had hurt – and it had hurt like a *bitch* – the pain was nothing compared to what he felt when the fire continued burning into his skull and began to melt the Bluetooth receiver. Krista screamed in his head, a high-pitched electronic shriek, and then she began shouting error messages and giving a rapid rundown of the system damage she'd sustained before falling silent.

Grace had been running around, spewing streams of flame everywhere, and as ArtWorks began to burn, Stuart bailed. He shoved his way through the front door, left hand pressed to his head in a useless effort to stop the pain. He felt drained of energy, barely able to walk. He headed slowly for his Camaro, intending to get inside, get the hell out of there, and find a place to hole up for a while where he could see what, if anything, he could do to repair Krista. He needed her. As much as he hated to admit it, she was the source of his power, and without her he'd never beat the other freaks that wanted to get their hands on Sierra. He didn't know what the fuck *that* was about, or where they'd come by their powers, and he didn't care. He only cared about himself. If he'd been a more self-reflective person, he might've realized this last thought encapsulated everything that was wrong with him. But he wasn't, so he didn't.

As he moved down the sidewalk, half walking, half shuffling, he heard the sound of glass shattering. He looked back and saw Mandy leap out of the window and land on the sidewalk in a crouch, as if she were a big cat of some kind, a tiger or panther or some shit like that. She was singed around the edges – the tips of her hair smoldered and her blouse and skirt were scorched in several places – but she appeared unhurt for the most part. She raised her head, sniffed the air, then she stood and started running in the opposite direction from him. When she reached a side alley, she turned and disappeared from view.

A few seconds later, Randall Kovach walked out of the front door. He looked different now. His head had shrunk somewhat, and he had a suggestion of ears and a nose. His mouth and eyes looked more normal, and his skin was a lighter shade of yellow. His head injury – which before had been a bloodless divot – was now bleeding freely. He looked up and down the sidewalk, and when he saw Stuart looking back at him, he headed the other way. He continued past the alley entrance where Mandy had turned and kept going.

Stuart wanted to go after the fucker and pay him back for

stabbing him between the shoulder blades. Krista had done her best to repair the damage, but the area still hurt. But the burns he'd suffered hurt worse, and he figured fuck Randall. He'd settle up with the asshole later.

He continued toward his Camaro, but before he could reach it, a woman ran out from a coffee shop called CaffeNation and almost ran into him. He realized that sirens were blaring, and he figured their noise had drawn the woman outside to see what was happening. She was African-American, with scarlet-dyed hair, wearing a white dress with horizontal pink stripes. She took one look at Stuart, and her eyes widened in surprise.

"Oh my god! Are you all right?"

Stuart smiled. "I will be."

He opened his mouth, intending to shoot his charger at her forehead, but the cable only ejected partway and hung limply from his mouth.

"You've got to be shitting me," he said, the words partially garbled.

Stuart took hold of the charger, intending to jam it manually into the woman, but the cable disconnected from the port beneath his tongue. He tried to reinsert it, but he found only wet, mushy flesh where the port had been. It was gone.

"Krista! What's happening?"

There was no immediate reply, but then he heard the pop and crackle of static in his head, followed by Krista's voice, her words almost inaudible.

"Fire…damage…system…non…func…tion…al…."

Her voice trailed away to nothing.

"Krista!" Stuart shouted, then louder, "*Krista!*"

He looked at the smart watch that had merged with his wrist, and he saw the screen was black. No app icons, no power indicator, nothing. It was dead. *Krista* was dead.

The woman who'd come out of the coffee shop had had enough of Stuart's strange appearance and even stranger behavior. She turned and fled back into the café.

"Fuck!"

Stuart hurled the useless charger after her. It bounced off

CaffeNation's glass door and landed on the sidewalk. He left it there and continued toward his Camaro, moving more unsteadily than before.

The pain from his burns was so intense that his vision blurred and his head swam with vertigo. He thought he might pass out, but he made it to the car. The door didn't open for him automatically, so he grabbed the handle and opened it the old-fashioned way. He practically fell into the driver's seat and managed to close the door behind him as a fire truck zoomed past.

Stuart knew he had to get out of there before the cops arrived. He put his hands on the steering wheel and waited for his body to connect with the vehicle. But his hands didn't merge with the steering wheel as they should've. He furrowed his brow – which hurt like a motherfucker, given his burns – gritted his teeth and concentrated so hard that his body began shaking. He thought it wasn't going to work, but slowly his hands and the steering wheel became one. He felt his mind connect to the Camaro, although the link was nowhere near as strong as before. Still, it was enough. The Camaro started, and he pulled away from the curb. He did a U-turn in the middle of the street and headed away from the Historic District as fast as his vehicle would take him. A paramedic van and a couple cop cars passed him going the other way, but none of the drivers so much as glanced in his direction.

At first he drove aimlessly. It took all his waning energy to deal with the pain of his burns, and he could barely think, let alone choose a destination. But the longer he drove, the more he kept remembering Sierra's face as she walked toward ArtWorks' entrance, blowtorch held tight in her hand, can of paint thinner in the other. He hadn't expected her to confront them like that, didn't know she had it in her. He thought she'd intended to attack Mandy after what she'd done to Karolyn – and hadn't that been some seriously sick shit? – but she'd ended up setting Grace on fire, which in turn had led to him getting the left side of his head crispy-fried. So Sierra was ultimately responsible for what had happened to him. Worse, she'd killed Krista, who – despite being a bit of a control freak – had been the best friend he'd ever had.

He'd gone to ArtWorks in the first place to teach Sierra a lesson in respect. Instead, he'd discovered others who'd been transformed like him, and in the process of trying to deal with their bullshit, Sierra had ended up making him look like an asshole – again! He wasn't sure how the others had come to be changed. Hell, he didn't know how and why it had happened to him. But he didn't care about them. All that mattered to him was finally making Sierra realize that she was *his*, that she was nothing without him, *less* than nothing.

And with that, he knew where he wanted to go.

"Krista, can you—"

He broke off, remembering that he was alone now. Krista was gone, and he couldn't use her tracking app to locate Sierra. But he didn't need Krista to find her, did he? They'd dated long enough for him to get to know everything about her, and he knew what she did whenever she was faced with a serious problem. Before her brother died, she'd talk to him, but after he was gone, she went to her parents, and that's where she'd go now. He was sure of it.

He'd driven in the opposite direction from the Sowells' neighborhood, but it wouldn't take him long to get there, not in his car. And while he might not be as strong without Krista, he figured he was still strong enough to show Sierra why it was a bad idea to disrespect him.

A very bad idea.

⋆ ⋆ ⋆

When Mandy hit the sidewalk, she scented the air, trying to pick up Sierra's trail. But the stink of the fire was too strong for her to smell anything else. Frustrated, she took off running, intending to go back to her convertible, hit the streets, and see if she could get Sierra's scent again. But she heard emergency vehicles approaching off in the distance. Her hearing was far sharper than it had been, and she knew she had several moments before they arrived, but she ducked down an alley anyway. Better to take a more roundabout route to her car and avoid being seen by the police. They'd take one look at her, see the scorch marks on her clothes and the burns on her skin – not to mention the blood that had splattered onto her when she killed Karolyn – and immediately want to question her about what had happened at ArtWorks. At the very least, they'd insist she accept medical attention from the paramedics on scene. But as much as she loved a man – or woman – in uniform, she wanted to avoid the hassle.

All in all, she'd escaped ArtWorks relatively unscathed. She had a few burns here and there, but she found the pain stimulating rather than debilitating. Same for the stab wound to her breast. The waves of agony that pulsed outward from the injury were almost indistinguishable from the sensations of building orgasm. She thought if she reached up and dug a finger into the wound, the resulting pain would cause her to explode with orgasm. She was tempted, but she decided against it. Not only couldn't she afford the distraction right now, but with each passing moment, the pains of her injuries lessened. She was healing at an extraordinarily rapid rate, so fast that soon it would be like she hadn't been injured at all.

She wished she'd had the opportunity to kill Grace for what the bitch had done to her, but Sierra had taken that pleasure from her. Admittedly, it had been amusing to watch the old crone thrash around as she burned, vomiting gouts of fire everywhere. Mandy wasn't clear on why there were other people connected to Sierra who'd undergone their own significant alterations. She'd recognized them all. Sierra had mentioned them to her during the weeks after her brother's death – her brother who was no longer quite so deceased – when she'd sought emotional comfort from Mandy. Deep down, Mandy had wanted to make a move on Sierra then, but she never would've allowed herself to consciously express such a desire. Thank Christ that version of her was gone.

She suspected that there was something larger in scope going on here than just her wanting to fuck the shit out of Sierra, some kind of master plan that she was only a part of. But she didn't care. So long as she got what she wanted – Sierra – nothing else mattered. Part of her – a part that was rational and orderly and saw the world in terms of factors to be calculated and problems to be solved – thought this single-mindedness might prove to be a mistake in the long run, and a costly one at that. But Mandy was all impulse, desire, and hunger now. She had an appetite for Sierra, and that appetite must be sated, regardless of the cost.

She continued running through alleys, her body healing, and imagined all the things she was going to do to Sierra when she finally got the cute little bitch alone.

★ ★ ★

Randall hadn't realized how badly he was bleeding until he was behind the wheel of his Lincoln Town Car and looked at himself in the rearview mirror. He had returned completely to his normal self – his *hated* self – once more, and the left side of his head was a blood-soaked mess. Blood ran down his neck and onto his chest, and he'd likely left a trail of it on the sidewalk for the police to follow straight to him. Best to start driving and get the hell out of here while he still could. People were starting to come out of businesses up and down the street, lured by the sound of approaching sirens. Every one of them was a potential witness, and he needed to go before they noticed his vehicle or – worse yet – thought to take a picture of it with their phones.

But he didn't start the engine, just sat there, staring at his reflection. It was hard to tell with all the blood, but it looked as if his head had a small dent in it. Had Jeffrey damaged his skull when he'd backhanded him? No, he thought. Jeffrey had somehow made a portion of his skull cease to exist. What he was looking at wasn't a cut. It was an opening in his head, a newly made hole.

He reached up with shaking hands and gently probed the injury. He brushed away some blood with a thumb and found himself looking at a small section of brain tissue. There was a concavity in it, as if Jeffrey's touch had erased part of his brain, along with the skin and bone that protected it.

Cold fear lanced through him, and he wondered just how seriously he'd been injured. He felt almost no pain. He figured Jeffrey's touch must have destroyed the nerve endings in the affected area, basically anesthetizing the wound. But just because it didn't hurt didn't mean he could dismiss it. His goddamned brain was exposed to the fucking air!

I need to go to a hospital.

He turned on the Town Car's engine, put the vehicle in gear, and drove away from the curb. Bishop Hill didn't have a hospital of its own. The nearest one was in Ash Creek, about a twenty-minute drive from here. He briefly debated going back and letting the paramedics tend to him. Paramedics always came out to the scenes of fires, didn't they? But how could he explain what had happened to him?

There was this young man who grew up across the street from me. He died in an automobile accident last year, but for some unknown reason he returned from the dead today, and his touch causes things to decay. Why was I at ArtWorks? After killing several people earlier – including my own wife – I wanted to kill the dead boy's sister because she insulted my Chucks this morning.

If he told them this, they'd send him off to a psychiatric hospital after patching his wound. No, that was wrong. The police would send his clothes out to be tested because of all the blood on them, and they'd learn the blood belonged to people who had been hacked to death with a knife. He'd end up in a *prison* for the criminally insane.

Maybe that would be best. After everything that had happened today, he was no longer sure what was real and what wasn't. He'd accepted that he'd somehow become a Chuck – although it seemed ridiculous now – but he was having trouble believing that four others, Jeffrey included, had undergone similar transformations. One such transformation was a miracle. A dark one, for sure, but a miracle still. But *five*? It was too much.

Rather than being dismayed by this line of thought, Randall felt a glimmer of hope. If he was crazy, then maybe none of this – him being a Chuck, the killings, the others who'd been changed – was real. If he was mentally ill, he could be treated, maybe even fully recover. And then he could put all of this behind him, a waking nightmare that had no more reality than the sort that plagued one's sleep. But how could he know for certain that what he'd experienced today had been only delusions?

He could think of one way to prove it. He could go home, walk into his kitchen, and see if Erika's corpse lay on the living room floor. If it didn't, if she was still alive and going about her day, then he'd know he was mentally ill, and he'd ask her to take him to the hospital. But if he found her body....

He tried not to think about that possibility. No need to borrow trouble.

Feeling better now that he had a plan of action, he took his right hand off the steering wheel and put it into his pants pocket so he could feel the reassuring solidity of his Chucks. He needed to remain positive if he was going to get through this, and nothing was more positive than a Chuck.

"Chuck says keep your chin up," he said, forcing himself to sound cheerful. "Things are going to get better!"

In the rearview mirror, just for an instant, he thought he saw a large yellow smiley face wink at him. Then it was gone, and he concentrated on driving, gripping the Chucks so tight his hand hurt.

⋆ ⋆ ⋆

Sierra pulled Ladybug into her parents' driveway and parked. She and Marc sat there for a moment, both too tired and emotionally wrung out to move. But then Sierra got out of the car, and Marc followed.

"What are you going to tell them?" Marc asked.

"I have no idea. Maybe I'll try the truth, as insane as it is, and just see how they react. I'll have you to back me up on it, so that might make a difference."

"Maybe," Marc said, but he didn't sound convinced. Sierra didn't blame him. She doubted there was a chance in hell that her parents would believe their story, but she didn't know what else to do.

Her parents lived in a safe neighborhood and usually left their front door unlocked during the day. Sierra had a key, but she didn't remember the last time she'd needed to use it. She opened the door and stepped inside, Marc following.

"It's weird to be back," he said. "I haven't come here—"

"Since after Jeffrey's funeral," Sierra said.

"Yeah."

Walter and Dana Sowell were good people, if not particularly imaginative. Both were retired, but Walter had owned and managed a carpet store in town called Gotcha Covered, and Dana had worked as a dental hygienist. Sierra had no idea where she'd gotten her artistic nature from, but it certainly hadn't been from them. Their house was nicely if blandly furnished, and the place was always clean and tidy. She suspected that her mom might have more than a touch of OCD, but she'd only laughed the one time Sierra had suggested it to her.

Who cares? she'd said. *So long as the house is clean.*

The living room – which was never used – was to the right of the foyer. Sierra led Marc into the hall, then toward the kitchen. It was the homiest place in the house, decorated in warm earth tones with framed watercolor paintings Sierra had done in college hanging on the walls. She found the paintings embarrassing. She was capable of producing much better work now, but her parents loved them. There was a breakfast nook in one corner where her parents spent a great deal of their time, drinking coffee, reading, talking, or just looking out the window and watching birds in the backyard. When she'd been a kid, Sierra had thought her mom and dad were the dullest people on the planet, but now she thought the idea of them doing simple things together and enjoying each other's company was sweet. She hoped she could have a relationship like that one day.

They weren't at the table, though.

"Mom? Dad?"

No answer.

Maybe it was because so many bad things had happened today, or maybe it was some primal instinct, but she had the sudden sick feeling that something was wrong.

She ran through the kitchen, into the dining room, and then into the family room. This was where Walter and Dana Sowell did most of their living – when they weren't sitting at the breakfast nook table, that was. It was also, unfortunately, where they'd done their dying. Her mother's body lay facedown on the couch, one arm hanging down, fingers touching the carpet. Her father lay next to the fireplace, his body twisted at the waist so his head and torso faced the ceiling and his trunk and legs were on their sides. Sierra had no doubt they were both dead. They'd sustained numerous stabs wounds, so many that it looked as if someone had dumped several gallons of red paint on them, and then splashed a few more gallons around the general vicinity for good measure. She knew who'd killed them too, for several dozen goddamned Chucks were scattered around the room, some of them – the *shuriken* kind – embedded in her parents' flesh.

Even though she knew there was no point to it, knew that her mom and dad were beyond help, she wanted to run to them, shake them, shout their names until life came back into their glassy eyes. She wanted them to look at her, smile, and say, *It's okay, sweetie. Everything's going to be all right.* Except it wasn't and it wouldn't be. Not now and never again.

She fell to her knees, a great wracking sob convulsing her body. For a moment she couldn't breathe, and she thought that was okay, that she didn't want to breathe, wanted to lie down, close her eyes, and wait for her heart to stop beating. Then Marc was kneeling next to her. He wrapped his arms around her, and she drew in a shuddering breath and began to cry. She wasn't surprised when Marc started crying with her.

⋆ ⋆ ⋆

Stuart pulled up to the Sowells' house and parked on the street. Sierra's Beetle – had a dumber-looking car ever been made? – sat in the driveway. He allowed himself a moment of smug satisfaction. He'd been right about where she'd go. Of course he had. Who knew her better than he?

The burns on the left side of his head still hurt like hell, but he decided to use the pain to fuel his anger. He felt almost totally drained of energy now. If only his fucking charger hadn't crapped out on him when he'd needed it. But if wishes were horses, then fuckety-fuck.

He tried to remove his hands from the steering wheel, but they refused to budge. They remained enmeshed with the substance of the steering wheel, and no matter how hard he concentrated, he was unable to separate himself from the car. He tried pulling himself free, but while the steering wheel shook, his flesh and bone remained fused with it, and all he succeeded in doing was sending jolts of pain shooting through his wrists.

"Fuck!"

He would've pounded his fist on the dashboard if he'd had a hand free. But he didn't, and it looked as if he wasn't going to separate himself from the car anytime soon.

There had to be a way, though. Krista might be dead – or offline or whatever – but his body hadn't returned to its previous flesh-and-blood state. He was still more machine than man. He could *feel* it. There had to be something he could do, some kind of augmentation he could use—

Panels in his forearms slid open, and a pair of metal coils swayed up into the air like twin serpents. But instead of fangs, these serpents had tiny round discs with very sharp edges in place of heads. Stuart imagined he could almost hear Krista in his mind.

"How badly do you want to get to Sierra?"

"Pretty goddamned badly," he said.

The rotary saws began whirring then, spinning so rapidly they made high-pitched sounds, as if they were alive.

Eeeeeeeeeeeeeeeeeeeeeeeeeeeeee....

The coils extended and the saws lowered toward his wrists and began their work. Stuart screamed as silver blood splattered the inner windshield.

* * *

Sierra told Marc she thought she was going to throw up. He started helping her toward the downstairs bathroom, but she refused to go there, didn't want to stay on the same floor as her parents' ravaged bodies. Marc helped her to the upstairs bathroom. She flipped on the light and told him to call 911 and give her a couple minutes of privacy. For a moment she thought he might protest, but he nodded and went back downstairs.

She closed and locked the door. She put her hands on the sink, leaned close to the mirror, and inspected her reflection. Her eyes were red from crying, and her cheeks were puffy. Jeffrey used to tease her about being an ugly crier, and she'd always denied it, although she'd known he was right.

She understood almost nothing that had happened this day, but she knew one thing: somehow she was at the center of it all. *Her* brother had returned to life on the first anniversary of his death. And people that *she'd* interacted with today – Grace, Randall, Stuart, and Mandy – had become monsters obsessed with her in one way or another. She was the one common factor in this insanity, and if that was so, there only one way to make the madness stop.

She opened a drawer in the sink cupboard. Inside were various devices her mother used – curling iron, hair straightener and such – but what she wanted was a much simpler tool. She removed a pair of styling shears and held them up to the light. They were nowhere near as large as the fabric scissors Mandy had used on poor Karolyn, but they were long enough, and more importantly sharp enough. Before going to college to get her degree in dental hygiene, her mother had worked in a hair salon. While she wasn't foolish enough to try to style her own hair, she used to cut Sierra's and Jeffrey's when they were young, and she'd cut her husband's. She would give herself a bit of a trim now and then, though. The styling shears weren't a straight razor, but Sierra felt confident that they'd serve well enough to open her wrists. She'd climb in the bathtub, do it quick, and then bleed out before Marc could do anything to save her. Once she was gone, the monsters would have no one to chase anymore, and maybe they would stop killing people and go away.

And maybe they wouldn't. Whatever happened, it wouldn't concern her anymore. She'd never have to feel pain ever again, never have to miss her brother, never have to run from monsters that had once been people in her life. Annoying, troublesome people, yes, but *human*. It would be over. It would *all* be over, and all it would take is a little bit of cutting.

She inserted her fingers into the loops of the shears' handles and opened the blades. She looked at the way the metal shone in the bathroom light. It was quite beautiful, really.

She started toward the tub, but then she stopped. There was a scent in the air, heavy, cloying, *exciting*....

There was a soft knock on the door. Sierra didn't want to unlock it, but she did it, and when she opened the door she saw Mandy standing there, giving her a seductive smile.

"You know your parents leave the back door unlocked?" she asked.

Sierra didn't answer. She was mesmerized by the desire blazing in Mandy's eyes, and her vagina grew so wet a damp spot spread on the front of her leggings. The styling shears slipped from her fingers and clattered to the floor, forgotten. She stepped forward, put her arms around Mandy's neck, and inhaled the sweet heady aroma of the woman's musk mingled with the smell of smoke from the fire. The combination was intoxicating. Mandy put her arms on Sierra's waist and the women kissed.

⋆ ⋆ ⋆

"Yes, that's right. Please hurry."

Marc disconnected and put his phone in his pants pocket. He stood in the living room. Its pristine, unused atmosphere gave it a calm, neutral feeling, something he desperately needed right now. If only he hadn't seen Jeffrey walking on the sidewalk, if he hadn't been so stupid as to get out of his car and chase after the ghost of his dead lover. But he had, and he knew he'd do it again given the same circumstances. Who wouldn't?

He felt awful for the people who had lost their lives today, more, he suspected, than Sierra and he knew about. And poor Sierra, coming to her parents' house only to find they'd both been murdered. And he felt sorry for himself too. After the things he'd seen – emphasis on *things* – he was lucky he hadn't gone on a permanent mental vacation. But most of all, he grieved for his sweet love. Jeffrey, by some unknown force, had become a mockery of the man he'd been. *His* Jeffrey would never have hurt anyone, let alone an entire building full of people. Something had twisted Jeffrey's body and mind, turned him into a monster that could kill with a touch. He knew Jeffrey would never have wanted to become such a creature, and he wished to god he knew a way to free him from the horror of his current existence.

He heard a voice then, a man's, amused and mocking, but when he looked around he didn't see anyone.

"It's your lucky day, Marc. You're about to get your chance."

The front door opened and Jeffrey stepped inside.

Marc's breath caught in his throat when he saw his love. His right hand was missing, and his face was dotted with small wounds from where Randall's *shuriken* Chucks had hit him. He stank of smoke from the fire in ArtWorks, and he was burned in several places, patches of his hair missing. His eyes were weepy ruins, and as he turned to look at Marc he squinted, and glops of clear fluid squeezed from his eyes like sloppy tears.

"Marc? Is that you?"

"Stay away! Don't come near me!"

"It's all right," Jeffrey said, his voice filled with sorrow. "I'm thinking clearly now. I won't hurt you."

He stepped into the living room.

Marc wanted to believe that his Jeffrey was back, that the man he'd loved and lost to a tragic accident one year ago today was now sane and lucid once more. But after what he'd seen this day, he feared he couldn't take that chance.

"If you love me, you'll stay where you are."

Jeffrey took one more step, hesitated, then stopped.

"I just wanted to say how sorry I am," Jeffrey said. "For everything. I don't know what happened to me or why my touch is so deadly. The man in the black suit did it, but I don't know how or why."

Marc didn't know what Jeffrey was talking about or who the man in the black suit was, and he didn't care. The nonsense was proof that Jeffrey's mind wasn't functioning as well as he said it was. It was proof that he was still dangerous.

"Where's Sierra?" Jeffrey asked. "I want to apologize to her too. After that, I'll go and I'll never bother either of you again."

"She—"

Marc broke off, unsure what to do. He didn't want to tell Jeffrey that his sister was in the upstairs bathroom. He didn't want

Jeffrey to attempt to give her his horrible gift. Killing his beloved sister would be the final damnation for Jeffrey – *his* Jeffrey, who he hoped was still inside that rotting carcass somewhere. He couldn't let that happen, not only for Sierra's sake but for the sake of the man he still loved.

He remembered when Randall had cut off Jeffrey's hand, how it had crumbled to dust when it struck the floor. It was as if the dark power Jeffrey now wielded – his deathtouch – could affect him too.

Jeffrey had one hand remaining.

Marc had an idea, one that was absolutely, totally bugfuck insane, but he figured, what the hell? It had been that kind of day.

He walked toward Jeffrey, surprised at how calm he felt. His heart should've been pounding, and he should've been shaking like the proverbial leaf. But his pulse was steady, his body still. He'd made his choice, and he was going to see it through.

Jeffrey didn't move as Marc approached. He continued squinting, doing his best to see. When Marc reached him, he stopped. He stood only a few inches away from the man whose body he'd known as well as, if not better than, his own. A body that was now gray-fleshed, black-veined, and stank like rotting garbage. He reached for Jeffrey's undamaged arm, took the hand by the wrist, lifted it up, and pressed it to Jeffrey's chest. Could Jeffrey's own power be turned against him? Marc was about to find out.

At first nothing happened, but then Marc felt agonizing pain begin to spread through his body.

"No," Jeffrey said. "*No!* You shouldn't have touched me!"

Through gritted teeth, Marc said, "It was worth a try."

He released Jeffrey's hand, put his arms around his love, and leaned in to kiss him. His lips crumbled to dust as they pressed against Jeffrey's, and then he slid through his lover's hands as his body disintegrated. He lay on the floor, a pile of dry, dead dust, and now the Sowells' living room was no longer quite so tidy.

CHAPTER THIRTEEN

Randall was feeling fairly optimistic as he turned onto his street. He'd convinced himself that he would find his Erika whole and healthy when he got home, and then he could put all of this insanity behind him and start getting the mental health care he so obviously….

As he drew near his house, he saw a Camaro parked in front of the Sowells' place. He also saw Stuart staggering across the lawn. His hands were missing and silver blood dribbled from his wrists onto the grass.

"That boy's quite a mess," Randall said. "A real. Fucking. *Mess*."

He gripped his steering wheel so tight his knuckles turned white. Then they turned yellow. He angled his Town Car toward the Sowells' lawn and tromped on the gas.

Chuck was back, and he was *pissed*.

* * *

Stuart was in rough shape.

His head still throbbed from the burns he'd received at ArtWorks, and now his wrists felt like *they* were on fire. He'd managed to get free from the steering wheel, although he'd paid a high price to do it. He didn't really know anything about how his half-human, half-machine body functioned, so he was unsure if he might bleed to death from his open wounds. The silver shit that came out of him was thicker than blood and oozed more slowly, so he thought he at least had some time before he was in danger of passing out. Enough time to reach Sierra and settle accounts with her once and for all. Although now that he thought of it, he wasn't sure what he was going to be able to do to her without hands. He hadn't thought that far ahead.

Fuck it, he thought. *I'll figure something out.*

He continued on and was halfway across the lawn when he heard a car approaching. He paid it no attention, figured it was just someone passing through the neighborhood. But then he heard the engine roar, following by the *ka-thump* as the car jumped the curb. He whirled around in time to see a Lincoln Town Car barreling toward him across the lawn, Randall's yellow smiley face behind the wheel.

He tried to dive out of the way, but he was too low on energy and couldn't move in time. The car smashed into him, the impact sending him flying through the air. He slammed into a large oak tree in the yard, bounced off, and hit the ground. Randall kept coming, and this time old-fashioned human adrenaline gave Stuart the boost he needed. He rolled out of the way, and the Town Car roared past and hit the oak. The front end of the car crumpled and the engine died.

Stuart rose painfully to his feet. His left leg was bent at a sickening angle, and he couldn't stand straight. He bled silver from a number of fresh wounds, and sparks shot forth from several of them as well.

Randall got out of his car and looked over the top of the vehicle's roof at Stuart.

"That settles *that* question," he said cheerily. "I Chuck, therefore I am."

Stuart had no fucking clue what the hell the old man was babbling about, and he didn't care. The fucker had stabbed him in the back at ArtWorks, had just rammed his car into him, and worst of all, he wanted to have Sierra for himself when she was *his*.

Stuart knew he didn't have much power left, but he hoped he had enough. The panels in his forearms slid open once more, and the rotary saws emerged. The sharp discs began whirring, and Stuart grinned as he started hobbling toward Randall. If he'd possessed the strength, he would've attacked the fucker at a run, but a limping walk was all he was capable of right then. That was okay, though. Walking slowly and menacingly toward an enemy looked badass. Randall came around the car to meet him. He still had a dent in his head, and his hands were empty.

Stuart grinned wider.

"Too bad I melted your knife, old man. Looks like you got nothing to fight with. I'm going to enjoy cutting that stupid-ass smiley face of yours to ribbons."

"Despite appearances, you foul-mouthed little shit, I am far from unarmed. You see, I don't need a weapon. I *am* a weapon."

Randall raised his right arm, and as Stuart watched, the man's yellow hand turned a copper color, and then the fingers merged and lengthened into a blade so long it was practically a sword.

Stuart was taken aback by Randall's sudden manifestation of so large a weapon, but he told himself that he had his twin rotary saws, and he was younger than Randall. He should be able to take out the asshole with ease.

Then Randall was running toward him, his curve of a smile wide, and his blade arm held high. Stuart stepped forward to meet the man's charge, but then Randall swung his arm, Stuart felt a jolt, and suddenly the world was spinning, spinning. He felt an impact, rolled, and came to a rest at an angle. He was on the ground, looking up at Randall, who stood next to Stuart's headless body. Silver blood and sparks fountained up from the neck stump, and then Randall used the tip of his knife arm to knock the body over. It hit the grass, and the rotary saws spun to a stop. Randall started toward Stuart, or rather, toward Stuart's *head*, because that's all he was now. A fucking head lying in the fucking grass, waiting for a fucking smiley-faced fuck to finish him off.

Fuck my life, Stuart thought.

Randall reached him, lifted a foot, and brought it crashing down on Stuart's head. He did this several more times before Stuart was finally gone.

★ ★ ★

Randall looked down at Stuart's head. He'd stomped on the damn thing until it had cracked like an egg, revealing a mixture of brains and electronic components.

"Goddamn kids and their technology," Randall muttered.

He wiped silver crap off his shoe in the grass, then he turned away from Stuart's head and started walking toward the Sowells' front door. He'd thoroughly enjoyed his previous visit here today, but he thought this one was going to be even better.

* * *

Sierra had no memory of moving to her parents' bedroom, but there she was, lying naked on the sheets, hands clutching double fistfuls of Mandy's hair as she pressed the woman's head against her cunt. Mandy was also naked, and she used her tongue as if it were a finely tuned musical instrument and she a virtuoso, giving a performance for an extremely appreciative audience of one. Sierra had never been with another woman before, but so far it was fantastic. *I could get used to this*, she thought. She knew it was probably inaccurate to think of Mandy as a woman, or even human, though. Those were only words, ineffective labels that couldn't come close to expressing everything that Mandy was. She was a primal force, like a volcano or a hurricane, and it was all Sierra could do to hold on for dear life and hope she survived the ride. But if she didn't, what a way to go.

Wave after wave of pleasure shuddered through her, each more intense than the last. *How much more of this can a human body take?* she wondered. A lot, she hoped.

The bedroom was suffused with the powerful odor of Mandy's musk, and although Sierra believed pheromones were supposed to be invisible when released into the air, a haze filled the room, one that was growing thicker with each passing moment. She wondered if by the time they were finished, the bedroom would be so full of the stuff they wouldn't be able to see each other.

A voice – *her* voice, but speaking so softly it was difficult to hear – whispered in her mind.

This isn't right. You didn't choose this.

She began thrusting her pelvis against Mandy's face even harder. She didn't want to hear what the voice had to say, didn't want it to spoil her fun, but when it spoke next, it was louder.

She's making you do this. She's raping you, using you like a life-sized human sex toy.

She thrust harder. Mandy slipped a pair of fingers into her vagina and began sliding them in and out rapidly, still continuing to lick her clitoris with fast, circular motions of her velvet-soft tongue. Sierra had never been so wet before, and each time she climaxed, she gushed fluid over Mandy's face and hand. Mandy lapped up Sierra's juices as if they were the finest of wines.

She's a monster, just like the rest of them, the voice said. Her method of feeding might be more pleasant than what the others did, but that was only a lure, like the bioluminescence that predators in the darkest parts of the world's oceans employed to attract their prey. Sierra pictured Mandy with a mouthful of angler-fish teeth, large and curved, tips sharp as steel needles. The image was as ridiculous as it was frightening, and she couldn't stop herself from letting out a small laugh. If Mandy heard it – which was doubtful given how much noise her ministrations were causing – she ignored it, likely assumed it was simply another way Sierra expressed her pleasure. Sierra had dated a guy in college who'd always giggled when he came. He'd warned her about it, but it had still caught her by surprise every time.

The image of Mandy with an angler-fish mouth helped Sierra distance her mind from her body, so while she still felt everything that Mandy was doing – *god*, how she felt it! – she was able to think a little more clearly while her body kept responding to Mandy as if it was on autopilot. She needed something to use as a weapon. The bedroom light wasn't on, but enough illumination filtered through the sheer white curtain over the window for Sierra to see. She turned her head toward her mom's nightstand. Mom loved mystery novels and kept a stack of hardback books next to her side of the bed. She read every night before going to sleep, at least half an hour and usually more. Sierra had learned to love reading from her, and like her mother, she had a soft spot for mysteries.

No help there, not unless she wanted to smack Mandy on the head with a book. Somehow, Sierra didn't think that would stop the woman. If anything, she'd probably think that Sierra was engaging in rough play and be turned on even more.

Sierra turned to look at her dad's nightstand. He wasn't a big reader, but when he did read, he preferred nonfiction, usually biographies, and he read only one book at a time. A thick tome on Abraham Lincoln lay on top of his nightstand, and while it would pack more of a wallop compared to one of Mom's slimmer volumes, she didn't think it would prove any more effective on Mandy. There were lamps on both nightstands, but they were small things made of plastic, and they'd make even worse weapons than the books. Beyond Dad's nightstand, propped up against the wall in the corner, was a wooden baseball bat. Dad had always been uncomfortable with the thought of having a gun in the house with two small kids, so he'd gotten the bat for home protection, and he'd kept it even after his children had grown and moved out. He'd never had a reason to use it, as attested to by the thin layer of dust clinging to the wood. Sometimes Sierra and Jeffrey had teased him about it, called him Sowell the Slugger, and he'd laugh good-naturedly. The bat would be an excellent weapon, but it was so far out of her reach, it might as well be on fucking Mars.

Looking at her parents' nightstands caused her to remember that they were dead, killed by Randall. Once more she saw their bodies lying in the family room, their clothes soaked with blood. She tried to hold onto the image of her dead parents, but Mandy's scent – already strong – grew stronger still, as if her body sensed Sierra wavering and was determined to keep her full attention where it should be – on her.

Mandy lifted her head from between Sierra's legs.

"You're starting to dry up, hon," she said. "Want to try something else?"

"Sure."

Grinning, Mandy came up into a kneeling position and scooted forward. She slid one leg under Sierra's, and one leg over. She then put her hands on Sierra's hips to angle her pelvis just so and started grinding her cunt against Sierra's, her body rippling like a serpent's, large breasts bouncing and slapping against her chest. All that remained of the wound she'd suffered when Grace had forced Karolyn to stab her was a small puckered scar on her left tit, and even that seemed to fade as Mandy continued thrusting. She reached down to take hold of Sierra's nipples between her thumbs and forefingers and squeezed hard.

Sierra's body responded with a tiny climax, brief but intense. If felt so good that her thoughts became mushy again, and she knew she was on the verge of surrendering completely to the inhuman levels of pleasure that Mandy could generate in her body. And if that happened, she didn't think she'd have the mental strength to pull herself back to reality again. She doubted she'd have the physical strength either. With each passing moment, she felt herself growing weaker, while Mandy appeared to gain strength and vigor the longer they kept fucking, as if she was a goddamned sex vampire.

Sierra was beginning to feel suction building at the point where their vaginas met, almost as if Mandy's cunt were pulling at her, preparing to literally devour her. She wanted to believe that this was a ludicrous thought, but after the things she'd seen today, no idea seemed too far out to her anymore.

Mandy increased the speed of her thrusting until she was going so fast Sierra thought they were in danger of breaking the bed. She fought not to respond, but the heady tang of Mandy's musk filled her nose and lungs, and her blood sang with her body's insatiable need to be one with Mandy, to let the woman devour her and swallow her whole.

The scar on Mandy's breast was gone now, the skin smooth and unmarked.

Sierra felt her identity, her very self, fading away, and she knew that if she couldn't find a way to break free from Mandy's spell in the next few moments, she'd be lost.

She still had trouble believing the transformation Mandy had undergone since they'd spoken on campus earlier in the day. Outwardly, she appeared much the same. The true change had taken place inside, and it had been so dramatic it was as if she were an entirely different person. Mandy was dead; long live Mandy.

She wondered what Mandy would think the next time she went to her office on campus and saw the photos of dead and bloody fetuses tacked to the door. Would she remember being the Mandy that had put those images up, the one who'd founded a campus organization to combat sex in all its forms, but most specifically gay sex? Or would that Mandy seem like a stranger to her, someone she couldn't imagine ever being?

The photos....

Sierra had always hated looking at the goddamned things. They were a crude and blatant attempt at emotional manipulation, and there was something cruel about putting them on display like that. She'd always suspected Mandy got a sick thrill at the thought of all the people walking by her office seeing those images and being disgusted. Mandy didn't care half so much about the issues of abortion – if she cared at all – as she did about hurting people she thought deserved it. *That's* what Sierra hated most about those photos, and it was what she hated most about Mandy too. Sierra grabbed hold of that hatred and held on to it tight, as if she were a drowning woman and it was a life preserver.

Her body went rigid as she reasserted control over it. No matter how desirable Mandy was, or how much pleasure her body could give, she was an ugly person on the inside – perhaps through no fault of her own – and while Sierra could pity her, she most definitely did not want to keep screwing her.

Mandy sensed something had changed between them. She stopped thrusting against Sierra and gave her a questioning look.

Sierra smiled, recalling something she and Jeffrey used to say to one another when they were kids.

"You're not the boss of me."

One of Mandy's eyebrows rose in surprise.

"Really? Well, if that's how you feel about it, I suppose I'll just cut to the chase and take you now. Too bad. I was *so* enjoying you. Oh well. It was fun while it lasted, but Momma's tank is close to empty and it's time to fill up. Goodbye, Sierra."

She closed her eyes, threw back her head, and then Sierra felt agonizing pain as Mandy's cunt began to eat her.

⋆ ⋆ ⋆

Randall came upon Jeffrey in the Sowells' family room, silently regarding his parents' bodies.

"Some of my finest work, I'd say."

Jeffrey turned to face him. It was impossible to gauge any

emotion in his damaged eyes, but his lips drew back from his teeth in a snarl.

"Why?" he demanded.

"Why the fuck not?" Randall countered. "Besides, what do you care? You're dead. They're dead." He nodded toward Jeffrey's parents. "As soon as I kill Sierra, you'll be one happy dead family. Won't that be nice?"

Jeffrey's remaining hand shot toward Randall's throat, but Randall swept his knife arm up and lopped off the boy's hand. Like the other that Randall had cut off, this one burst into dust when it hit the carpet.

"That's two for two," Randall said.

Jeffrey didn't react to the loss of his hand. Instead, he jammed the wrist stump, which oozed clear fluid, against the side of Randall's arm blade. Randall yanked the blade away from Jeffrey, but some of the goo clung to the metal, and as Randall watched, the copper beneath it blackened. It felt like his arm was being eaten away by acid, and he cried out in pain. The black spread up and down the blade, and an instant later, it fell away to dust.

Jeffrey grinned. "One for me."

Randall couldn't believe the bastard had taken his whole fucking arm. Worse yet, he'd taken the Chuck blade – again! Well, he still had an arm left, didn't he? He concentrated and his left arm became a long copper blade, just as the other had been. His last blade hadn't been damaged as it sliced through Jeffrey's hand, only after Jeffrey had smeared that clear glop on it. So long as this blade didn't remain in contact with Jeffrey – or his clear blood – for very long, it should remain intact. That meant he had to strike fast and strike hard.

As soon as the change was accomplished, Randall attacked. He hacked off Jeffrey's entire right arm, and it broke apart into dust before it hit the carpet. Randall took this as a sign that the boy's power was starting to fade. Time to finish this.

He swung his blade arm toward Jeffrey's neck, intending to decapitate him, just like that little fucker Stuart. But Jeffrey was able to bring up his remaining arm in time to block the blow. The blade sliced through the forearm and kept going, sinking into the juncture between Jeffrey's neck and shoulder. But Jeffrey had managed to slow the blade's momentum, so it only cut his head halfway off. Randall tried to pull the blade free, but it was lodged tight.

"Fuck!"

Clear fluid oozed from the wound in Jeffrey's neck, and he smiled grimly.

"Want to see a trick?" he asked. "I learned it from Grace."

He made a sound like he was trying to bring up a giant wad of phlegm, then he spat clear goo all over Randall's face.

Randall screamed as the substance began eating away at his flesh, unmaking him wherever it touched. He wanted to try and wipe it off, not that it would have done any good – but he had only one arm, and that one was stuck in Jeffrey's neck. Besides, the goddamned thing didn't have any fucking fingers.

The death-blight spread swiftly. Randall's scream died away when his mouth crumbled to dust, and once his head was gone, the rest of him went fast. Within seconds, Randall's body, blade arm included, had been reduced to scattered bits of dust on the carpet.

⋆ ⋆ ⋆

Jeffrey kicked the dust and watched as it drifted in the air.

"Fuck you and fuck your Chucks," he said.

He heard a loud thump then, coming from upstairs.

"Sierra!"

He ran from the family room, his head wobbling unsteadily on his neck. He prayed he'd remain intact long enough to reach her.

⋆ ⋆ ⋆

Sierra felt her spine buckling as Mandy's body pulled at her, and the flesh of her pelvic area felt strangely insubstantial, as if it were becoming watery. She knew she had only seconds left, if that, and she struggled to lift arms that felt fragile as dead twigs and take hold of Mandy's waist. The woman wasn't grinding against her now. She was motionless, her body tense, head back and eyes closed. Whatever she was doing to Sierra, she was putting all her energy into it, was completely focused on herself. Sierra saw her chance and took it.

She gripped Mandy's waist as hard as she could and twisted beneath her. Mandy was strong, stronger than Sierra was now, but she hadn't been expecting any resistance from her doomed lover, and Sierra took her by surprise. Mandy toppled off the side of the bed, Sierra rolled with her, and they hit the floor in a tangle of arms and legs. Sierra felt so drained of energy that all she wanted to do was close her eyes and let Mandy finish what she'd started, but she knew the next few moments would tell whether she lived or died, and if she wanted to do the former, she needed to get her ass in gear. She'd thrown them down on the floor in front of her father's nightstand, and she pushed herself to her feet and lunged toward the corner where the baseball bat was propped up. She was so weak that her head swam with vertigo and her vision blurred. She feared she was going to pass out, and for an instant her vision did go black, but then her hand closed around the reassuringly solid wood of the bat's handle. She felt a scrap of hope then, and it gave her a burst of renewed strength.

Mandy had pulled herself to a sitting position.

"Sierra, what the hell are you—"

Sierra picked up the bat, got both hands around the handle in a strong grip, then spun around and hit Mandy as hard as she could on the side of the head. There was a sickening crunch of bone, and Sierra felt the jolt of impact shudder up her arms. Mandy was knocked against the side of the bed, and she bounced back. Before she could fall to the floor, Sierra raised the bat and brought it down on top of the woman's head. This time the noise it made when connecting with Mandy's skull was even more nauseating, and for an instant the woman's gaze met Sierra's. Wordless understanding passed between them – not between Sierra and a monster, but between two very human women – and then Sierra hit her again. And again. She kept hitting her, and with each blow she felt a measure of her strength return, as if she was reclaiming it from Mandy.

When she was finished, the end of the bat was smeared with

blood, hair, and bits of brain matter, and there were splatters of crimson on the bed sheets and on Sierra's naked body. Mandy lay on the carpet, her head a grotesque blood-slick mass of torn skin and splintered bone. But she wasn't dead yet. Her eyes stared up at the ceiling, but she drew in shallow breaths through a mouth that was now missing most of its teeth. The scent Mandy gave off had changed from an enticingly tangy musk to a sour ammonia stink that reminded Sierra of cat piss. Sierra was physically and emotionally spent, and she didn't want to hurt Mandy anymore. As injured as she was, the woman was no longer a threat. Sierra could walk away and leave her like this for the police to deal with when they arrived. But she thought of the stab wound on Mandy's breast, the one that had become a scar before finally disappearing altogether. Mandy was injured far more seriously now, but if she had the power to heal a stab wound, could she recover from the damage Sierra had inflicted? And could she do so before the police arrived? As dangerous as Mandy was, Sierra feared she couldn't take any chances. Too many people had died today, and she didn't want to be responsible for allowing Mandy to recover enough to harm the police and paramedics who responded to Marc's 911 call.

She had to finish this.

She thought then of how Mandy had killed Karolyn, of the way she'd rammed the fabric scissors up between Karolyn's legs over and over, blood spilling onto the floor of ArtWorks in thick, dark gouts. Mandy lay with her own legs splayed open, and Sierra saw a picture in her mind, an image of herself kneeling in front of Mandy and shoving the bat into her body and then pounding it in and out, in and out, reducing her insides to jelly.

An eye for an eye, she thought. *Or in this case, a cunt for a cunt.*

She almost did it. But in the end she was simply too fucking tired. She brought the bat down on Mandy's head one more time, and the woman stopped breathing.

A great weariness came over Sierra then, and she dropped the bat to the floor next to Mandy. If this had been a cheap horror movie, the woman would've sprung to life, taken hold of the bat, and killed Sierra. But it wasn't, and Mandy lay there, nothing more now than a slowly cooling corpse.

Sierra met Jeffrey on the stairs. She hadn't thought to put her clothes back on before leaving the bedroom, but she wasn't ashamed of her nakedness. Jeffrey was her brother, and he'd never made her feel ashamed in his life. He looked worse than ever, his skin an ashen gray that looked too much like the color of the dust his deathtouch created. One arm was completely gone, and the other now ended at the elbow. His head leaned to one side, and she saw a deep wound on his neck, one that oozed clear fluid. Add to this the Chuck wounds on his face and his damaged eyes, and he was, not to put too fine a point on it, a goddamned mess.

"Are you all right?" he asked. "I heard noises...."

"I'm okay. Mandy, not so much."

Jeffrey was older and taller than her, but standing as they were, she found herself gazing down at him, as if she were literally his big sister. The role reversal felt strange and uncomfortable.

"Randall won't be bothering you anymore," he said. "From dust he came, and to dust he returned."

"Marc?" she asked.

"No." It was all Jeffrey needed to say.

Sierra felt only a distant sadness at this bad news. She was too numb to feel much more right now, but she knew she would grieve more fully later.

"I...." she began, but then trailed off. She had too much to say and didn't know where to begin.

"It's going to be all right," Jeffrey said. His voice had a liquid rattle to it now, due to his neck wound, Sierra guessed. "*You're* going to be all right. I love you."

"I love you too."

She moved to put her arms around him, but before she could touch him, he fell away to dust and was gone. She was sad to lose him again, but she hoped this time he would remain at peace.

She heard approaching sirens then – a lot of them – and she knew that Marc had managed to complete his 911 call before he'd died. She didn't know if there was an afterlife, but if there was, she hoped Jeffrey and Marc would be together there.

She turned around and headed back upstairs. She'd dealt with enough shit today, and if she was going to have to talk to cops, she at least didn't want to do it naked. She returned to her parents' bedroom and went inside. She avoided looking at Mandy's body as she gathered her blouse and leggings from where she'd thrown them before climbing into bed with Mandy. She went out into the hallway to put them on, feeling somewhat foolish for not wanting to dress in front of Mandy. Then she went downstairs, careful to avoid stepping on her brother's remains on the way down.

She'd decided to tell the police the truth. They'd undoubtedly think she was crazy and throw her ass into a mental hospital, but that was okay. She felt that lying would be dishonoring the memories of the innocent people who had died this day. Besides, she could use the rest she'd get in a hospital.

When she reached the bottom of the stairs, she stopped. Something wasn't right, but she couldn't—

And then it hit her. It was quiet. The sirens had stopped.

She went to the front door, opened it, and looked outside. She saw Randall's car in front of the oak tree in the yard, its front end crumpled. Stuart's Camaro was parked on the street, the driver's side door hanging open. Stuart's decapitated body lay in the yard, his head some distance away. When the hell had all this happened? Probably when she'd been in bed with Mandy. A nuclear bomb could've detonated outside then and she wouldn't have noticed. One thing she didn't see: police vehicles. Maybe the sirens she'd heard hadn't been coming here. Maybe Marc hadn't managed to call 911 before he died after all. She'd have to do it herself. She'd left her phone at ArtWorks, and it was so much molten slag now. Her parents still had a landline, though. The phone was in the kitchen, and she could call from there.

She closed the door and headed for the kitchen, but when she entered it, she stopped and stared. A man with long blond hair dressed in a black suit sat in the breakfast nook, two mugs of fresh coffee sitting on the table before him.

"Nice to finally meet you, Sierra. My name is Corliss, and we have a lot to talk about."

★ ★ ★

Corliss gestured for her to take the other seat at the small table. Her mom's seat. He was sitting in her father's.

She didn't move.

"You have no need to fear me," Corliss said. "I have no intention of harming you. In fact, I've come to help you. And you needn't worry about the police arriving and interrupting us. I've frozen time, so we can talk as long as we wish undisturbed."

Still she didn't move.

"I can explain everything that's happened today. More, I can tell you how to fix it. But first, you need to sit down, sip some coffee – I made yours with cream and sugar, just the way you like it – and listen to what I have to say."

He gestured once more to her mom's empty seat.

Sierra considered for a moment, but then she started forward. What was one more weird experience on top of everything else that had happened today?

She sat, but she didn't touch the coffee. It smelled wonderful, though, and she felt guilty for reacting like that. How could she enjoy anything after all the death she'd witnessed?

"Because life goes on," Corliss said, as if reading her thoughts. "Well, *your* life anyway. You're the last soldier standing, Sierra. If this were a slasher film, you'd be considered the final girl. But you're so much more than a mere survivor. Or at least, you could be."

Sierra looked at her coffee. Not only would it taste great, but as weary as she was, she could use the energy boost.

Fuck it.

She picked up the mug and took a long, satisfying drink. After she was done, she held onto the mug with both hands. Its warmth was comforting.

"I dreamed about you last night," she said. "I watched you bring Jeffrey back. And I saw you earlier, on the street across from ArtWorks. Before the fire."

"Yes."

Despite his urging that she should drink her coffee, he hadn't touched his.

She had a difficult time not staring at the man's jacket. It was almost as if instead of being made from cloth, it was fashioned out of space, of distance. Looking at it was like looking into a night sky where stars had never shone. Its darkness seemed to go on forever, and part of her wanted to join with that nothingness, to hurl herself into its oblivion and travel through the silent dark for all eternity. The effect was beyond hypnotic, and she had to keep tearing her gaze away from the jacket and focusing on Corliss's eyes.

"Who are you and what the hell do you want?" she demanded. "Are you responsible for all this fucking insanity? Did you resurrect Jeffrey, and if so, why?"

Corliss smiled, and she didn't like the look of his sharp lizard teeth.

"Those are a lot of questions. I did indeed restore your brother to life – of a sort – and I initiated the transformations your other friends experienced. They made their own choices after that, although I admit I manipulated events now and again to help things along. As for who I am, I've already told you. I'm Corliss. My people are known by many names in many places. The Unhallowed, the Children of the Gyre, Nightfears, the Darkblooded, and more. But we refer to ourselves simply as the Multitude. It is our sacred purpose to help break down reality so that it can more swiftly and efficiently be processed into nonexistence. In short, we predigest Entropy's food for it."

Sierra looked at him for a moment, then said, "I have no idea what the fuck you're talking about."

Corliss shrugged. "It's a difficult concept to grasp at the best of times, and you've been through a great deal today. Unfortunately, you're not finished yet. My people are powerful, but we're not immortal. How could we be? We serve Entropy, do we not? In the end, the Gyre takes all, even us. So from time to time, when our ranks grow thin, we go on a recruitment drive, for lack of a better term. We identify potential candidates who might make effective additions to our ranks, and then we conduct field tests to determine their suitability. You are one of those we've chosen, Sierra, and today is your test."

Sierra's head was spinning.

"You're saying everything that's happened today – people

becoming monsters, people *dying* – was all part of some fucking *job interview*?"

"Essentially."

Anger blazed hot and sudden in Sierra. As she'd feared, she was the center of all the blood, pain, and horror of this day, but she never could've imagined it would be for so ridiculous a reason.

"What makes you think I'd make a good…whatever the hell you are?"

From the way he'd described it, it sounded like his people were nothing more than a race of cosmic maggots feasting on the corpse of the universe.

In response, Corliss reached across the table and gently touched his index finger to her forehead. A memory rose from the depths of her mind then, one she'd buried long ago and never wanted to unearth.

"No," she whispered, but she couldn't stop it from coming.

CHAPTER FOURTEEN

Sierra is six years old.

Her parents have brought her to her grandmother's house in the country. She's not sure where it is compared to her house in Bishop Hill. All she knows is that it takes forever to drive here. She supposes it could be all the way on the other side of the world.

Jeffrey didn't come this time. He's in Boy Scouts, and his troop went camping this weekend. She wanted to go too, go *so bad*, and she cried before he left and cried even more after he was gone. It isn't fair that she couldn't go. Just because 'Scouts' has the word 'Boy' in front of it is a dumb reason to leave little sisters behind.

Her parents are inside the house, which doesn't look much different to her house in town despite being in The Country. She wishes Grandma and Grandpa lived on a farm with animals and a lot of land. Then it would've been fun to visit. But they don't. Their backyard isn't much bigger than hers, and while they have bigger trees on their property, there's no barn and no animals, except Rusty, a stray cat her grandmother feeds whenever he comes around and who always runs away when she tries to pet him. There are houses on either side of theirs too. It seems to her that The Country isn't much different to Bishop Hill, except it's even more boring.

It's summertime, but instead of being sunny, the sky is overcast. It rained this morning, and Mom said it'll probably rain again and Sierra is supposed to come back inside if it does. But the grown-ups are playing cards at the kitchen table – and drinking what her dad calls 'adult beverages' – and that's no fun. Grandma and Grandpa don't have any video games for her to play, and Mom won't let her watch TV or use a computer without grown-up supervision. So she'll stay outside even if starts raining – as long as the adults let her get away with it, that is.

The air is humid from the rain, and the grass is damp. Sierra is wearing flip-flops and she likes swishing her feet through the wet grass, likes the way the moisture feels on her bare skin. She does this for five minutes, tracing a figure eight in the yard, before she tires of it. She wanders around the yard, trying to find something – anything – interesting. She's at the side of the house, looking at a large sticker bush that's grown up against the foundation and wondering what it would feel like to wrap her hand around it and squeeze as hard as she can, when she sees the toad.

It's crouched near the drain spout, hunkered down as if trying to make itself invisible. It's big, about the size of her hand, and she wonders if she can catch it before it can hop away. She's never tried to catch a toad, never even seen one in real life, but she instinctively knows that if she moves too fast, she'll scare it. She inches forward. Closer. Closer. She reaches out her hand.... She expects the toad to leap away at the last instant, but it doesn't. It remains still as a stone, and when she wraps her fingers around it she makes an excited *squeeee* sound.

She lifts the toad up to her face to examine it. She's surprised by how light it is, and how squishy too, especially its sides. It feels like the toad is a little warty bag filled with water. She wonders what would happen if she squeezed it, really hard. Would it pop like a water balloon? What would come out of it? Blood? Guts?

She squeezes it, just a little, just to see what happens. Nothing does. The toad looks at her with its black-marble eyes. She wonders what it thinks when it sees her. Does it think she's a giant? Does it think she's a monster?

Something happens inside her then. She doesn't know what it is, can't put words to it, but somewhere in her mind something switches off. Or maybe on. She looks at the toad, and she doesn't see an animal now. She sees an object, a thing, a play toy with which she can do whatever she wants.

And she wants to see the toad fly.

She carries the toad into the backyard, and when she reaches a suitable place – one where the grass isn't tall or thick – she stops. She looks at the toad one more time, then she hurls it straight up into the air. She expects it to spin around as it soars upward, but it remains level with the ground, as if it's levitating under its own power. When it reaches the apex of its flight, it hangs there for a split second, just long enough for Sierra to think it might stay there. But of course it doesn't. It plummets, tumbling on its way down, and it hits the ground with a sound like a beanbag. It bounces, but not as much as she expects, and then comes to a rest on its back and doesn't move.

She feels nothing.

She walks over to the toad and kneels to inspect it. She's only six, so she didn't throw it all that high, and the toad has survived its landing. She can see it breathing, but it doesn't right itself, doesn't try to escape. It's almost as if it wants to be thrown again.

Sierra obliges.

She throws it three more times, and each is the same. Up, pause, down, *thwack*. And after the last time the toad's left side is swollen and bulgy, and gray goop is leaking from its mouth. She's impressed that the toad can take so much punishment and still be alive. She wonders how much more it can take. Not much, judging by its current condition. One more throw, maybe two, and it will be over.

For the merest fraction of an iota of an instant, she sees someone standing close by – a man dressed in a strange black suit with long blond hair. He smiles at her approvingly and then disappears, having come and gone so quickly her conscious mind doesn't register his presence. But her subconscious mind? That's a different story.

She reaches for the toad, intending to send it skyward for what might well be the final time, when whatever switch was flipped inside her flips back. She freezes, stunned by the realization of what she's done. A maelstrom of emotions rips through her. Shame, revulsion, self-hatred, sorrow.... Tears stream down her face, and she sobs so hard she can barely breathe. Her hand trembles as she picks up the toad and carries it back to the spot near the drainpipe where she found it. She puts it down gently, hoping that it will recover from what she's done to it, knowing that it won't.

"I'm sorry," she whispers. "I'm so sorry."

Then she turns and runs away. She doesn't go into the house, doesn't seek the comfort of Mom and Dad, Grandma and Grandpa. If Jeffrey was here she'd go to him. He might be her big brother and he can be a real pain sometimes, but when she's upset, when she really *hurts*, he's always there, and he always listens, and he never judges.

But he's not here, so she runs down the driveway, onto the road, and keeps running. It will be a half hour before the adults realize she's missing and call 911. A state trooper will find her an hour later, walking because she's too exhausted to run anymore. But she'll still be crying, and she'll be whispering "I'm sorry" over and over.

* * *

When Sierra came out of the memory, she was shaking as if in the grip of arctic cold.

"I was just a kid," she said. "I didn't know what I was doing. I didn't *mean* it!"

"Of course you did. Despite what people like to believe, none of us are born with empathy. We innately understand the true nature of existence, that in the end everything is nothing but food for the Gyre. We have to be taught to believe otherwise, to pretend that other lives matter as much as our own, that others' pain is our pain. It's only a comforting illusion, of course, but one that helps most people get through their lives and fulfill their ultimate purpose with the least amount of fuss. It's sad, really, but if it keeps the cattle content...." He trailed off then finally took a sip of his coffee. "Like the majority of people, you've created a shell identity around your true self. But unlike most, your core remains intact. It's a spark that can, under the right circumstances, be fanned into a glorious dark flame."

Something else about the memory of the toad came back to her then.

"You were there," she said. "I saw you, just for an instant."

Corliss smiled and nodded.

"We research our recruits most thoroughly. So, let's discuss what comes next. If you want events to continue from this point on, I'll allow time to restart and go on my way. The police will arrive and you'll have quite a bit of explaining to do. Your shell personality will remain intact, and whatever the rest of your life holds – I'm betting on a long prison stay, given the way you bashed in Mandy's head – you will still be you, and you will never hear from me again."

"I sense an *or* coming," Sierra said.

"Or you can move on to the last phase of the test. If you do, you'll have a chance to prevent the events of this day from occurring, saving numerous lives in the process."

"Are you serious? You can do that?"

"I am indeed serious, but only *you* can do it, Sierra. If you so choose, I will send you back in time exactly one year, and you'll have a chance to stop the accident that claimed Jeffrey's life from ever happening."

Sierra couldn't believe what she was hearing. Save Jeffrey's life, and by doing so save everyone else who'd died today? Her parents, Marc, Karolyn, and all the rest? How could she say no to that?

"Well, you won't be saving *everyone*," Corliss said. "In order to save your brother, you will need to kill Grace, Stuart, Randall, and Mandy, but as they were a year ago. Perfectly ordinary humans with no idea of what they'll become one day. But the seeds of their monstrous selves will be inside them, and by killing them, you'll prevent them from ever becoming those creatures – which means everyone they killed today will still be alive. But let me make this very clear: killing the four of them is the *only* way you'll get a chance to save your brother. If you try to do it without killing the others first, all your attempts will fail. You still might fail even if you *do* kill them, but that's the only way saving Jeffrey will be possible."

Sierra had allowed herself to feel hope when she'd first heard Corliss's offer, but now she realized she'd been a fool to listen to him.

"This is bullshit. It's all part of the sick game you've been playing since this all started."

"*Sick* depends entirely on one's point of view, but I assure you my offer is a legitimate one. I'm not guaranteeing you success, but I *am* giving you the opportunity for it."

"If you're so fucking powerful, why not go back in time and change things so all this madness never happens?"

Corliss smiled wide, revealing his disturbingly sharp teeth once more.

"Because that, my dear, is not the deal. You have two choices and two choices only. Do nothing and things remain as they are, or go back and kill the others and have a chance at saving Jeffrey and preventing all the deaths that have taken place this day. That's it, and you need to choose now. As they say in commercials, this is a limited time offer."

Sierra wanted to tell Corliss to go fuck himself, but she didn't. Instead, she found herself considering what he'd told her. She believed everything he'd said, about who and what he was, and what he could do. She'd experienced too many bizarre things today to disbelieve him. And deep down, maybe in that cold emotionless core he'd spoken of, she recognized the truth of his words. So the question wasn't could he make good on his offer. The question was could *she* do it? Could she kill four people to save dozens of others, among them her brother and parents? From what Corliss said, if she succeeded, the events of this day would never occur. And it wasn't as if she'd never killed anyone. Mandy's blood was still literally on her hands, as well as other parts of her body. But she'd killed Mandy in self-defense. If she went back in time one year, Mandy – along with Stuart, Grace, and Randall – wouldn't be monsters. They'd be innocent people, and *she'd* be the monster stalking and killing them. But she wouldn't be killing them for her own pleasure. She'd be doing it to protect those who they would kill one day. It would be a preemptive strike. She recognized this line of reasoning as bullshit, though. Killing was killing, regardless of the reason. But if she had the chance to prevent people dying, didn't she have the moral responsibility to take it, regardless of the cost?

She continued like this, thoughts going around and around, mind like a dog chasing its own tail, catching nothing and getting nowhere. There was no good decision to be made here. She had only two choices, both of them bad. So she chose the one that would do the least bad for the most people, and god help her.

"I'll do it."

Corliss displayed no outward reaction to her decision. He stood, walked to a corner of the kitchen, and raised one of his hands. His fingers lengthened into ebon claws, and he slashed the air close to the wall. A line appeared, as if he'd made an incision in reality itself. He inserted his hands into the rift and pulled it open until it was wide enough for a person to step through. When she looked inside the rift, she saw the kitchen, only the view was opposite, like she was looking in a mirror, only one that didn't reflect her or Corliss.

"I placed the rift here so it would be out of the way. If you succeed and restore your parents to life, they won't accidentally blunder into the rift scar over here. Touching one can cause… unfortunate aftereffects."

He looked at her expectantly, and she realized he was waiting for her to thank him. Well, he would have to wait until the goddamned sun burned itself to cold ashes.

Corliss scowled, but he didn't make her lack of gratitude an issue.

"You have one shot at this," he said, "and while this may sound like a joke, I assure you it isn't: time is not on your side."

She nodded to him, rose from the table, took a deep breath, and stepped through the rift.

* * *

When she was gone, Corliss sealed the rift and returned to the breakfast nook to finish his coffee. His own test, which had taken place so long ago he didn't like to count the years, had been equally as cruel as the one Sierra was facing. He'd succeeded, although not without difficulty, and had become one of the Multitude. He'd never regretted the dark path he'd chosen, and he was rooting for Sierra. He believed she had what it would take to pass the last part of her test, provided she found a way to break through her façade of humanity and access the monster that everyone harbored inside them. She'd killed Mandy, which was strong evidence that his faith in her wasn't misplaced, but she'd resisted violating the woman's body at the end. That aversion to giving in completely to her darkest self troubled him. If she couldn't give herself over to the monster inside her, she would fail.

No use in brooding on it, he decided. He'd know the outcome soon enough.

He sat back and sipped his coffee.

★ ★ ★

Sierra stepped into her parents' kitchen and was momentarily disoriented. It was as if she'd walked toward the wall and had been turned around without realizing it. She looked behind her and saw the rift close. It didn't disappear entirely, though. If she looked closely, she could see a slight shimmer in the air where it had been. *That must be the rift scar*, she thought. She didn't go any nearer to it, mindful of Corliss's warning about it causing unpleasant aftereffects.

At first the kitchen didn't look any different than the one she'd left, and she wondered if Corliss was playing a trick on her. But then she noticed some things weren't the same. Some of the items on the counters were different, most notably the microwave. Dad had gotten Mom a new one for Christmas last year, one that he'd purchased from Electronics Emporium at Stuart's recommendation. It had all the latest technological bells and whistles, most of which her mom never used. But that microwave wasn't here. The old one, a square white thing that looked like it was made in the Eighties, was still in its place. And the clock on it said it was 4:03 p.m. She hadn't checked the time before she'd left the future, but that sounded about right. Corliss had said he'd send her *exactly* a year into the past, and he had – which meant she had little time to prevent Jeffrey's accident.

Time is not on your side, Corliss had said. Talk about an understatement.

There were other signs she was in the past. The sky outside the kitchen window was dark, heralding the approach of what would turn out to be one hell of a storm. The house felt different too. There was a calmness to it, a placidity, and Sierra knew this was because this version of her parents' home had yet to know violence and death. And if she succeeded, it never would.

She experienced an impulse to race through the house and check the family room, her parents' bedroom, the stairs, and confirm for herself that there were no bodies or piles of gray dust. She almost did it, but then she heard the garage door opening. It was Mom and Dad. They'd gone out somewhere – maybe to pick up groceries for dinner – and had returned home. She figured it likely they were both in the car. Her parents liked to do things together, even running everyday errands. *We enjoy each other's company*, her mother had once said. Sierra doubted her parents would enjoy entering their kitchen and seeing their daughter standing there, blood all over her. She wouldn't be able to explain her presence, let alone all the blood, and she couldn't afford to waste time.

She hurried to the front door – which was of course unlocked – opened it and stepped outside. A strong wind was already blowing, tearing leaves off the trees and tumbling them away, and the first drops of rain began to fall. Randall's Town Car wasn't on the lawn, and Stuart's Camaro wasn't parked at the curb. In a sense, they *were*, she supposed, just a year in the future.

She closed the door and started across the lawn. She glanced back in time to see the garage door close. Good. With any luck her parents would never know she'd been there. She walked straight across the street to the Kovachs' house. She tried not to think about what she intended to do once she got there, tried not to think at all. Corliss had said her deepest self was cold and emotionless, and she intended to let it take the wheel for a while – if she could.

The rain was coming down steadily by the time she stepped onto the Kovachs' porch. She appreciated the rain. Not only did it feel refreshing on her skin, it washed most of the blood from her face and hands. It was no help for the stains on her clothes, but she supposed you couldn't have everything.

She stepped up to the front door and rang the bell. It was September, but she had an absurd impulse to shout *Trick or treat!* when the door opened to reveal Mrs. Kovach. She wore a white sweatshirt with a cardinal on the front, along with a pair of gray leggings.

"Sierra? What you doing out in the rain? Is something wrong?"

You mean aside from your husband murdering a lot of people – including my mom and dad – a year from now? she thought. Out loud, she said, "It's important I speak to Mr. Kovach. Is he home?"

Erika frowned, not only because the request was so odd, Sierra thought, but because of how she looked. But Erika opened the door wider and stepped back to allow Sierra to enter her home. Sierra smiled gratefully and walked inside. Erika shut the door then turned to Sierra.

"He's down in the basement." She paused, and then added with an edge of distaste, "Working on his Chucks."

Sierra could almost hear Erika mentally add *goddamned* before *Chucks*.

Sierra had never realized it before, but Erika didn't like her husband's hobby any more than the rest of Bishop Hill did.

"You can wait in the kitchen, and I'll go down and get him, all right?"

"Thank you."

Sierra followed Erika to the Kovachs' kitchen, and she stood next to one of the counters while Erika went to the basement door, opened it, and started downstairs.

Now that she was here, Sierra didn't know if she could go through with it. For one thing, she hadn't counted on Erika being here. How could she kill Randall without also harming Erika, maybe even having to kill her too?

I should leave, she thought. *I should run out of here and go to Jeffrey, beg him not to have dinner with Marc tonight, make him stay with me all night long so he won't go driving in the storm. He'll never encounter Courtney Marsh, never swerve into the ditch and launch his truck into the air like a fucking flying coffin.*

But Corliss had told her if she attempted to contact Jeffrey, it wouldn't work. He'd still get into his pickup, still drive out of town, still meet Courtney Marsh, still crash, still die.

You only have his word on that, she thought.

Corliss was running this whole show, this fucking *test*. He made the rules, and if he said the only way to save her brother was to kill Randall and the others, then that was it. She either did it or she didn't, saved Jeffrey or allowed him – and all the people Randall, Mandy, Grace, and Stuart would kill in the future – to die.

There was a butcher's block on the counter next to the stove. She gripped the handle of the butcher knife and slid it free. It might not be copper or have a Chuck on the handle, but she thought it would do the job. She hid the knife behind her back, faced the open basement door, and waited.

She heard shoes clomping up the basement steps, and then Randall emerged into the kitchen. He smiled broadly – of course – when he saw Sierra. He wore a brown flannel shirt and jeans, but otherwise looked the same as he would a year from now. Erika followed him out of the basement.

"It's good to see you, Sierra!" Randall said as he approached her. "It's been too long. You should've brought an umbrella with you, though. You're soaked." He turned to Erika. "Can we get her a towel?"

Erika's smile was strained, probably by the way he said *we* when he clearly meant *her*.

"Sure."

Erika left the kitchen, and Sierra was so grateful she could've cheered. Now that Erika was momentarily out of the way, she could do what she had to.

"So what brings you to our humble home on this stormy Monday?" Randall asked. He noticed her clothes for the first time, and he frowned. "Did something happen?"

Corliss had said the seeds of the monsters Randall and the others would become were already in them, but when she looked at Randall, she didn't see a smiley-faced killer. She saw a well-meaning, if eccentric, older man who simply wanted to make the world a nicer place. How could she kill a man like that?

"Did Erika tell you what I was up to down in my secret workshop?"

He spoke brightly, his previous concern for her gone, as if it had never existed. He reached into his pocket and pulled out a Chuck.

"This is the first one of a new batch, fresh off the production line. I want you to have it." He held it out to her. "Chuck says good girls don't visit neighbors wearing dirty clothes."

She brought the knife around and rammed it into his stomach. He let out an *oof* of air, and the Chuck fell from his fingers and clattered to the floor.

Sierra stabbed him three more times in quick succession before he collapsed. Then she knelt, put the blade to his throat, and set about carving him a second smile, this one permanent.

She was so intent on her work that she didn't realize Erika had returned until she heard the woman scream.

Sierra rose and turned toward Erika, who stood staring at her husband's dead body in horror, a neatly folded towel held in her hands.

"It's all right," Sierra said, gripping the blood-slick blade. "I know you won't believe me, but I just saved a lot of lives."

Erika gaped at her, then she dropped the towel, turned, and ran. Sierra pursued her without thinking, and she wasn't thinking when she brought her down in the living room and did the same thing to her as she'd done to Randall. She was breathing heavily by the time she was finished, and when she stood, she looked down at Erika. The woman lay on her back, the cardinal on her sweatshirt now just one more splotch of red on the white.

"I'm sorry, Mrs. Kovach. But I couldn't let you call the police. I couldn't take the chance that they'd stop me before I can save my brother."

Erika didn't answer her, of course, but Sierra thought she might've understood if she knew the full story behind what was happening. Funny, she thought she'd feel...well, *something* after killing two people. Three if you counted future Mandy. But she felt no more than she did on that long-ago day when she'd hurled the toad high into the air. Maybe it would hit her later, but right now, she had more work to do. She needed a car, and she'd seen a wall mount for keys on the kitchen wall near the Kovachs' refrigerator. She'd have preferred driving her Ladybug to using Randall's Town Car, but she'd make do.

She hurried back to the kitchen.

★ ★ ★

Sierra's apartment building was the next closest stop, and she drove there as fast as she thought she could without drawing a cop's attention. If she got pulled over, she'd have a difficult time explaining the blood on her face, hands, and clothes, some of it Mandy's, some of it Randall's and Erika's. The rain was coming down harder now, and she had the Town Car's wipers running at high speed. Wind buffeted the car, and she had to fight to keep it from swerving.

Grace's Lexus was in its usual parking place, but Sierra's Beetle wasn't there. Where had she been a year ago? Cleaning up after an afternoon class at ArtWorks? Maybe. She'd been in her apartment when she'd spoken to Jeffrey on the phone. When they'd argued. *That* she'd never forget. It was trippy to think that there was another her out there somewhere, one who was a year younger and didn't know her brother was going to die this night. She envied that woman and wished she could go back to being her, if only for a little while. But you couldn't go back – her current foray into the past excluded. You could only go forward.

She parked Randall's car next to Grace's, grabbed the butcher knife off the passenger seat, and got out. Again, the rain washed her face, hands, and weapon clean, but it did nothing for her soul. She knew that part of her would never be clean again.

She went inside the building, walked to Grace's door, and knocked. After a moment, she heard Grace's muffled voice.

"Who is it?"

Sierra concealed the knife behind her back and kept her face turned away from Grace's peephole.

"Liquor delivery," she said. "I've got two bottles of Maker's Mark for you."

A moment's hesitation as Grace likely tried to remember if she'd placed an order for booze, but then she unlocked the door and opened it. She was smiling, but her smile faded when she saw who it was.

"Sierra?"

A year had made a real difference in Grace's appearance. This

Grace was an alcoholic, but she was still employed, still had her shit together, more or less. She was thin, but at a much healthier weight than the last time Sierra had seen her, and her face didn't have the sallow complexion it would in a year's time. Grace wore professional attire – a gray suit jacket, white blouse, gray slacks – and Sierra figured she'd just gotten home from work. Sometimes she left the bank a little early so she could get a head start on the night's drinking.

This Grace had listened to Sierra complain about Jeffrey's boyfriend from time to time, but she'd yet to comfort a Sierra who was grieving the loss of her brother. At this point, Sierra didn't come over often, so Grace looked at her with a certain amount of puzzlement.

"Is something wrong?" she said.

"Everyone keeps asking me that," Sierra said.

She brought the knife forward and stepped toward Grace.

* * *

When she was finished, she found Grace's phone – which, ironically enough, was in her purse – and Sierra took it with her when she departed. She left bloody fingerprints on the doorknob, and probably inside the apartment too, but she didn't care. She didn't have time to clean up the scene. She had two more people to kill and not a lot of time to do it.

As she drove away from the building, she used Grace's phone to call Stuart. He answered after the fifth ring.

"Hello? Who is this?" Stuart sounded guarded, suspicious.

"It's Sierra."

"Hey! I didn't recognize the number you're calling from."

"Yeah, my phone's on the fritz, so I had to borrow a friend's."

"Come on by the store, and I'll set you up with a new phone, top of the line. I'll even give you my employee discount."

At this point in time, they'd only been dating for a couple months, and Stuart was still careful to conceal his need to control her. But she knew it was there, and she could detect a hint of it in his tone now. He wasn't *asking* her to come by. He was *telling* her.

"Sounds good. I need to drop by the college first, so I might be a little while."

"No problem. I'm not going anywhere. And after we get you set up with a new phone, you want to go have dinner or something?"

To Stuart, *or something* always meant *fuck*.

"I'd love to," Sierra said. "See you soon."

She disconnected and kept driving toward Riverbank Community College.

⋆ ⋆ ⋆

Sierra couldn't remember what Mandy's teaching schedule had been a year ago, but since she didn't know where the woman lived, she thought the school was her best bet to find her. She had one thing going for her. She knew that Mandy had a tendency to stay late in her office on campus, grading homework and tests, answering emails, meeting with students, attending committee meetings. She was one of those people who believed in not going home until they'd completed the day's work, all of it.

The rain was still coming down when Sierra pulled into the faculty parking lot. She looked for Mandy's Mustang and was relieved when she saw it there. She had to park on the other side of the lot, and when she got out, she slipped the knife into the back of her leggings and concealed it beneath her blouse. It wasn't the most comfortable way to carry a knife, and as wet as her blouse would be, when she walked into the building where their offices were, you'd be able to see the blade through the cloth. But she couldn't simply carry the knife onto campus, not unless she wanted to get shot by security.

She saw a woman walking across the street toward the faculty lot then, huddled beneath a black umbrella that looked like it might be blown away by the wind any moment.

It was Mandy.

Sierra felt a certain grim satisfaction upon seeing her. Encountering her here in the lot would save her time. But that was all she felt. Was this what Corliss had told her about? Was this her true self, all cold, ruthless calculation? Or was she merely suppressing her emotions in order to do what she had to? She wasn't sure one was better than the other.

She hurried toward Mandy and met the woman on the edge of the faculty lot. This was pre-Corliss Mandy, hair up in a tight bun, conservative business attire, blouse buttoned all the way to the throat. The woman radiated icy control but now that Sierra had gotten to know sex vampire Mandy – in *so* many ways – she could detect the raging sexuality barely controlled by the woman's carefully maintained persona. She doubted even Mandy was aware of it.

Mandy stopped and looked Sierra up and down, frowning with disapproval.

"What have you done to yourself? You look like you've been wallowing in mud like a pig!"

"It's not mud," Sierra said.

Mandy leaned closer to inspect the stains on Sierra's clothes, and at that moment lightning flashed, followed an instant later by a deafening crack of thunder. The storm was becoming violent, deadly. Sierra knew just how it felt.

She leaned toward Mandy without a word, and before the woman could react, Sierra kissed her. Mandy stiffened in shock, but then Sierra put her arms around the woman and slid her tongue between her lips. Mandy resisted for several more seconds before her body relaxed and she began kissing Sierra back. These weren't gentle kisses either. They were passionate, almost desperate kisses. Sierra wasn't certain given the rain, but she thought Mandy might be crying.

Sierra reached behind her back and drew her knife.

⋆ ⋆ ⋆

She left Mandy where she lay. The woman deserved better than that, but Sierra didn't have time to give it to her. She ran back to Randall's Town Car, got in, and roared out of the faculty parking lot, swerving around Mandy's body. She turned onto the street.

Three down, one to go.

She looked at the car's dashboard clock.

5:12.

Jeffrey and Marc would be heading for Temptations to eat dinner, might already be there for all she knew. She pressed the accelerator to the floor and raced through the raging storm toward Electronics Emporium. On the way, she couldn't resist driving past ArtWorks. It was a relief to see the building intact and to know that Karolyn was inside, alive and happy in her work. She prayed she'd be able to keep her that way.

* * *

Sierra didn't have time to fuck around. She pulled up to the curb in front of the store and started honking the horn.

Stuart's manager, Alton, stepped outside to see what the hell all the commotion was about. Sierra rolled down the passenger-side window.

"Can you tell Stuart to come out here, please? It's an emergency."

Alton frowned doubtfully, but he nodded and went back inside. A moment later, Stuart came out. He stood in the store's doorway to keep out of the rain, but given the way the wind was blowing, it didn't help very much.

"Sierra? Whose car is that?"

The accusation in his tone was subtle but unmistakable to Sierra. What Stuart really wanted to know was if the car belonged to a man, and if so, why was she driving it?

"That's not important right now!" Sierra had to shout to be heard over the wind and rain. "Hurry up and get in the car!"

Stuart looked taken aback by her words, and why not? He was used to giving commands in a relationship, not taking them. But after a moment's hesitation, he dashed through the rain, opened the Town Car's passenger door, got inside, and closed it behind him. Once in the car, he tried to reassert dominance.

"I don't know what you want, but it had better be important, I just got soaked running—"

Sierra laid his throat open with a single swift swipe of her blade. Blood sprayed the dashboard, Stuart's eyes went wide, and he clapped his hands to his throat in a futile attempt to keep his blood inside his body where it belonged. He turned to look at Sierra, an expression of utter bafflement on his face, as if all the laws of the universe as he knew them had just upended.

"Sorry," Sierra said. "But you *are* an asshole."

She reached past him – getting even more blood on herself in the process – opened the door and shoved him out onto the sidewalk. He wasn't dead yet, but she felt confident he would be in short order. She pulled the passenger door shut, put the car in drive, and pulled away from the curb, the Town Car's rear end fishtailing on the wet pavement.

She glanced in the rearview mirror and saw Alton run out of the store and kneel next to Stuart. If she'd had any hope of saving Jeffrey without the cops knowing what she'd done, it was gone now. Not only had she left evidence at the scenes of her crimes – her *murders* – there now was a witness. One who could identify the vehicle she was driving. How long before Bishop Hill's finest put out an all-points bulletin on Sierra Sowell, last seen driving a Lincoln Town Car? Not long enough, she thought.

She'd done what Corliss said she had to, so that meant she could save Jeffrey now. She picked up Grace's phone and called his number. She wasn't sure what she was going to say, but all she needed to do was prevent Jeffrey from driving away from Temptations while he was upset. She'd tell him that she needed his help. It was true enough. He'd met her somewhere and while she couldn't tell him the truth – he loved her, but there was no fucking way he'd believe her insane story – it didn't matter what she said, so long as she kept him away from County Road 25A and Courtney Marsh.

His phone rang a half dozen times and then went to voicemail.

"Hey, this is Jeffrey. I'm probably doing something amazing right now, but I'll return your message once the excitement dies down."

There was a beep and the phone began recording. She understood why Jeffrey hadn't picked up. He was on the phone with her, the *other* her, the one from today, who instead of supporting her brother when he was hurting chose to lecture him about his lousy taste in men.

She spoke fast before the phone cut her off.

"Jeffrey, it's Sis. Wherever you're at, pull over now and wait out the storm! I can't explain why it's important you do this, but it *is*. Please do it! I'll explain when I—"

Another beep. She'd run out of time. In more ways than one, maybe. What were the odds that Jeffrey would listen to her message before the accident? Zero, she thought. They'd been arguing on the phone not long before the accident happened. He'd be too mad at her to listen to any message she left.

She began to come out of the nearly emotionless state she'd functioned in since arriving in the past, and she felt despair take hold of her. She'd killed five people, and by doing so, she'd saved the lives of all those they would've killed in the future, but it hadn't been enough to help her save the life of the person who mattered most to her in the world. But maybe, just maybe, that wasn't true. Not yet, anyway. If the accident hadn't happened yet, then it could still be stopped. *She* could stop it. If she could get there in time.

She had one more monster to kill, the biggest monster of all.

Lightning flashed, thunder cracked, and Sierra drove like a maniac as she headed out of town.

⋆ ⋆ ⋆

Courtney Marsh wished she had listened to her teacher. Mrs. Olivetti had practically begged her not to go out into the storm, but it hadn't been *that* bad when her oboe lesson had ended. Yes, it had been raining, but the thunder and lightning hadn't started yet. Mrs. Olivetti had checked her phone's weather app, and she said the storm was going to get worse – a *lot* worse – before Courtney could make it back to Bishop Hill. But she'd believed she could beat the storm, at least that's what she'd told herself. She had tennis practice tonight, and while Coach Balmer wouldn't take them outside to practice in the rain, she'd have the team practice in the gym. They could work on their serves, practice backhands and lobs. You didn't need a net and a regulation court for these things. She knew if the storm got too bad – like, *apocalyptic* bad – Coach Balmer would send the team a group text canceling practice. But

Courtney had her phone out and resting on her Altima's passenger seat, and so far, no text. Until she received one, she'd assume practice was still on.

Jagged bolts of lightning crisscrossed the sky, followed almost immediately by multiple peals of thunder. Courtney jumped in her seat, and the motion caused her to jerk the steering wheel to the left. Her car edged over the line, not much, and she quickly pulled back into her lane.

"You're an idiot, you're an idiot, you're an idiot," she said to herself, unaware that she spoke these words out loud. Between the frantic *whap-whap-whap* of the windshield wipers, the sound of the rain, and the now-regular bursts of thunder, she couldn't hear her own voice.

This wasn't the first time her drive for perfection – some of the other students at school might call it an *obsession* – had gotten her in trouble, but it was the worst. She told herself she should pull over to the side of the road and wait for the storm to let up. That would be the safe thing to do. The *smart* thing. And she prided herself on being smart, didn't she? Smart was what it was all about. Smart was her ticket out.

Her parents had split up when she'd been a baby, and her dad left her with her mother. She hadn't seen him in years, only talked to him on the phone on holidays – if he remembered to call. He lived in California with his new wife and kids. He was a physician, an ENT to be precise, and he sent regular child support, no problem there. Courtney figured he probably had an accountant write the checks for him. The problem was Courtney's mom.

Her mother had worked to help support her husband while he was in medical school. The deal was that when he was finished, it would be her turn for college. She had her sights ultimately set on law school. But Courtney had come along during Mom's freshman year of undergrad (surprise!) and Dad divorced her at the beginning of her sophomore year. She struggled along for the rest of that semester, but going to school, working, and being a single mother had been too much. She dropped out of college and never went back. She'd worked a series of low-paying, high-stress jobs, had dated a series of spectacularly useless men, and ended up with a severe case of depression. Courtney didn't blame her mother for any of this. She'd caught some bad breaks and she'd done the best she could to deal with them. But instead of seeing a doctor and getting a prescription for an antidepressant, her mom had chosen to self-medicate. And her drug of choice was heroin.

She'd been able to hide her addiction for a while, was able to keep working and keep being a mother. But the more her body acclimated to the drug, the more she needed to get the same effect, and so on and so on. Now she was barely functional, was sick all the time, and she was living solely off the child support payments Courtney's dad sent. And most of that money went to pay bills – if there was any left over after her mom bought drugs, that is.

Courtney had tried to talk her mother into getting help numerous times. She'd researched rehab programs on the internet, read articles on how to talk to a loved one who was addicted, what to say to get through to them. Every one of her attempts failed. Not only wouldn't her mom listen to her, she became so angry that she barely wanted to have anything to do with her daughter anymore. She'd already overdosed twice, would've died if the EMTs hadn't given her Narcan each time. Courtney knew it was only a matter of time before heroin claimed her mom's life, before her long, slow suicide attempt was finally successful.

So Courtney worked her ass off at school, intending to get as many scholarships to college as possible, maybe even a free ride to the school of her choice if she was lucky. She planned to go to med school and become a doctor. Not because she wanted to be like her dad – although in truth that *was* a small part of it – but because she wanted to help people like her mom, and because she never wanted to have to worry about money again for the rest of her life. She'd seen firsthand what happened when one partner didn't fully support another.

But there was more to getting into a good school besides academics, which was why she played oboe in the school orchestra and why she was on the tennis team. She wanted to make herself the most attractive college candidate possible. And that meant not missing a single fucking practice. No exceptions.

She wasn't like either of her parents. She wasn't a quitter. When she started something, by god, she finished it, and she wasn't going to let a rainstorm, no matter how bad, keep her from—

A pair of headlights materialized out of the darkness in front of her, close and headed straight for her car. She barely had time to scream.

★ ★ ★

Jeffrey had stopped crying, but it hadn't impaired his vision much. As hard as the rain was coming down, his wipers couldn't keep the water off the windshield, not even at their highest setting.

It's like the whole world is crying, he thought, and then laughed.

"Drama queen," he said.

He'd been so fucking angry when he'd left Marc at Temptations, and he'd gotten even angrier after calling Sierra. He knew better than to talk to her about problems he was having with Marc. Sierra couldn't *stand* him. Oh, she claimed to have nothing against him personally, said that she thought he was too jealous and insecure to make a good partner for him, that as his sister it was her job to look out for him. That there was truth in this, he had no doubt. He also knew it wasn't the *whole* truth. Throughout their childhood, on into high school and through college, they'd been more than brother and sister. They'd been best friends. They'd both dated before, but neither of them had really gotten serious about anyone until Jeffrey had met Marc. Yes, their relationship could be volatile at times, but for the most part it was good, better than it ever had been with anyone else. Sierra felt threatened by how close he and Marc had become. Jeffrey saw Sierra a lot less these days, spoke on the phone to her more rarely. They still texted now and then, but they weren't in almost constant contact like they'd once been. Jeffrey missed being close to his sister, but he thought a little distance would be good for both of them. They'd become too enmeshed over the years. They needed some space to be able to build their own lives. Since he'd been seeing Marc, she'd started dating a guy named Stuart. Jeffrey thought he was an ass, and he hadn't been shy about telling her so. But lately, he'd tried to rein in his criticism of Stuart. If Jeffrey wanted her to lay off him about Marc, he had to do the same for her when it came to Stuart.

But as much as he hated to admit it, Sierra might be right about Marc. Jeffrey loved him, he had no doubt about that, but he couldn't live with Marc's jealousy any longer. He needed to have a talk with him. Not tonight, and maybe not tomorrow, but soon, once the emotional aftertaste of tonight had passed. He'd tell Marc he loved him, but if he wanted them to stay together, he would have to learn to handle his insecurities better, maybe see a therapist. Jeffrey would offer to go with him if it would help. Hell, maybe they could do couples therapy. Whatever it took. And if Marc tried and it didn't work – or if he refused to even make the attempt – Jeffrey would know he'd done all he could and that it was time to move on. But if it *did* work, then he'd stay. He hoped it would work. He really did.

He felt calmer now, more settled, and as he began to think more clearly, he realized that he had done an extremely foolish thing rushing out into the storm the way he had. He needed to find somewhere he could turn around so he could head back to town. Or maybe he should find somewhere to pull over, somewhere he'd be far enough off the road so somebody wouldn't come along, not see his car, and hit him.

That decided, he started to ease off the gas – and that's when he saw the headlights emerge out of the storm's darkness. It looked like the other driver had swerved over the centerline and was coming straight for him. Adrenaline surged through him. He gripped the steering wheel tighter and prepared to hit the brake and yank the wheel to the right.

But then he heard a sound over the thunder. It was…a car horn? And it was coming from behind him.

He saw headlights in his rearview mirror. This car was coming up on him *fast*. The driver swerved around Jeffrey's truck, roared past, and headed straight for the oncoming car. Whoever was behind the wheel didn't hit their brakes, didn't slow down. If anything, it looked like they continued accelerating.

The crash was spectacular.

The sound of the collision drowned out the thunder, and the

vehicles – a Lincoln Town Car and a Nissan Altima – spun on the wet pavement in opposite directions, tipped, and rolled.

Jeffrey slammed on his brakes and his pickup hydroplaned. For a sickening instant he thought he was going to lose control of his vehicle too, but he didn't. He came to a stop fifty feet from where the accident happened, and he sat there, engine running, windshield wipers snapping back and forth, thunder booming, rain pounding on the roof of this truck. He tried to draw in a breath. It took a moment, and when he was finally able to pull air into his lungs, he did so in a ragged, sudden gasp.

That could've been me, he thought. *Would've been me.* If the driver of the Town Car hadn't intercepted the Altima.... Because that's what it had looked like, like the Town Car's driver had purposely driven past him in order to hit the Altima. But that was ridiculous. Who would do such a thing? More likely the Town Car's driver had wanted to pass him, and because of the storm, hadn't been aware of the other driver. It had been an accident. A stupid, meaningless accident, nothing more.

Hand shaking, he pulled his phone from his pocket and called 911.

CHAPTER FIFTEEN

Sierra opened her eyes with a start. The last thing she remembered, she was heading straight for Courtney Marsh's car and then – nothing.

She stood on a road, cornfields on either side of her. It was late in the day, and the sun was near the horizon, but there was still plenty of daylight left. She held out her arms to examine them, looked down at her chest and legs. She appeared uninjured. More than that, her clothes were clean, not a drop of blood on them.

From behind her came the sound of clapping, and she turned to see Corliss standing there. He was smiling, but his eyes glittered like two chips of ice.

"Well done," he said.

"I don't suppose you're going to tell me that none of it really happened, that it was all a dream."

"I'm afraid not. Everything happened, and the consequences are now permanent. Jeffrey is alive. Mandy, Randall, Grace, Stuart, and Erika are not. Neither is Courtney Marsh, poor girl. But all the others who died – including your parents and Marc – they're still alive. Or if they aren't, they've died natural deaths in the year since you drove Randall's car into Courtney's."

"And me?" she asked.

"You died too. In this world, you've been dead for a year. Exactly one year. You're also known as the woman whose mind snapped and for some unknown reason went on a killing spree. You can imagine your family's reaction, especially Jeffrey's, when they learned you were behind the wheel of Randall's car that night."

Assuming Corliss was telling the truth, she had taken lives and saved lives, and while her brother now lived, she was dead, and Jeffrey and their parents believed she was a murderous lunatic. Bad enough to lose a family member in a car accident, but to live with the knowledge that their daughter and sister had been a monster? She'd destroyed their lives too, just in a different way.

She felt a distant echo of an emotion that might have been sorrow, but it soon faded and she gave it no more thought.

"Did I pass the test?" she asked.

"With flying colors," Corliss said. "Welcome to the Multitude. Only one task remains unfinished. You know what to do."

She did.

Corliss knelt in the road and she stepped toward him, her hands becoming ebon claws. She took hold of Corliss's head gently, almost lovingly. He gave her a final smile, this one peaceful, almost beatific.

"I now perform my final service to Entropy," he said. "Praise Oblivion."

"Praise Oblivion," Sierra echoed, then jammed her clawed thumbs into Corliss's eyes. She pushed inward, penetrating his brain, and once her thumbs were deep enough, she began moving them in slow circles, stirring shit around in there.

Corliss remained silent the entire time she did this, but his body spasmed as if he was having a seizure – which, all things considered, he probably was. When she withdrew her thumbs, Corliss slumped to the road, dead. She licked her thumbs clean as she watched his head and hands slowly withdraw into his suit. His arms and legs went next, and when his body was gone, the suit folded in on itself again and again, each time growing smaller, until at last it was gone.

Interesting. She'd have to look into getting herself an outfit like that.

She then raked the air, making her first rift. She stepped through and sealed it behind her.

This could be the end.

But it isn't.

★ ★ ★

"I don't understand how you can be so…so…."

"Handsome?" Jeffrey offered.

"Not sad," Marc said.

The two men sat side by side on their new couch. They'd picked it out last month when Marc had moved into Jeffrey's apartment. The couch was the first real purchase they'd made together, the first thing they had that wasn't Jeffrey's or Marc's but *theirs*.

Both of their phones lay atop the glass coffee table. They'd been off all day because of the reporters who kept calling. They all wanted an exclusive interview with Jeffrey on the one-year anniversary of the day his sister had viciously murdered five people – four with a butcher knife and one with a car she'd stolen from one of her victims. Jeffrey and Marc had both taken the day off work for the same reason, so that reporters couldn't find them at their places of employment. A few had tried knocking on their apartment door throughout the day, but they eventually gave up and left. Marc had suggested they leave town for a week or so, maybe take a trip somewhere peaceful and relaxing, but Jeffrey had wanted to remain in Bishop Hill. Mostly so he could be here for his parents. He'd spoken with them earlier. They'd been doing their best to avoid the media too, and they'd planned a quiet night at home, just like Jeffrey and Marc had.

"I know," Jeffrey said, "but I can't escape the feeling that what she did at the end, ramming Randall's car into Courtney's—"

"She did to save your life," Marc finished. "Do you know how crazy that sounds?" He froze, eyes wide. "Oh my god, I shouldn't have said that."

"Said what?"

"You know – the *C* word."

Jeffrey smiled.

"Yes, I know it sounds *crazy*, but the thought gives me some comfort. I'll never know why Sierra killed those people. None of us will. She didn't leave a note behind, and there were no signs that she was going to hurt anyone. She'd never been violent before. But the idea that she saved my life, even if she did a terrible thing to do it, means that the sister I knew was still somewhere inside her. Remember that voicemail she left? She was warning me that I was in danger. Even in her darkest moment, she was still capable of love. Maybe it's not much, but I'll take what I can get, you know?"

Marc put his hand around Jeffrey's shoulders, and Jeffrey leaned against him. They sat like that, quiet, for a long time.

★ ★ ★

Jeffrey and Marc's apartment was located on the ground floor of a building much nicer than the one where Sierra had lived. She stood outside their patio window. The blinds were drawn so they couldn't see her – or her them – but her senses were much sharper now, and she had no trouble hearing them speak from out here.

She smiled.

"I'd murder the world for you, bro."

Then she turned and sliced open a rift. On the other side lay a vast dark plain. In the distance, things larger than any mountain on earth moved in a stately procession, their mindless journey without beginning or end. Above them the sky was filled with winged creatures born from the fevered dreams of the mad and the dying. They dipped and darted, endlessly searching for prey. And high above the world, colors swirling slowly around a circle of infinite blackness – the same color as Corliss's suit, incidentally – was the Gyre, the End of All Things.

Sierra had never seen anything more beautiful. She was looking forward to serving it alongside her new family.

She stepped into her future and was gone.

FLAME TREE PRESS
FICTION WITHOUT FRONTIERS
Award-Winning Authors & Original Voices

Flame Tree Press is the trade fiction imprint of Flame Tree Publishing, focusing on excellent writing in horror and the supernatural, crime and mystery, science fiction and fantasy. Our aim is to explore beyond the boundaries of the everyday, with tales from both award-winning authors and original voices.

•

Other titles available by Tim Waggoner:
The Mouth of the Dark

Other horror titles available include:
Thirteen Days by Sunset Beach by Ramsey Campbell
Think Yourself Lucky by Ramsey Campbell
The Hungry Moon by Ramsey Campbell
The Haunting of Henderson Close by Catherine Cavendish
The House by the Cemetery by John Everson
The Devil's Equinox by John Everson
The Toy Thief by D.W. Gillespie
Black Wings by Megan Hart
Stoker's Wilde by Steven Hopstaken & Melissa Prusi
The Playing Card Killer by Russell James
The Siren and the Specter by Jonathan Janz
Wolf Land by Jonathan Janz
The Sorrows by Jonathan Janz
Savage Species by Jonathan Janz
The Nightmare Girl by Jonathan Janz
The Dark Game by Jonathan Janz
House of Skin by Jonathan Janz
Dust Devils by Jonathan Janz
Castle of Sorrows by Jonathan Janz
Will Haunt You by Brian Kirk
Creature by Hunter Shea
Ghost Mine by Hunter Shea

•

Join our mailing list for free short stories, new release details, news about our authors and special promotions:

flametreepress.com